Students' Book

the *Beginners'* CHOICE

Sue Mohamed and Richard Acklam

Longman

UNIT	STRUCTURES	KEY VERB	VOCABULARY	ENGLISH IN ACTION
11	• *Very/not very* • Object pronouns: *me/you/her/him/it/us/them* • Past Simple (*Be*): *was/were* • Past Simple + *ago* • *I think/I don't think* . . .	• *Be* • *Do*	• Describing people	Writing and answering 'Wanted' advertisements
12	• Likes and dislikes (2): *love/hate* • Adverbs of frequency (2): *How often . . .?* + *once/twice;three/four times a week* • Prepositions (4): *a long way from/far from/near/opposite* • *Some/any* + countable/uncountable nouns • *How far is it?/How long does it take?*	• *Like* • *Be*	• Food • Meals • Describing places • Transport	Applying for a holiday job
13	• *What's it like? It's* + adjective • Present Continuous (now) • *This/that/these/those*	• *Do* • *Be*	• Weather • Seasons • Expressions for special occasions	Sending greetings cards
14	• *To be* + born • Comparatives + *than* • *Should/shouldn't* (advice)	• *Be* • *Have got*	• Health and feelings • Illnesses	Going to the doctor's
15	**Consolidation** • Thinking about learning: listening and reading • Across cultures: celebrations • Language in context: puzzle page			
16	• Superlatives • *I agree/I don't agree* • Imperatives: *go/turn/take* (street directions)	• *Be*	• Size and weight • Street directions	Inviting a friend to stay
	Survival • A board game			
17	• *A/an/the* or (–) + places • Present Perfect Simple (experience) • *Been* vs *gone*	• *Have* • *Be* • *Do*	• Points of the compass • Geographical place names (*city, town,* etc.)	Having an interview for a job
18	• *Quite* vs *really* + adjectives • Present and Past Simple *have to/don't have to* (obligation) • Regular adverbs ending in *-ly* • Irregular adverbs • *Too* vs *very* + adjectives	• *Have to*	• Clothes /shoe sizes • Expressions for shopping	Buying shoes and clothes
19	• *Will* (future prediction) • Present Continuous (descriptions) • Question words (review) • *First/then* . . .	• *Do* • *Be*	• Everyday actions (2) • Types of accommodation • Rooms of the house	Exchanging holiday homes
	Photo finish • Completing the story			
20	**Consolidation** • Thinking about learning: speaking and writing • Across cultures: education • Language in context: school			

An extended map of the contents of *The Beginners' Choice* can be found at the front of the Teacher's Book, featuring:

• the pronunciation syllabus
• the skills work, unit by unit
• the detailed contents of each Consolidation unit

3 Match the words to the pictures.

1 Listening   5 Grammar
2 Speaking   6 Vocabulary
3 Reading   7 Pronunciation
4 Writing

E

A   Telephone

...two to tango. **taxi** *Martin drives a* **taxi**. *He takes people
...nething that to a place in his car, and they pay him.*
...ot of liquid or **telephone** *noun* **1** *Lisa is using the*
...re is a water **telephone**. *She lives in London, but she is*
...the roof of our *speaking to her friend in Paris.* verb
...The petrol **tank** **telephoning, telephoned, telephoned 2**
...ar is empty. *to speak to someone using a* **telephone**
...un **1** *Sugar has Robert* **telephoned** *his brother in London.*
...et **taste.** *verb* **Phone** *is another word for* **telephone.**
...g, **tasted**, **tasted** **television 1** *We have a* **television** *in our*
...ke this food. It *house. It's a* **colour television. 2** *Peter*
...good. *and his sister like watching* **television.**
"What's on **television** *this evening?" -* **TV** *is a short*

F

amo   *ich liebe*
amas   *du liebst*
amat   *er/sie/es liebt*
amamus   *wir lieben*
amatis   *Sie lieben*
amant

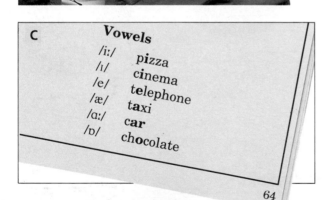
B

G

C   **Vowels**

/iː/   p**i**zza
/ɪ/   c**i**nema
/e/   t**e**lephone
/æ/   t**a**xi
/ɑː/   c**a**r
/ɒ/   ch**o**colate

64

NB   **Useful classroom language for reference**

What's this?
What's this in English?
How do you spell that?   C. I. N. E. M. A.

How do you pronounce that?   /sɪnəmə/

How do you say *Gracias* in English?
              Thank you

Sorry, I don't know.
Sorry, I don't understand.

What does it mean?
Can you say that again, please?

D

*2/ but now I work in a
bank. I work from
8.30 a.m. to 5.30 p.m. So*

1 Good morning!

O

L

Breakfast food and drink;
and/or

F

H

P

D

I

N

J

C

Q

B

G

E

M

A

K

1 Vocabulary: breakfast food

1 Match the names of the food to the pictures.

Example: hot chocolate – *D*

marmalade – Q   coffee – A   tea – B   sugar – C
bread – I   orange juice – F egg – G   bacon – H
croissant – J   milk – E   butter – K cereal – L
cheese – M   ham – N   toast – O   jam – P

2 🖥 Listen and check your answers.

2 Pronunciation: word stress

**1 🖥 Listen and repeat the breakfast vocabulary.
Where's the stress?**

☐
Example: coffee

2 Write the breakfast vocabulary, like this:

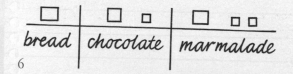

3 Speaking

1 Ask and answer with other students.

What do you have
for breakfast?

Tea and toast.

NB *and/or*

Tea + coffee = Tea *and* coffee.
Tea/coffee = Tea *or* coffee.

What do you have for breakfast, tea or coffee?

An office

A café

4 Listening

1 📼 **Listen to three conversations. Match the conversations to the pictures above.**

Conversation 1 is in . . .
Conversation 2 is in . . .
Conversation 3 is in . . .

2 Listen again. Tick (✓) the drinks they have.

Conversation	1	2	3
coffee		✓	✓
tea	✓	✗	✓
hot chocolate			
orange juice			✓

3 Listen again. How many drinks do they have?

Conversation 1: How many teas? 1, 2 or 3?
Conversation 2: How many coffees? 1, 2 or 3?
Conversation 3: How many teas? 1, 2 or 3?
How many coffees? 1, 2 or 3?

4 Offer another student a drink, like this:

A restaurant

Tea?
Yes, please.

Milk and sugar? No, thank you.

NB Black or white coffee?

In Britain, a (white) coffee is with milk.

In Britain, a black coffee is without milk.

Do you have coffee with (+) or without (−) milk?

7

5 Grammar: nouns

Singular	Plural
a + noun *an* + a, e, i, o, u	noun + *s*
a restaurant *an* egg	2 restaurant*s* 3 egg*s*

1 Complete with *a* or *an*.

Example: . . . restaurant – a restaurant.

1 an egg
2 a black coffee
3 an orange juice
4 a tea
5 an office
6 a café

2 💻 Listen and repeat the vocabulary with *a* or *an*.   /ə/ /ən/

3 💻 Listen and complete the conversation in the café.

CUSTOMER: I.t.C.a. fee black coffees and Orange juice please.
WAITER: Anything else? no Tomat.
CUSTOMER: .No Thank you

4 **Practise the conversation with another student.**

ENGLISH IN ACTION

You are in the Grosvenor Hotel restaurant.

1 Read the breakfast menus and answer these questions.

1 Which is the big breakfast – the English breakfast or the Continental breakfast?
2 Which is the small breakfast – the English breakfast or the Continental breakfast?
3 How much (£) is the English breakfast?
4 How much (£) is the Continental breakfast?
5 Would you prefer the English or the Continental breakfast?
6 Would you prefer tea, coffee or hot chocolate?

2 Now order your breakfast.

Example: YOU: A coffee and a croissant, please.
WAITER: Certainly, madam.

Good Morning

The Express Continental Breakfast
is now available in the lounge

£4.25

Help yourself to

Continental Breakfast

Tea, coffee or chocolate
Chilled orange juice
Selection of cereals

Croissants, toast, jam and butter

Full English Breakfasts are available in the Clarence Restaurant from 07.00 - 10.00

Breakfast
at the Grosvenor Hotel

◆

FULL ENGLISH BREAKFAST

£8.50

Tea, coffee or chocolate
Chilled orange juice
Selection of cereals

Croissants, toast, jam and butter

Grilled bacon, sausage, tomato, scrambled and fried eggs, sauté potatoes

Served by the waiter

PRICES ARE INCLUSIVE OF VAT AT 17½%

071 968 4435

6 Pronunciation: numbers

1 Look at the menus on page 8.

1 What is the telephone number of the Grosvenor Hotel?

2 What is the code for central London?

2 Work in groups of three students, A, B and C.

STUDENT A: Look at the telephone numbers on this page. Say the <u>underlined</u> number.

STUDENT B: Look at the telephone numbers on page 126. Listen for a number on your list. Say the number next to it.

STUDENT C: Look at the telephone numbers on page 127. Listen for a number on your list. Say the number next to it.

Student A

Hear	Say
453 6419	601 3788
	<u>249 3491</u>
223 3927	735 5566
204 6419	234 8122
491 2598	993 8630

3 Ask another student – *What's your telephone number?*

7 Vocabulary: countries

1 🖳 Listen. Match the countries to the codes.

2 Listen again. Repeat the countries and codes.

3 Ask and answer with another student – *Where do you come from?*

Where do you come from?

Where in Spain?

Spain.

Madrid.

NB Double numbers and letters

071 968 4435 = 'Oh', seven, one – nine, six, eight – *double four*, three, five.

Egg = *e double g.*

How do you spell co*ff*ee?
How do you say 0225 399 661?

INTERNATIONAL DIALLING CODES	
Argentina	010 90
Brazil	010 54
France	010 33
Greece	010 39
Italy	010 55
Japan	010 30
Spain	010 81
Turkey	010 34

Alb
Bu
Ge
Hu
Ja
Nc
Sw
Un

Key verb: *to be* (singular):
I/you/she/he/it

GROSVENOR HOTEL

PHONE MESSAGES

Date: 2 October   Time: 9.30 a.m.

For: Mark Andrews

From: Mrs Mary

Please Phone Back   Yes ☑   No ☐
Phone number

Paris

8 Listening

1 🖾 **Listen to the telephone conversation. Complete the message above.**

9 Grammar: *to be* (singular)

I'm sorry, *he's* not here.

1 Look at the example above. Complete the chart.

I am	= I'm
you are	= you' . . .
he is	= he' . . .
she is	= she' . . .
it is	= it' . . .

2 Describe the pictures above to another student. Point and say the correct sentence.

1 He's a receptionist.
2 She's Mary Bryant.
3 It's a telephone.
4 She's in Paris.
5 He's in the Grosvenor Hotel.
6 It's the Eiffel Tower.

Speaking

Talk to other students. Write their names and telephone numbers, like this:

Sorry, I don't know your name.

How do you spell that?

And what's your telephone number?

I'm Hans Schmidt.

H.A.N.S. S.C.H.M.I.D.T.

Sorry, I haven't got a telephone.

NAME Grosvenor Hotel
TELEPHONE 071 968 4435

Language review 1

1 Nouns

Singular	Plural	Plural ending in o/s/ss/ch/x
a restaurant an egg	2 restaurants 6 eggs	3 sandwiches 4 potatoes

a Name the food and drink in the picture.

Example: an orange, 3 eggs *, 4 coffees, 1 sandwich,*
5 croissants, 2 pizzas,

2 And/or

Bread + jam = bread and jam
Tea/coffee? = tea or coffee?

b Complete this dialogue with *and, or, yes, no,*
please, thank you.

A: Tea *or* coffee?
B: Tea *please.*
A: With milk?
B: *Yes,* please.
A: *Or* sugar?
B: No, *thank you.*
A: A biscuit?
B: *No,* thank you.

3 Adjectives

Adjectives come before nouns.

A *big* breakfast.
3 *black* coffees.

c Answer these questions.

Example: A: Do you have black or white coffee?
    B: Black coffee.

1 Do you have a big breakfast or a small breakfast?
2 Do you have an English breakfast or a Continental breakfast?
3 Do you have hot chocolate, tea or coffee for breakfast?

4 Verbs

• **Key verb: *to be* (singular)**

I am I'm	Mark.
You are You're	Mary.
She is She's	a student.
He is He's	a waiter.
It is It's	a hotel.

d Put these words in order.

Example:
Hans am I Schmidt – I am Hans Schmidt.

1 student you a are.
2 in she café is a.
3 is a big it office.
4 for what have breakfast you do?
5 Mary am I Jones.
6 Japan in is he.
7 don't sorry I name your know.
8 spell how you do that?
9 your number what telephone is?
10 come you where from do?

5 Question words

Questions	Answers
What do you have for breakfast?	*Tea and toast.*
How many sugars do you have?	*2*
Where do you come from?	*America.*
How do you spell that?	*A.M.E.R.I.C.A.*

About + numbers 10-12, 15, 30, 45;
What time is it?; am/pm

1 Revision

1 Make a list.

Breakfast this morning

tea
eggs

2 Answer this question – *What time do you have breakfast?*

About six

About eight.

About seven

About nine.

2 Vocabulary: the time

1 Match the times to the clocks.

B seven o'clock   five o'clock · G   eight fifteen ➤ H
F nine thirty   six forty-five ➤ E   ten forty-five ➤ C
A eleven thirty   twelve fifteen ➤ D

2 Work with another student. Point at the clocks on this page. Ask and answer, like this:

What time is it?   Seven o'clock.

3 Tell another student. What time is it now?

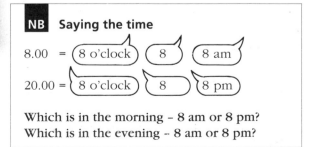

NB **Saying the time**

8.00 = 8 o'clock   8   8 am

20.00 = 8 o'clock   8   8 pm

Which is in the morning – 8 am or 8 pm?
Which is in the evening – 8 am or 8 pm?

OPENING AND CLOSING TIMES IN BRITAIN

BANKS
Mon – Fri   09.30 to 15.30
Sat   09.30 to 12.00
(Not all banks open Sat.)

OFFICES
Mon – Fri   09.00 to 17.30

POST OFFICES
Mon – Fri   09.00 to 17.00
Sat   09.00 to 13.00

PUBS
Mon – Sat   11.00 to 23.00
Sun   12.00 to 14.00
             then 19.00 to 22.30
(Some pubs close in the afternoon,
between 14.00 and 17.30.)

SHOPS
Mon – Sat   09.00 to 17.00
(Many are open until 20.00 every
day, and some open on Sundays.)

TOURIST INFORMATION CENTRES
Mon – Fri   09.00 to 17.00
(Many are open until later, and open
at weekends in the summer.)

SEPTEMBER

MONDAY		7	14	21	28
TUESDAY	1	8	15	22	29
WEDNESDAY	2	9	16	23	30
THURSDAY	3	10	17	24	
FRIDAY	4	11	18	25	
SATURDAY	5	12	19	26	
SUNDAY	6	13	20	27	

3 Reading

1 📼 **Before you read, listen and say the names
of these places.**

post offices   pubs   shops   offices   banks
Tourist Information Centres

**2 Read the leaflet above on opening and closing
times in Britain. Answer these questions.**

Example: What time are shops open from
Monday to Friday? – From 9 am to 5 pm.

1 What time are post offices open on Saturday?
2 What time are banks open from Monday to
  Friday?
3 What time are pubs open on Sunday?
4 What time are offices open from Monday to
  Friday?
5 What time are Tourist Information Centres
  open on Tuesday?

**3 Look at the calendar above and complete the
days of the week.**

Sat.   = . . . ⎫
Sun.   = . . . ⎬ the weekend

Mon.   = . . . ⎫
Tues. = . . . ⎪
Weds. = . . . ⎬ the weekdays
Thurs. = . . . ⎪
Fri.   = . . . ⎭

4 💻 **Listen and say the days. Where's the stress?**

**5 Work with another student. Test your spelling,
like this:**

Example: A: How do you spell Monday?
           B: M.O.N.D.A.Y.

4 Grammar: *to be* (plural)

This shop It	is open from 9 am to 9 pm.
Generally, shops They	are open from 9 am to 6 pm.

1 Work with another student. Make sentences like the ones above about these places.

pubs   Tourist Information Centres
banks   post offices

2 Complete the chart.

Singular	Plural
I am	we are
you are	you are
she/he/it is	they are

5 Writing

Look at *Opening times in Australia* below.
Write a text like this about your country,
changing the <u>underlined</u> words.

6 Grammar: prepositions 1

at, from, to, on + time

I have breakfast *at* 7 o'clock. Shops are open *from* 9 am *to* 5 pm.

1 Look at *Opening times in Australia* again. Complete these sentences.

1 Shops are open from Monday to Friday.
2 Offices are closed on Sunday.
3 Banks are closed at the weekend.

2 🖵 **Listen and check your answers. Is the stress on the preposition or the days of the week?**

3 Tell another student about opening times in your country. Is your information the same or different?

DARWIN

AUSTRALIA

PERTH

ADELAIDE

BRISBANE

SYDNEY
CANBERRA
MELBOURNE

OPENING TIMES IN AUSTRALIA

IN <u>AUSTRALIA</u>, shops are open from <u>9.00 am</u> to <u>5.30 pm</u>, <u>Monday to Friday</u> and <u>9.00 am</u> to <u>4.00 pm</u> on <u>Saturday</u>. Offices are generally open from <u>9.00 am</u> to <u>5.00 pm</u>, <u>Monday to Friday</u>. The weekend is <u>Saturday</u> and <u>Sunday</u>. Banks are open from <u>9.00 am</u> to <u>4.00 pm</u>, <u>Monday to Thursday</u>, and <u>9.30 am</u> to <u>5.00 pm</u> on <u>Friday</u>. They are closed <u>at the weekend</u>.

Go/get + to; Present Simple questions (1)

get home

go home

get to work/the office

go to work/the office

get to school

go to school

Go and get + to

1 Write the places below in the correct column.

go/get	go to/get to	go to the/get to the
		post office

post office   work   bank   shops
home   school   pub   office
restaurant   hotel   café   cinema
Tourist Information Centre

2 Tell another student about your work or school routine, like this:

> On Monday, I go to work at about 8 o'clock and get there at . . .

7   Listening

1 💻 Listen. Jon is at home talking to his friend Rob. Where does Jon work?

2 Listen again and write Jon's times on the chart.

Questions	Jon	You	Your partner
1 . . . go to work?	3.30	8.00	8.00
2 . . . have breakfast?	3.15	10.15	4.00
3 . . . get to work?	4.00	4.30	1.00
4 . . . go home?	7.15	5.00	5.00
5 . . . get home?	7.45	5.30	5.30

3 Write your times on the chart.

4 Make questions from the chart, like this:

What time do you go to work?

5 Ask another student the questions. Write their times on the chart.

15

ENGLISH IN ACTION

Prepare to go shopping in Britain.

1 **Work with another student. Match the things in the picture to the places. Ask and answer, like this:**

A: Where do you go for a beer?

B: To a pub.

a bank   a shop   a pub   a post office
a Tourist Information Centre

2 **Work with another student. Ask for things from the picture.**

Example: A: Can I have a stamp, please?
         B: Yes, here you are.

3 📼 **Listen to this conversation.**

1 Where are the two people?
2 What does the customer buy?
3 How much are they?

4 **Listen again. What question does the customer ask?**

5 **Complete these dialogues.**

IN A PUB

A: *Can* I have a whisky and *an* orange juice, please?
B: Yes, here you are. Anything else?
A: No, thank *you*
B: That'll be £2.30, *please*
A: Thank you.

IN A TOURIST INFORMATION CENTRE

A: Can *I* have *a* map of London, please?
B: Certainly. Anything *else?*
A: *Yes*, please. A list of hotels and restaurants, please.
B: Anything else?
A: No, *thank* you.

6 **Practise the dialogues with another student.**

You are in a street in Britain.

7 **Go to the pub, the post office, the shops, the bank, and the Tourist Information Centre. Ask for different things.**

Language review 2

1 Verbs

• **Key verb: *to be* + nouns and adjectives**

Positive

I	am	
She/he/it	is	a student
You/we/they	are	hot

• **Key verb: can – asking for things**

Can	+ Subject	+ Main verb	+ Object
Can	I	have	a coffee, please?

• **Key verb: auxiliary *do* in questions**

To make questions add auxiliary verb *do*.

	Auxiliary	Subject	Main Verb	
Positive Question	Do	You you	go go	to school. to school?

a Complete the sentences with *is* or *are*.

Example: Susan *is*. at school – Susan is at school.

1 The bank *is*. closed on Saturday.
2 Ali and Mohamed *are* at home.
3 Sumiko and I *are* in the classroom.
4 Pedro *is* a receptionist.
5 Post offices *are* open at 9 o'clock.

b Change the nouns in the sentences in exercise a to *she, he, it, we* or *they*.

Example: Susan is at school – She is at school.

c What do you say in a post office to ask for:

3 postcards?
7 stamps?
1 airmail letter?
1 map of London?

Example: Can I have 3 postcards, please.

d Make questions.

1 Where/you/come from?
2 How/you/spell/your surname?
3 What time/you/go/school?
4 What time/you/get/home?
5 When/you/go/cinema?

e Answer the questions in exercise d in complete sentences.

Example: 1 – I come from Brazil.

2 Prepositions

• **With certain verbs**

come *from*	I come *from* Switzerland.
go *to*	I go *to* work at 7 am.
get *to*	I get *to* the office at 7.30 am.

• **With places**

In	**At**
in Australia	*at* home
in London	*at* work
in a hotel	*at* school

• **With time**

What time do you have breakfast?
At 7 o' clock *in* the morning.

What time are the shops open?
From 9 am *to* 5.30 pm, from Monday to Saturday.

What day are they closed?
On Sunday.

f Complete this text about Maria with *to, at, from, in* or *on*.

On Monday I go *to*. the office *at* 8 o'clock. I get there *at* about 8.15 am. I work *in* the same office as Duncan Edwards. He comes *from* Scotland. *From* 9 o'clock *to*. 12.30 pm, I write letters and answer the telephone. Then we go *to*. a café for lunch. *At* 2 o'clock, I go back *in* the office. I go home *at* about 6 o'clock and read a book before I go *to*. bed.

g Now write a similar text about you.

The family, plural nouns

A nuclear family
Son, father, daughter, mother.

A single parent family
One parent and one or more children.

An extended family
Father, grandmother, uncle, cousins, grandfather, aunt, mother, brother, sister.

1 Revision

🖳 Listen and tick (✓) the pronunciation of the final *s*.

	/s/	/z/	/ız/
hotels		✓	
cigarettes	✓		
offices			✓
stamps	✓		
pubs		✓	
oranges			✓
shops	✓		
eggs		✓	
postcards		✓	
schools		✓	

2 Vocabulary: families

1 Work with another student. Put the family vocabulary from the photographs above in the correct column.

👩 Women/girls	👨 Men/boys	👩👨 Both
mother aunt sister grand-mother daughter	Father uncle grandfather brother son	cousins ~~one~~ parent children

2 🖳 Listen and check your answers. Mark the stress.

NB	**Spelling of plural nouns**

Singular	Plural
person	people
man	men
woman	women
family	families

What is the plural of *child*?
What is the plural of *baby*?

3 Grammar

Possessive *'s*

1 Look at the photograph of the single-parent family. Use this information to name the people.

Jon comes from Australia. He's a single parent with two children, a girl called Alison and a boy called Alex.

2 Complete these sentences.

Example: Jon is . . . father. – Jon is Alex's father.

1 Alex is Jon's son.
2 Alex is Alison's brother.
3 Alison is Jon's daughter.
4 Alison is Alex's sister.
5 Jon is Alex and Alison's father.

3 Look at the photograph of Jon's family. Ask and answer about the objects below like this:

A: Whose is this?
B: Alison's.

4 Now ask and answer about things in your class.

4 Speaking

> Jon *has got* 2 children.
> The average family in the world *has got* 3.9 children.

1 Look at the map. What do you think – how many children has the average family in these places got? Complete the chart below.

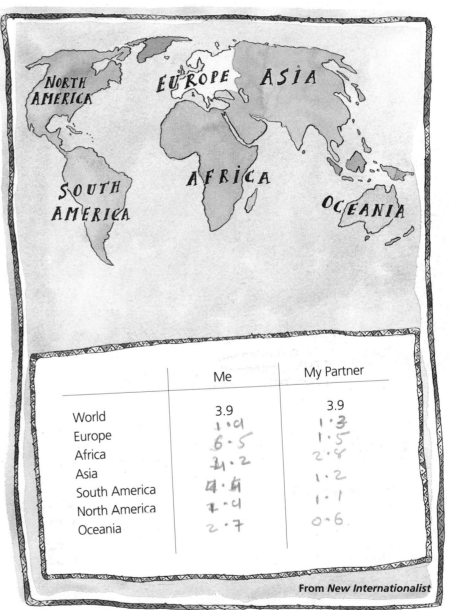

	Me	My Partner
World	3.9	3.9
Europe	1.9	1.3
Africa	6.5	1.5
Asia	21.2	2.8
South America	4.5	1.2
North America	7.9	1.1
Oceania	2.7	0.6

From *New Internationalist*

2 Ask another student. Write what she/he thinks.

3 Now look at the map on page 126. Are you correct? Is your partner correct?

4 Work with other students. Name two countries in each continent.

SPIRITUALS

The Spiritual is one of the most famous

forms of American folk music. In the

1800s black workers on plantations often

sang this type of religious song.

He's got the whole world in His hands
He's got the whole world in His hands
He's got the whole world in His hands
He's got the whole world in His hands

5 Listening

1 **Read the words of the song above and answer this question: Who is *He*?**

2 **[cassette] Listen and number the subject of each verse.**

the whole world . .*1*.   brother . .*2*.   daughter . . .
mother . . .   father . . .   baby .*3*.
all of us .*4*.   son . . .   sister . .*?*.

Pronunciation: /h/

1 **[cassette] Listen and repeat.**

/h/   /h/   /h/ /h/
He's got the whole world in His hands.

2 **Practise the words and sing the song.**

6 Grammar: inverted questions

Have got

| How many children *has* he *got*? | He *has* He's | *got* | 2. |
| How many children *have* you *got*? | I *have* I've | *got* | 3. |

1 **Ask other students about their families.**

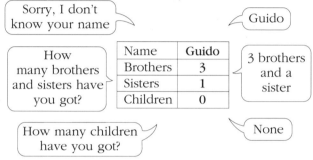

Name	Guido
Brothers	3
Sisters	1
Children	0

2 **Tell the class about other students, like this:**

Guido has got three brothers, one sister and no children.

To be

	My family	*is*	small.
	Is	your family	small?
How big	*is*	your family?	

1 **Complete these personal questions.**

1 What . . . your name?
2 What . . . your address?
3 What . . . your telephone number?
4 *Are* you married or single?
5 . . . you a student?

2 **Ask and answer these questions with another student.**

Numbers: teens and tens;
Key verb: *to be* + ages

Caroline and Nick Evans
are proud to announce
the arrival of their new baby girl
Sarah
Date of birth 7th May 1985
Time 5.00a.m. *Weight* 4 kilos
Colour of eyes Blue
Colour of hair Brown
Mother and baby are fine.

7 Reading

1 Read the card above and answer these questions.

1 What's the baby's first name?
2 What's the baby's surname?
3 Is the baby a boy or a girl?
4 Is the baby big or small?
5 What colour are her eyes?
6 What colour is her hair?
7 Is the baby OK?

2 Ask other students – *How are you?*

Fine

OK

Not too good

8 Pronunciation: ages

1 Look at the card again. How old is the baby now?

2 ▣ Listen and repeat these numbers.

2	12	20
3	13	30
4	14	40

3 Now predict how you say these numbers.

5	15	50
6	16	60
7	17	70
8	18	80
9	19	90

4 ▣ Listen. Are you correct?

5 ▣ Listen. Which number do you hear?

1 Michelle is thirteen/thirty.
2 Elena and Paloma are fourteen/forty.
3 Craig is fifteen/fifty.
4 Andrew and Tony are sixteen/sixty.
5 Alfonso is seventeen/seventy.
6 Françoise is eighteen/eighty.
7 Abdullah and Mohamed are nineteen/ninety.

9 Writing

1 Look at the sentences below. What does each *'s* mean?

a possessive *'s*
b the verb *has*
c the verb *is*

My brother**'s** name is Paul. He**'s** thirty-four.
He**'s** married and he**'s** got three children.

2 Write about someone in your family.

3 Read your partner's work and ask questions.

Example: A: How old are your children?
B: They're six and twelve.

> **NB Age**
>
> Age = *to be* + number
>
> Carmen *is* twenty-five.
> How old *are* Eduardo and Roberto?
> They *are* thirty-seven.
>
> How old are you?

21

Homestay New Zealand
New Zealanders are known as friendly, happy, hospitable people. On farmstay and homestay visits you can share the li...

Host Farms and Homestays
To experience the real Australian lifestyle, you can stay as a pavi... guest with friendly ...

Ireland Welcomes You
Stay with an Irish family in a town or country home for a ...rm welcome ...d com-

---

You go to an English-speaking family

for a week.

1 Look at these advertisements. Where do you go? You decide.

2 What do you think? What questions do the family ask you? Make a list with another student.

Example: Where do you come from?

3 🔲 Listen to the family. How many of their questions are on your list?

4 Listen again. Write the other questions. Answer all the questions.

5 Write questions to ask people in the family. Here are their answers. What are the questions?

Example: My mother's name is Mary. – What's your mother's name?

1 My big brother is fourteen.
2 I've got two children.
3 Both my parents are nearly ninety.
4 My grandchildren's names are Steve and Jane.
5 Jane is six and Steve is fourteen.
6 My daughter has got two children.
7 My sister is only six. years old

6 Discuss with another student.

How many people are in this family? Who are they?

7 You've got five presents. Match the presents to the parcels.

Example: A – 4

1 Perfume   2 Pen   3 Book

4 Box of chocolates   5 Flowers

8 What do you give to each person?

Example: The flowers are for the grandmother.

Language review 3

1 Nouns

• **Plurals**

Irregular nouns		Nouns ending in *y*	
Singular	**Plural**	**Singular**	**Plural**
person	people	baby	babies
man	men	family	families
child	children		
woman	women		

a Change these sentences to the plural.

Example: I am a student – We are students.

1 She is an old woman. *They are old women.*
2 You are a baby. *You are babies.*
3 It is a big family. *They are big families.*
4 He is a good person. *They are good person People.*
5 She is a small child. *They are small children.*

2 Verbs

• **Key verb: *to be* + age**

Questions	Answers
Are you ten?	No, I'm eight.
How old is he?	He's thirty.

• **Key verb: *to be* in questions**

Positive

I	am	
You/we/they	are	late.
She/he/it	is	

Question

Am	I	
Are	you/we/they	late?
Is	she/he/it	

• **Key verb: *have got***

Positive

I/you/we/they	have	got	a big family.
She/he/it	has		

Question

Have	I/you/we/they	got	a big family?
Has	she/he/it		

b Make questions from the sentences in exercise a above.

Example: I am a student – Am I a student?

c Here are some answers. Write the questions.

Example:
I've got three children. – How many children have you got?

1 . . .? Toast and coffee.
2 . . .? No, he's married.
3 . . .? I'm thirty-four.
4 . . .? Two, a girl and a boy.
5 . . .? No, I come from Australia.
6 . . .? I'm fine.

d Look at this family tree. Complete the sentences with the correct verb.

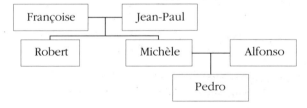

Françoise and Jean-Paul . . . married. They . . . . . . two children, Robert and Michèle. Michèle . . . married to Alfonso. They . . . . . . a son, Pedro.

3 Possessive *'s*

Questions	Answers
Whose pen is this?	It's Susan*'s*
Whose parents are they?	They're George*'s*

With two or more names, write *'s* with the last name only.

Whose child is she?   She's Alison and Martin*'s*.

e Complete these sentences with names from the family tree in exercise d above.

Example:
Jean-Paul is . . . grandfather. – Jean-Paul is Pedro's grandfather.

1 Françoise is . . . mother.
2 Michèle is . . . daughter.
3 Alfonso is . . . father.
4 Robert is . . . son.
5 Françoise is . . . grandmother.

4 It's a small world

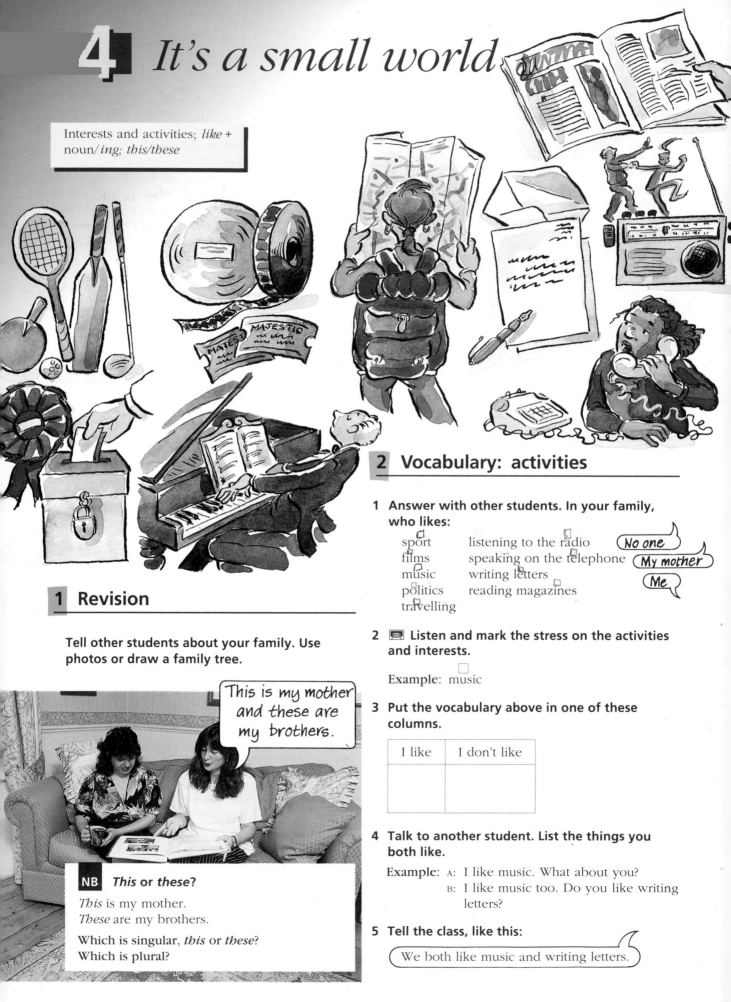

1 Revision

Tell other students about your family. Use photos or draw a family tree.

> This is my mother and these are my brothers.

NB ***This* or *these*?**

This is my mother.
These are my brothers.

Which is singular, *this* or *these*?
Which is plural?

2 Vocabulary: activities

1 **Answer with other students. In your family, who likes:**

sport   listening to the radio   No one
films   speaking on the telephone My mother
music   writing letters   Me
politics   reading magazines
travelling

2 ▣ **Listen and mark the stress on the activities and interests.**

Example: music

3 **Put the vocabulary above in one of these columns.**

I like	I don't like

4 **Talk to another student. List the things you both like.**

Example: A: I like music. What about you?
         B: I like music too. Do you like writing letters?

5 **Tell the class, like this:**

> We both like music and writing letters.

24

3 Writing

1 Look at these examples then complete the sentence below.

+ and +	I like tea *and* coffee.
− or −	I don't like tea *or* coffee.
+ but −	I like tea *but* I don't like coffee.
− but +	I don't like coffee *but* I like tea.

I like listening to the radio . . . watching television . . . I don't like
going to the cinema . . . the theatre.

2 Write three short sentences about your likes and dislikes.

**3 Use *and/but/or* to make one long sentence from your three
sentences.**

4 Grammar: *-ing* form

1 Write the verbs from these activities.

Activity	Verb
reading magazines	read
writing letters	write
listening to the radio	listen
speaking on the telephone	speak
travelling	travel

2 Match the verbs below to the pictures on this page.

watch television   wash   cook   do housework   sleep   eat   work
    5   1   4   6   7   2   3

3 Now write the activities from these verbs.

**4 Talk to another student. How many hours a day do you spend
on these activities?**

Example: Watching television? About an hour a day.

5 What do you think? In a lifetime, the average American spends:

15   23   3   7   6   4

7 years washing
6 years eating
4 years doing housework
23 years sleeping
15 years working/studying
3 years cooking

**6 Read the results from an American magazine survey on page
127. Are you correct?**

Miss Yolanda Kuipers
Mondriaanlaan 27, LG
Mussellianaal, G381,
Netherlands

In the 18-25 age group,
Yolanda, a student,
would like to correspond
with people from France.
Her interests are
volleyball, reading,
surfing and going to
discos.

Mr Dieter Giese
Bahnofstr Beiseforth. 6
4026 Malsfeld, Germany

Would like to correspond
with people between
ages 20 to 40. Mr Giese
is in the 20-40 age group
and his interests are
music, travelling, reading
and sport.

Natasa Visar
Matla Belic 16.41236
Ljubljana Yugoslavia

Aged 18, Natasa would
like to correspond with
people from anywhere in
the world. Her interests
are foreign countries,
pop music, sports,
dancing, travelling and
films.

Mr Alberto Lovana
PO Box 1462 08080
Barcelona. Spain

Would like to be a friend
of other BBC listeners in
other countries Aged 27.
Interested in reading,
film, travel and music.

motorbike owners in
other countries. Aged
27. Also interested in
ballet and the arts.

Ms Azeb Daramola
PO Box 32106 Addis
Ababa Ethiopia

Aged 25, Azeb would
like a male penfriend
from anywhere in the
world. Interested in
reading, travel, sports
and music.

Danuta Kubny
Ul.Puszkina /1 35-4
Rzezow, Poland

A student, enjoys
reading, talking to
people, writing letters.
Aged 21. Interested in
reading, travel and
music.

Paolo Schieso.
Via Corno 2-6,1. 19600,
Pisa Italy

He speaks Russian,
German, Chinese and a
little English. His interests are literature, travel
and correspondence.

Ali Bangura
c/o 25 Lower East Street
Freetown, Sierra Leone,
West Africa

Aged 18, interested in
cricket, listening to the
radio and writing letters.
Would like to correspond
with people all over the
world.

Dear
16

From BBC English

5 Reading

1 Read the page above from the magazine *BBC English* and complete the chart.

Name	Age	Country	Interests
Alberto Lovana	27	spain	reading and film travel and music
Azeb Daramola	25	ethiopia	read travel sports and music
Danuta Kubny	21	poland	all
Ali Bangura	18	Africa	cricket
Natasa Visar	18	yugoslavia	pop music, sports dancing, travelling and films.

2 🖥 Listen and repeat these questions.

1 How old is Alberto?
2 Where does he come from?
3 What does he like doing?

3 Work with another student and check your answers on the chart.

6 Grammar: Present Simple

Questions

1 Complete these questions with *do* or *does*.

Where . . . Alberto come from?
Where . . . you come from?

. . . he like music?
. . . you like reading?

2 Write three questions about your teacher.

Example: Where does she/he come from?

3 Ask another student your questions. Ask your teacher if you don't know the answers.

3rd person *s*

1 Look at this information about Danuta Kubny. Complete the sentences about you.

She comes from Poland.	I come from India.
She is 21 years old.	I am 23 years old
She likes reading and music.	I like reading and music.

2 🖥 Listen. Add the verbs to the correct column.

eats   sleeps   does housework
washes   works   studies
cooks   reads   listens

	/s/	/z/	/ɪz/
She/he	likes	comes	watches

3 Tell another student about your daily routine, like this:

I get up at 7.00. I wash and . . .

4 Tell the class about your partner's routine.

ALTA RICA
A bold
ADVENTURE
in TASTE

They come down from the high sierras. Bearing the finest arabica beans of Latin America. Across the most inhospitable terrain they trek until the precious cargo is safely delivered. Then the specially selected beans are high-roasted to create a rich, full-bodied coffee. A coffee with a distinctive aroma and character. A coffee we call 'Alta Rica'.

NESCAFE
ALTA RICA

Your promise of perfect coffees.

TESCO
SPANISH
WINES

perrier

I kneau what I like.

7 Listening

1 Look at these advertisements. What are they advertising?

1 Where do these products come from?
2 Which can you buy in the shops in your country?
3 Which are expensive? Which are cheap?

2 🖭 Listen to this shop assistant from a big American department store. Which products have they got?

- Perfume from France or perfume from Egypt?
- Oranges from America or oranges from Spain?
- Tea from Ceylon or tea from India?
- Coffee from Brazil or coffee from Kenya?
- Chocolates from Britain or chocolates from Switzerland?
- Flowers from Holland or flowers from Germany?
- Wine from Italy or wine from Portugal?

3 Listen again. Write the nationality words you hear.

Example: French.

4 Work with another student. What do they sell in the department store? Make a list.

Example: French perfume, American oranges . . .

NB   Position of adjectives

The shop assistant is *American*. He sells *Italian* wine.

Do adjectives generally go before or after nouns in your language?

---

8 Pronunciation

Nationalities

1 Work with another student. Write the countries.

Country	Nationality
Italy	Italian
Spain	Spanish
Portugal	Portuguese
Egypt	Egyptian
Germany	German
Japan	Japanese
Hungary	Hungarian

2 🖭 Listen and mark the stress on the countries and nationalities.

☐   ☐
Example: Italy – Italian

3 Add two or three other countries and nationalities to your list.

9 Speaking

1 Look at the information in *BBC English* on page 26 about Paolo Schieso. List the other languages he speaks.

He speaks Italian . . .

2 Ask and answer with another student. What languages do they speak in:

Australia? Argentina?
Brazil? Switzerland?
Algeria?

3 What languages do you speak? Ask other students.

4 Tell the class about other students. How many students speak the same languages as you?

ENGLISH IN ACTION

You would like a penfriend.

1 Read Paolo's letter to *BBC English*. What information is in the letter but not in the penfriend advertisement on page 26?

Via Como 2-6. 1
19600 Pisa
Italy

8 May 1991

Dear Sir/Madam,
        I am writing to ask for a penfriend. I am 18 years old and come from Italy. I speak Russian, German, Chinese, Italian and a little English. I like literature, travel and writing letters. Please put this information on the Penfriends' page in your magazine.

Yours faithfully,
Paolo Schieso

(P. SCHIESO)

2 Work with another student. Check how to write formal letters in English.

- Where do you write your address?
- Where do you write your name?
- Where do you write the date?
- How do you begin?
- How do you finish?

3 Now *you* write to *BBC English* and ask for a penfriend. Answer these questions in your letter.

- How old are you?
- Where do you come from?
- What languages do you speak?
- How big is your family?
- What are your interests?

4 ▣ Listen and write the address of *BBC English*. Send your letter to this address.

BBC English Magazine

Language review 4

1 Adjectives: nationalities

Country	Nationality
America	American
Argentina	Argentinian
Australia	Australian
Brazil	Brazilian
Britain	British
Greece	Greek
Holland	Dutch
Italy	Italian
Japan	Japanese
Portugal	Portuguese
Spain	Spanish
Turkey	Turkish

a Write three sentences about the people below.

Example: She/Holland.
She comes from Holland. She's Dutch. She speaks Dutch.

1 They/Brazil.   5 You/Argentina.
2 He/Japan.   6 You both/Turkey.
3 We/Italy.   7 Melissa and Doreen/America.
4 She/Portugal.   8 I . . .

2 *This* or *these*?

Singular	Plural
This is a pen.	These are pens.
This is a magazine.	These are magazines.

b Write two sentences for each picture.

Example: . . . Japanese radio.
This is a Japanese radio. This radio is Japanese.

1 . . . Dutch flowers.
2 . . . Spanish wine.
3 . . . Brazilian coffee.
4 . . . an Italian stamp.

3 Verbs

• **Present Simple: Key verb: *like***

Positive

I/you/we/they	like	tea.
She/he/it	likes	

Question

Do	I/you/we/they	like	tea?
Does	she/he/it		

c Put the words in the correct order and make questions.

Example: does eat what she? – What does she eat?

1 get up what does time he? whalt time does he get up
2 does work where she?
3 to shops the when he does go?
4 home do she does at what?
5 bed he go time to what does?
6 she sleep how hours does many?

• **– *ing* form**

Activities.
Read*ing* is one of my interests.
***Like* + verb + *ing*.**
I like read*ing*.

d Think of a person in your family and answer the questions in exercise d.

Example: My grandmother gets up at . . . Then she . . .

e Name the activities on the left.

f Look at the pictures in exercise e. Which activities do you like doing?

4 *and/but*

    +   +
I like tea *and* coffee.

    +   –
I like tea *but* I don't like coffee.

g Complete the sentences below with *and* or *but*.

Example: I'm English . . . I work in France.
I'm English but I work in France.

1 I'm Brazilian . . . I don't like Brazilian films.
2 He likes doing housework . . . going shopping.
3 I'm English . . . I don't understand all Americans.
4 I speak German, French . . . a little Italian.
5 She likes the cinema . . . she prefers television.

5 Consolidation

1 Across cultures: politeness

Revises:
Vocabulary: Polite expressions; places
Grammar: *Can I have*; Key verb: *to be*

1 Read this information about politeness in Britain. What do you think? Are British people polite?

2 Tell another student about politeness in your country. What is the same as in Britain? What is different in your country?

ARE THEY polite?

1 A bar of chocolate, please.

30p, please.

Thank you.

Here's 20p change.

Thank you.

Thank you, goodbye.

1 PLEASE AND THANK YOU

British people say *please* and *thank you* a lot but it is not necessary to reply with a special word when they say *thank you* to you.

2 SORRY

They also say *sorry* a lot. They say *Sorry, I don't understand* and *Sorry, I don't know*. They also say *sorry* when they mean sorry! For example, if they get to school at 10.15 and the class is at 10 o'clock, they say *Sorry I'm late*.

3 SIR/MADAM

Sir for a man and *Madam* for a woman are used in formal letters when the writer does not know the person's name and to customers in some hotels and restaurants.

Hello, Mike.

Hi, Clare.

4 NAMES

They use first names a lot. *Mr, Mrs, Miss,* and *Ms* are not used without the person's surname.

5 EXCUSE ME

British people say *Excuse me*, not *Sir* or *Madam*, to get another person's attention.

6 QUEUES

In Britain people queue in cinemas, shops, post offices, banks and lots of other places.

2

Good evening, Sir. **3**

Dear Sir or Madam,
Thank you
for your letter

4

Dear Mrs Downs,
Thank you for
your recent
application
for the
vacancy

Mr G. Telson,
48, Singleton Road,
London,
N4 1AB

5

Excuse me.

6

3 What do you say in these situations?

4 Choose one or two of these situations. Practise the complete conversation with another student.

2 You ask a woman in the street, the time.

1 You ask for two coffees and a tea in a café.

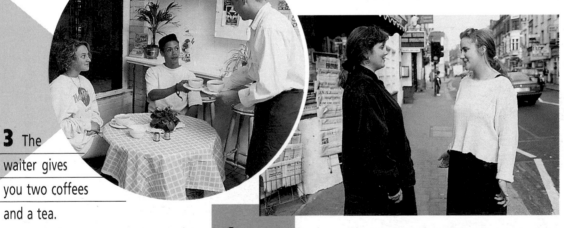

3 The waiter gives you two coffees and a tea.

4 Another person asks you *Where is the bank?* and you don't know.

5 You want to buy a book but the shop assistant is not looking at you.

6 Your friend is waiting at the cinema. You get to the cinema at 8.05 pm and the film is at 8 o'clock.

2 Thinking about learning: vocabulary

> **Revises:**
> Vocabulary: Places; breakfast food and drink; numbers; days of the week; families; countries; *to like*
> Grammar: Sentence formation

1 With another student, put the words below into these different groups.

1 breakfast food and drink
2 numbers
3 days of the week
4 family members
5 continents and countries
6 interests

tea	father	reading	twenty-five	coffee
ham	Monday	sport	hot chocolate	Sunday
cheese	Europe	music	grandmother	two
baby	sugar	toast	Thursday	films
son	Friday	daughter	Wednesday	seventy
butter	eggs	eight	Australia	brother
Asia	Africa	forty-five	Greece	France

2 Add other words you know to each group.

3 Work with another student. Organise the continents and countries like this:

post office

cinema — places — school — teacher

restaurant — student

4 Look at other ways to organise vocabulary. Which ways do you like? Which ways don't you like?

5 Choose ten words from the different groups. Mark the stress on these words.

6 Put your words in sentences. Show your work to other students. Look at their sentences. Are they in good English?

Translation
an apple – une pomme
an egg – un œuf
cheese – fromage
sugar – sucre
butter – beurre

Pictures
cigarettes
flowers
a book
a pen

Example sentences
My grandmother is my mother's mother.
My brother is my mother's son.

Grammar table

Singular	Plural
shop	shops
tomato	tomatoes
baby	babies
child	children

Opposites

hot / cold
black / white
big / small

3 Language in context: numbers

Revises:
Vocabulary: Alphabet; numbers
Grammar: Present Simple questions

1 📼 Listen to these football supporters, at a football match. What team do they support?

2 **Listen again and complete the chant.**

2, 4, 6, 8,
Who do we appreciate?
S c o t l a n d
' Scotland !

3 **Work with other students. Change the chant. Support your favourite team.**

4 📼 **Listen to three dialogues. For each dialogue, answer these questions.**

1 How many people speak?
2 Where are they?

5 **Listen again. Write the numbers you hear in each dialogue.**

Dialogue 1	Dialogue 2	Dialogue 3
a. 4 age	e. 6:45 Time	g 8:30 to 4 time
b. 12 age	f 37.14356 Telephone	h 5:30 "
c. 16 age		i 1:44 money
d 5:15 Time home		

15

6 **Work with another student. Which numbers refer to *money/time/age/a telephone number*?**

Example: a – age

7 **Listen again. Are you correct?**

8 **Listen again. Write the questions they ask about:**

• age
• the time children get home
• a telephone number
• bank opening times
• a map
• the price

9 **Work with another student. Practise the questions and answers.**

Check what you know!

Now turn to page 128 and complete
Check what you know 1.

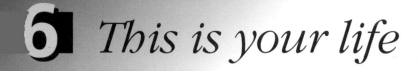

6 This is your life

Jobs; *a/an* + jobs; *What do you do?*

1 Revision

1 Name these jobs.

Example: a tesutdn – a student
a reetach
a aiwtre
a hsop tssasitan

2 🖥 **Listen. What is this person's job?**

3 Listen again. Which of these things does she do at work?

open the shop	answer the phone
read sports magazines	teach English
write letters	serve customers
cook	

Which of these things does she like doing?

2 Vocabulary: jobs

1 Write three sentences about your job or the job of another person in your family. Do not name the job! Think about these questions.

Where do you work? *wr. cd. srhs*
What do you do at work? *book are read*
What do you like doing at work? *phone si*

2 Read your sentences to other students. They guess the name of your job.

3 Ask other students about their jobs.

Example: A: What do you do?
B: I'm a teacher

4 Write what you remember. Ask again if necessary. Mark the stress on the jobs.

☐
Maria is a dentist
☐
Julio is a teacher

Pronunciation: *do*

1	2
/djʊ/	/duː/
What do you do?	

1 🖥 **Listen. Which *do* is stressed, 1 or 2?**

2 🖥 **Listen to these questions. Which word has got main stress?**

1 Where do you work/study?
2 What do you do at work/school/university?
3 What time do you start?
4 What time do you finish?

3 Ask another student the questions above.

3 Reading

1 Before you read, look at the pictures below. Find an astronaut, a politician, a soldier and a pilot.

2 Look at the pictures again. How many famous people can you name?

3 Read the History Quiz and match the dates to the historical events.

History Quiz

When did...

Petrograd change its name to Leningrad?
Cory Aquino become the President of the Philippines?
Pope John Paul II visit South America?
James Earl Ray assassinate Martin Luther King?
Amelia Earhart fly across the Atlantic?
Valentina Tereshkova become the first woman in space?
The French Revolution start? – 1489
The Second World War finish? –1945
Marie Curie discover radium? –1910
Columbus get to America? –1492
The Berlin Wall come down? – 1489
Napoleon win his famous victory at Austerlitz? – 1805

August 1945   November 1989

September 1910   February 1986

June 1963   January 1924

July 1789   May 1932

April 1968

December 1805

March 1983   October 1492

Vocabulary: months

1 🎧 Listen. Correct your answers to the History Quiz.

2 Listen again. Put the months in the correct stress columns. Which months look or sound the same in your language?

☐ March	☐☐ August	☐☐	☐☐☐	☐☐☐

3 Ask another student these questions.

1 Which months are hot/cold in your country?
2 Which month does the school year start/finish?
3 Which month do you usually go on holiday?

4 Grammar

Past Simple questions and answers

Did the French Revolution start in July 1789?	Yes, it *did*. No, it *didn't*

Test another student's history, like this:

A: Did Columbus get to America in August 1492?
B: No, he didn't.

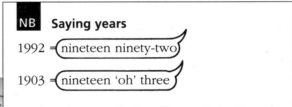

NB **Saying years**

1992 = nineteen ninety-two

1903 = nineteen 'oh' three

Look at the years in the History Quiz. How do you say them?

> Ordinal numbers; *on* + dates; *yesterday, today, tomorrow*; Possessive adjectives: *my, your, her, his*

5 Speaking

Work in groups. Guess what different students did at the weekend. Use the verbs below.

Example: Did you go to the cinema?

listen	read	write	watch	speak	have
go	get	visit	finish	start	buy
work	study	sleep	wash	eat	cook	do

6 Pronunciation: /f/, /s/, /θ/, /ð/

1 Complete this chart.

Write last Saturday's date.
Write yesterday's date.
Write today's date.
Write tomorrow's date.

Date	Month	Year
15	12	95

2 📖 **Listen and repeat the numbers.**

1st/2nd/3rd/4th/5th/6th/7th/8th/9th/10th

3 Predict how you say these numbers.

18th/21st/22nd/23rd/30th/31st

4 📖 **Listen and check your pronunciation.**

5 📖 **Listen and repeat these words.**

/ð/ /f/   /ð/ /s/   /ð/ /θ/
The first. The second. The third.

6 Say these tongue twisters.

It's 1st February 1345.
It's 2nd February 1345.
It's 3rd February 1345.

> **NB** **Saying dates**
>
> Write: 10th December 1995
>
> Say: *the* 10th *of* December 1995
>
> What's the date today?

HIS NUMBER'S UP!

King Henry IV of France was the 14th king of France and Navarre. By coincidence, he was born on 14 December 1553, and won his most decisive victory on 14 March 1590. But King Henry's luck finally changed after a papal ban was placed on him by Pope Gregory XIV – because the King died, the victim of assassination, on 14 May 1610!

From Clar

7 Reading

1 Read the text above. What number is important?

2 Read the text again. Answer these questions.

1 What was the King's name? *King Henry IV*
2 Where did he come from? *France*
3 When did he win an important victory? *14 march 1590*
4 What was the Pope's name? *Gregory XIV*
5 When did the King die? *14 may 1610*

Grammar: *my, your, her, his*

1 Complete this sentence.

When was the King's birthday?
His birthday was on . . .

2 📖 **Listen and answer this question.**

Whose birthday is it today?
Her birthday is on . . .

3 When is your birthday? Ask other students and write a list.

> Birthdays
> Gabriella – 14th February.
> Ulrich – 2nd March
> Spiros – 20th September

4 Tell the class who you spoke to. When is her/ his birthday?

> I spoke to Gabriella. Her birthday is on the 14th of February.

8 Listening

1 🖵 **Listen to an interview about Richard Branson, the British businessman. Complete these sentences.**

He finished school in 1967

He started work in 1967

He opened his first shop in 1971

He made his first £1,000,000 in 1973

2 Listen again. What questions did the interviewer ask?

3 🖵 **Listen to the pronunciation of these three regular verbs. Do they end with /d/, /t/ or /ɪd/?**

finished

started

opened

9 Grammar: Past Simple

Past Simple regular	
listened	visited
liked	washed
talked	closed
watched	worked

1 Look at the Past Simple forms above and answer these questions.

1 What is the infinitive of each verb?

2 How do you make the regular Past Simple form?

2 🖵 **Listen and repeat the verbs above.**

3 Tell another student which things above you did yesterday.

Example: I listened to the radio.

4 Match these irregular Past Simple forms to their present forms.

Present	Past
make	did
get	spoke
have	made
do	ate
speak	got
buy	went
write	was
read	gave
am/is	wrote
go	had
eat	read
give	bought

5 🖵 **Listen and check your answers.**

6 Write five sentences. Say what you did last week.

Example: I went to the cinema.

ENGLISH IN ACTION

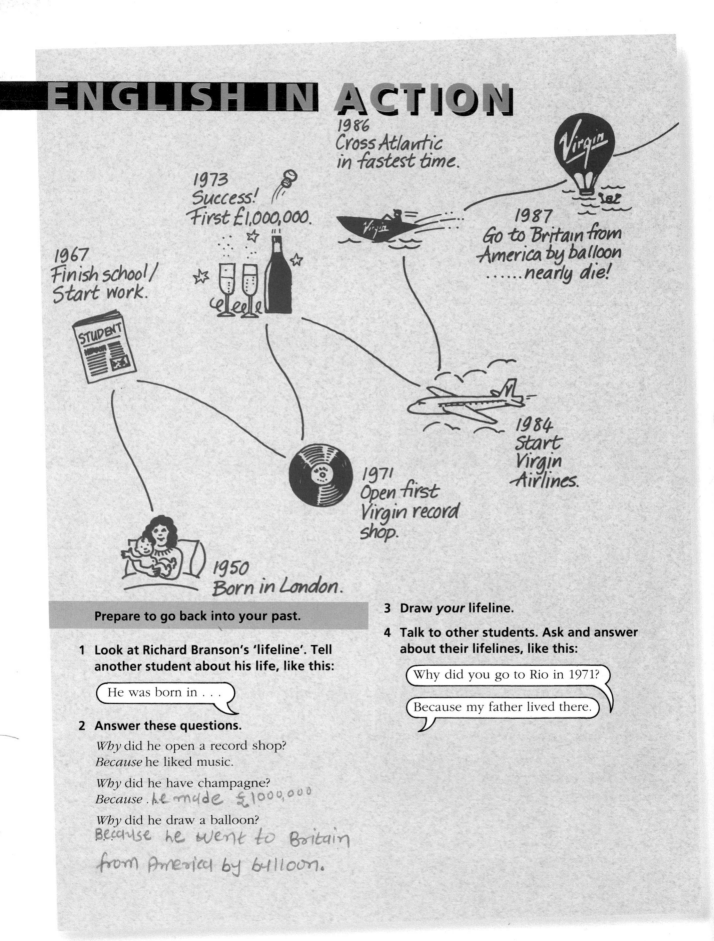

1986
Cross Atlantic
in fastest time.

1973
Success!
First £1,000,000.

1987
Go to Britain from
America by balloon
......nearly die!

1967
Finish school/
Start work.

STUDENT

1984
Start
Virgin
Airlines.

1971
Open first
Virgin record
shop.

1950
Born in London.

Prepare to go back into your past.

1 Look at Richard Branson's 'lifeline'. Tell another student about his life, like this:

> He was born in . . .

2 Answer these questions.

Why did he open a record shop?
Because he liked music.

Why did he have champagne?
Because .he made £1,000,000

Why did he draw a balloon?
Because he went to Britain
from America by balloon.

3 Draw *your* lifeline.

4 Talk to other students. Ask and answer about their lifelines, like this:

> Why did you go to Rio in 1971?

> Because my father lived there.

Language review 6

1 Possessive adjectives: singular forms

Subject pronouns	Possessive adjectives
I	my
you	your
she	her
he	his
it	its

a Complete the sentences with *my, your, her, his*.

1 This is my sister. . . . name is Maria.
2 Hello. What's . . . name?
3 I'm a teacher. I like . . . job.
4 Antony is an actor but . . . sister is a student.

2 Verbs

• Past Simple statements

Regular verbs (verb + *ed*)		Irregular verbs	
start	started	make	made
wash	washed	get	got
listen	listened	have	had
finish	finished	go	went
open	opened	speak	spoke
walk	walked	do	did
cook	cooked	write	wrote
work	worked	sleep	slept
remember	remembered	give	gave

• Past Simple questions and short answers

Question

Did	I/you/we/they she/he/it	remember?

Short answer

No,	I/you/we/they	didn't.
Yes,	she/he/it	did.

b Write what you did this morning. Begin like this:

I got up at . . .

c Answer these questions with short answers.

Example: Did you watch TV last night? – Yes, I did.

1 Did you get up before 8.00 this morning?
2 Did you have eggs for breakfast?
3 Did you read a newspaper?
4 Did you walk to school?

3 Prepositions: dates

I go on holiday *in* July.
I went to Belgium *in* 1977.
I start work *on* Monday.
It's my birthday *on* 2nd October.

d Complete with *in* or *on*.

1 School started . . . September.
2 They went on holiday . . . 20th June.
3 He got home . . . Monday.
4 We went to America . . . 1989.

4 Why/because

Why does he go to school? Because he's a teacher.
Why have I got presents? Because it's your birthday.

e Join a sentence from column A to a sentence from column B. Make one sentence using *and, but* or *because*.

Example: I know his name (but) I don't know his address.

A	B
1 I know his name.	a The students are friendly.
2 He speaks Arabic.	b I don't know his address.
3 They stayed at home.	c They watched TV.
4 They had champagne.	d She speaks Japanese.
5 She speaks Chinese.	e She passed her exams.
6 I like teaching.	f He lived in Egypt.

Yeni Hotel ★★★ Istanbul, Turkey

Yeni Hotel offers you 138 elegantly furnished rooms, each with direct telephone, minibar, 3-channel radio, TV with satellite. There is a restaurant, a breakfast room and an American bar with a comfortable and modern atmosphere.

. . . .

Yeni Hotel 138 odası, restoranı, kahvaltı salonu, Amerikan barı, odalarında telefonu, minibari, 3-kanal müziği ve uydu yayını ile size rahat, modern ve çağdaş bir ortam sunar.

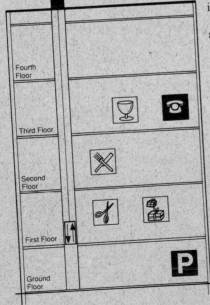

Fourth Floor

Third Floor

Second Floor

First Floor

Ground Floor

1 Revision

Ask other students about their holidays last year. Use these words to make questions.

1 Where/go on holiday last year?
2 Who/go with?
3 Have a good time?
4 Stay in a hotel?
5 What/do?

2 Vocabulary: hotels

1 Look at the symbols below and the Yeni Hotel brochure. Which things has the hotel got?

bathrooms with showers   a car park

a swimming pool   central-heating

twin-bedded rooms   a lift

colour televisions   a hairdresser's

2 Make a list. Which five things above are most important for you on holiday?

3 Talk to another student. Which three things are important for both of you?

3 Grammar: prepositions 2

Look at the diagram of the hotel. Where is the hairdresser's?

It's *above* the car park.   It's *in* the hotel.
It's *on* the first floor.   It's *next to* the shops.
It's *under* the restaurant.

1 Answer these questions with another student. Use each preposition above once only.

Example: Where is the lift? – It's on the first floor.

1 Where are the telephones?
2 Where are the shops?
3 Where is the car park?
4 Where is the bar?
5 Where is the restaurant?

4 Reading

1 Read the Yeni Hotel brochure.

1 Where is the hotel?
2 How big is it?

2 Read the brochure again. What facilities has the hotel got? Which sentences are correct, a or b?

1a There is a telephone in each room.
 b There are telephones only in reception.
2a There is 3-channel television in each room.
 b There is satellite television in each room.
3a There is bar service to each room.
 b There is a small bar in each room.
4a There is a special room for breakfast.
 b There is tea and coffee in each room.

5 Grammar: *there is/there are*

> *There is* a telephone in each room.
> *There are* telephones in reception.

1 Look at the example sentences above and answer these questions.

1 Is *there is* used with the singular or plural noun?
2 When do you use *there are?*
3 Is there a question form? What is it?

2 Look at the brochure again. Match the questions below to the short answers.

Example: Is there a bar in the hotel? – Yes, there is.

1 Are there many rooms in the hotel?
2 Is there a breakfast room in the hotel?
3 Are there banks in the hotel?
4 Is there a sauna in the hotel?

Yes, there is.   No, there isn't.
Yes, there are.   No, there aren't.

3 Draw a diagram of your perfect hotel.

4 Work with another student. Ask questions and draw your partner's hotel.

Example: A: Is there a bar in your hotel?
     B: Yes, there is. It's above the shops.

6 Listening

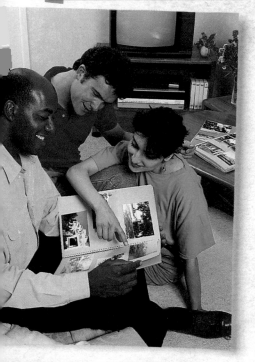

1 🖥 **Listen to this conversation. Simon and his wife Neesha are talking to their friend Rob about their honeymoon in Turkey.**

What was the most important thing for Neesha and Simon?

a A colour TV
b A private bathroom
c A double bed

2 Listen again. Are these sentences true (T) or false (F)?

1 They had a good time in Turkey. ✓ T
2 They went on Sunday evening. ✗ f
3 They got to the hotel at about 11.00 pm. ✗ f
4 They liked the receptionist. T
5 They slept in single beds. ✗ F
6 They had a black and white TV. ✗ F

7 Grammar: negatives 1

1 Read this question then complete the sentence below.

What was the problem when Neesha and Simon arrived at the hotel? The hotel had a twin-bedded room but it . . . a double room.

2 Complete the chart.

Present positive	Present negative	Past negative
I like	I don't like	I didn't like
You . . .	You don't buy	You didn't buy
She/he/it . . .	She/he/it doesn't eat	She/he/it didn't . . .
We go	We . . .	We didn't go
They finish	They . . .	They . . .

3 Write the full forms of *don't, doesn't* and *didn't*.

4 Look at the true and false sentences in Exercise 6 Listening. Listen to Neesha and Simon again. Why are some sentences false?

Example: Sentence 2 is false because they didn't go on Sunday evening. They went on Saturday evening.

5 Read this extract from Neesha's diary. Complete with *don't* or *doesn't*.

JUNE   Week 25

Monday 17

This evening I met Simon's friend, Rob. I know him very well. Simon likes Rob a lot but he _doesn't_ like Caroline, Rob's wife. Simon _doesn't_ like many people! He _doesn't_ go out or visit friends much. He prefers to stay at home. I _don't_. I'm completely different.

6 Read the diary extract again and answer these questions.

1 What doesn't Simon like?
2 What doesn't Neesha like?

8 Speaking

1 **Work with another student. Look at Neesha and Simon's honeymoon photographs and say what they did/didn't do.**

Example: They visited the Blue Mosque.

visit the Blue Mosque	buy souvenirs
watch folk dancing	go swimming
go to a Turkish bath	visit museums

9 Grammar: *our, your, their*

1 **Talk to another student. Who said this, Neesha or Rob?**

a How was *your* holiday in Istanbul?
b We went to reception and gave *our* names.
c We slept in *their* room.

Who does *your/our/their* refer to?

2 **Complete the chart.**

Subject pronoun	Possessive adjective
I	my
you	your
she	. . .
he	. . .
it	its
we	. . .
you	. . .
they	. . .

3 **Complete this conversation with *our*, *your*, or *their*.**

NEESHA: Where did you and Caroline go for *your* holiday?

ROB: We visited *our* friends, Gregg and Lauren, in Canada. They gave us *their* car for two weeks. We had a fantastic time.

SIMON: Did you take the children?

ROB: No, this was *our* holiday – just me and Caroline. The children stayed with *their* grandparents in Scotland.

NEESHA: So you had *your* second honeymoon while we had *our* first!

4 **Read the conversation again and answer these questions.**

1 Where did Rob and his wife go on holiday?
2 Who did they go with?

ENGLISH IN ACTION

You're going to have a holiday

with other students.

1 **Work in groups. Look at these advertisements. List the English-speaking countries they advertise.**

2 **Look at the advertisement for the Caribbean. Find examples of things it offers, using these expressions:**

  a *Would you like* + noun?
  b *Would you like to* + verb?

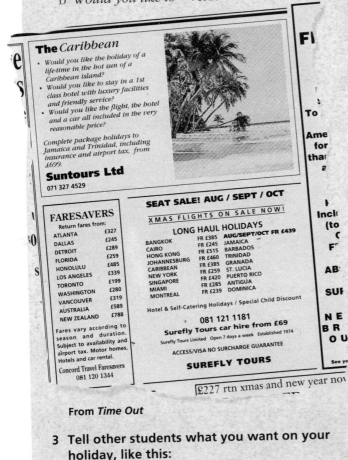

The *Caribbean*

- *Would you like the holiday of a life-time in the hot sun of a Caribbean island?*
- *Would you like to stay in a 1st class hotel with luxury facilities and friendly service?*
- *Would you like the flight, the hotel and a car all included in the very reasonable price?*

Complete package holidays to Jamaica and Trinidad, including insurance and airport tax, from £699.

Suntours Ltd
071 327 4529

FARESAVERS
Return fares from:
ATLANTA	£327
DALLAS	£245
DETROIT	£289
FLORIDA	£259
HONOLULU	£485
LOS ANGELES	£339
TORONTO	£199
WASHINGTON	£280
VANCOUVER	£319
AUSTRALIA	£589
NEW ZEALAND	£788

Fares vary according to season and duration. Subject to availability and airport tax. Motor homes, Hotels and car rental.
Concord Travel Faresavers
081 120 1344

SEAT SALE! AUG / SEPT / OCT
XMAS FLIGHTS ON SALE NOW!

LONG HAUL HOLIDAYS
BANGKOK	FR £385	**AUG/SEPT/OCT**	**FR £439**
CAIRO	FR £245	JAMAICA	
HONG KONG	FR £515	BARBADOS	
JOHANNESBURG	FR £460	TRINIDAD	
CARIBBEAN	FR £385	GRANADA	
NEW YORK	FR £259	ST. LUCIA	
SINGAPORE	FR £420	PUERTO RICO	
MIAMI	FR £285	ANTIGUA	
MONTREAL	FR £239	DOMINICA	

Hotel & Self-Catering Holidays / Special Child Discount

081 121 1181
Surefly Tours car hire from £69
Surefly Tours Limited Open 7 days a week Established 1974

ACCESS/VISA NO SURCHARGE GUARANTEE

SUREFLY TOURS

£227 rtn xmas and new year no[...]

From *Time Out*

3 **Tell other students what you want on your holiday, like this:**

  a *I'd like* + noun
  b *I'd like to* + verb

> I'd like a holiday in the sun.

> I'd like to stay in a 1st class hotel.

4 **Talk to other students. Plan your holiday to an English-speaking country.**

1 Where would you like to go? Why?
2 When would you like to go?
3 Which travel company would you like to fly with?
4 How much are the tickets?

5 **Tell the class what your group decide.**

6 **Prepare the information to give the hotel about your group. Think about:**

- the date and time of your arrival.
- the number of single, double or twin-bedded rooms you would like.
- if you would like a room with or without a bathroom.
- if there are any other facilities you would like.

Now book your rooms.

STUDENT A: Phone a hotel in the country your group would like to visit. Book rooms for your group.

STUDENT B: You are the receptionist. Ask questions to complete the information on this form.

The Park Hotel
Room Reservation Request

Please reserve (insert numbers of rooms):

☑ Twin Bedded   ☐ Double Bedded   ☐ Single

From night of .... 7 day night 25 Amy

to morning of .... 19......

☑ With breakfast   ☐ Without breakfast

Name .... Fabio

Address .. VA PIPPE N.23

.... N.23

.... ITAY CT

Telephone No: 306743

Approximate time of arrival: .... 1 Pm

44

Language review 7

1 Verbs

- **Key verb: auxiliary *do* in negative form**

Present Simple *afmnsiy*

I/you/we/they	don't	
She/he/it	doesn't	go

Past Simple *maisiy*

I/you/we/they She/he/it	didn't	go

- **Key verb: *like***

Offering	**Asking for things**
A: Would you like a drink?	A: I'd like a Coke.
B: Yes, please.	B: Here you are.

a Complete these sentences with *don't, doesn't* or *didn't*.

1 I don't understand what this word means.
2 She went home but she didn't see her mother.
3 They didn't watch television last weekend
4 I'm sorry I didn't come to the party.
5 He speaks Spanish but he doesn't speak Portuguese.
6 I don't like tea and she doesn't like coffee.

b Put the words in the correct order.

Example:
Coffee like you would a Sir? – Would you like a coffee, Sir?

1 new like I'd a cheque book please.
2 like to letter I'd send America to this.
3 tourist would town our of you like map a?
4 lemon it and you would with like ice?

2 *There is/There are* + short answers

Statement	Question	Short answer
There is a hotel.	Is there a hotel?	Yes, there is. No, there isn't.
There are 4 hotels.	Are there 4 hotels?	Yes, there are. No, there aren't.

c Write five sentences to describe your town.

Example: There is a cinema. There are three banks.

3 Possessive adjectives: plural forms

Subject pronoun	Possessive adjective
we	our
you	your
they	their

d Complete with *she, his, her, it, our, they, their*.

We visited our friends, Manuel and Carmelita last June. They usually go to see their grandmother every week-end. She .'s got a very big house in Madrid with 8 bedrooms. They like his . house very much; it .'s extremely comfortable and they can relax there. Manuel usually takes his . guitar and Carmelita usually does they homework.

4 Prepositions: *in, on, above, under, next to*

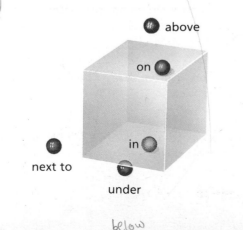

above
on
next to
in
under

below

e Describe this picture.

Example: There's an apple on the table.

Take-off!

Bar

WHISKY
Scotch and Bourbon

GIN

VODKA

BRANDY

RUM
Dark and light

BEER
Including light ales

CHAMPAGNE

WINES
*Specially selected
red and white wines*

MINERAL WATER

JUICES
Orange, Tomato

MIXERS & SOFT DRINKS
*Cola, Lemonade, Dry Ginger,
Diet cola, Tonic, Soda*

CORDIAL
Lemon, Lime

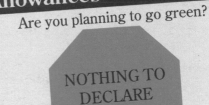

The Customs Allowances

Will you be going red?   **Are you planning to go green?**

NOTHING TO DECLARE

Go through the red channel   Go through the green channel

		Duty Free	Duty Paid
	Cigarettes **or**	200	300
	Cigarillos **or**	100	150
	Cigars **or**	50	75
	Tobacco	250 grammes	400 grammes
	Still table wine	2 litres	5 litres
	Spirits, strong liqueurs over 22% vol, **or**	1 litre	1½ litres
	Fortified or sparkling wines, some liqueurs, **or**	2 litres	3 litres
	An additional still table wine allowance	2 litres	5 litres
	Perfume	60cc/ml	90cc/ml
	Toilet water	250cc/ml	375cc/ml
	Gifts, souvenirs, other goods	£32 worth but not more than: 50 litres of beer 25 lighters	£265 worth but not more than: 50 litres of beer 25 lighters

No-one under 17 is entitled to tobacco or drinks allowances.

You are all now on the plane. You would like a drink before dinner.

1 Look at the bar menu above. Put this dialogue with the flight attendant (FA) in the correct order. Then order the drink you would like.

YOU: Yes please. 6

FA: And with or without lemon? 5

FA: Here you are. Have a good flight. 7

FA: With ice? ③

YOU: Without lemon. 6

FA: What would you like to drink? (1)

YOU: Thank you. 4

YOU: A gin and tonic, please. ②

You want to buy some duty free goods.

The flight attendant sells duty free drinks and other goods, cheaper than in shops.

2 Look at the duty free allowance for Britain above. Answer these questions.

1 How many litres of whisky can you take into Britain?
2 How many litres of wine can you take?
3 How many cigarettes?
4 How many cigars?

3 What do you want to buy? Write a list. Which channel do you go through – green or red?

4 Complete the landing card below.

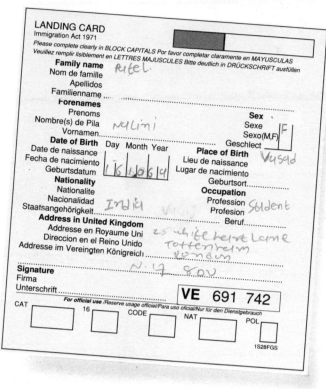

LANDING CARD
Immigration Act 1971
Please complete clearly in BLOCK CAPITALS Por favor completar claramente en MAYUSCULAS
Veuillez remplir lisiblement en LETTRES MAJUSCULES Bitte deutlich in DRÜCKSCHRIFT ausfüllen

Family name *Patel.*
Nom de famille
Apellidos
Familienname

Forenames *Nalini*   **Sex** *F*
Prenoms   Sexe
Nombre(s) de Pila   Sexo(M,F)
Vornamen.   Geschlect

Date of Birth Day Month Year   **Place of Birth** *Vusad*
Date de naissance *16 06 4*   Lieu de naissance
Fecha de nacimiento   Lugar de nacimiento
Geburtsdatum   Geburtsort

Nationality *India*   **Occupation** *Student*
Nationalite   Profession
Nacionalidad   Profesion
Staatsangehörigkeit   Beruf

Address in United Kingdom *25 white hert Lane*
Addresse en Royaume Uni   *Tottenham*
Direccion en el Reino Unido   *Londan*
Addresse im Vereingten Königreich   *N.17 8DV*

Signature *N.Patel*
Firma
Unterschrift

VE 691 742

CAT   16   CODE   NAT   POL
For official use /Reserve usage officiel/Para uso oficial/Nur für den Dienstgebrauch

1S28FGS

Grammar: *any* in questions

5 Study this grammar before you land and go through Customs.

a Have you got *a* cigarette?
b Have you got *any* cigarettes?
c Have you got *any* perfume?

What do you think? Does the Customs Officer ask question, a· or b? What's the difference?

6 Which can you count, cigarettes or perfume? Add *a* or *any* to this chart about questions.

. . .	+ singular countable nouns.
. . .	+ plural countable nouns.
. . .	+ uncountable nouns.

7 Put the words below in the correct columns.

Have you got	a	any
	. . .?	. . .?
	. . .?	. . .?

souvenirs   cigars   tobacco   bottle of wine
toilet water   cigar   book   whisky

8 Answer his questions.

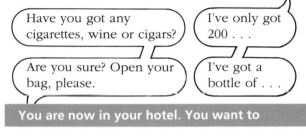

Have you got any cigarettes, wine or cigars?

I've only got 200 . . .

Are you sure? Open your bag, please.

I've got a bottle of . . .

You are now in your hotel. You want to

send a postcard to your English teacher.

9 On the card below write your teacher's address. Then write about your journey. Here are some questions to help you.

1 Where and what time did you arrive?
2 Did you have a good flight?
3 What happened in Customs?
4 What do you think of your hotel?

View of beach and mountains.

8 | *We're going to have a party!*

Colours and clothes

1 Revision

Check you know these colours. Complete the sentences.

Example: I'd like an . . . juice. – I'd like an orange juice.

1 Coffee without milk is *black* coffee.
2 Coffee with milk is *white* coffee.
3 Sarah, the baby on page 21, has got *blue* eyes.
4 Sarah has got *brown* hair.
5 At Customs, go through the *green* channel if you have got nothing to declare.
6 Go through the *red* channel if you have got things to declare.
7 White and *red* = pink
8 Yellow and *blue* = green
9 Black and *white* = grey

2 Vocabulary: clothes

1 **Look at this page from a clothes mail order catalogue. Match the descriptions to the clothes.**

2 **Check your answers with another student, like this:**

Example: A: What's J?
B: *It's* a pink shirt.
A: What's G?
B: *They're* green shoes.

> **NB** **Plurals for clothes**
>
> '*It's* a shirt' but '*they're* trousers.'
>
> Do you say *it's* or *they're* with these clothes?
> . . . a skirt   . . . shorts
> . . . jeans   . . . a sweater

SIZES
Small = S   Medium = M   Large = L

1   White jeans
(also available in blue and black)
S/M/L   £30.00   C

**2   Red and white T-shirt
(with mauve trimmings)**
(also available in blue/white)
S/M/L   £9.99   B

3   Brown sweater
(also available in black, green
and blue) S/M/L   £39.99   A

**4   Brown trainers with
orange laces**   D
(also available in black/white)
All sizes   £39.50

5   Green jacket   H
(also available in black)
S/M/L   £60.00

6   Yellow dress   I
(also available in red and white)
S/M/L   £50.00

7   Green shoes   G
All sizes and colours   £59.99

8   Red and white tie   K
(also available in green/white and
black/white)   £10.50

9   Dark blue trousers   L
(also available in black and dark
green) S/M/L   £49.00

10 Pink shirt   J
(also available in white and blue)
S/M/L   £24.99

11 Light blue blouse   E
(also available in white) S/M/L
£19.99

12 Dark blue skirt   F
(also available in black)
S/M/L   £37.49

3   Writing

**1   Look at the clothes catalogue again. Choose
four things to buy.**

1 What size are you? Small, medium or large?
2 What size shoes do you wear?

**2   Complete the order form. Tell another student
what you would like. How much does your
order cost?**

Order Form
Complete in **BLOCK CAPITALS** and return to the address above,
enclosing a cheque or postal order for the correct amount.

Name _____

Address _____

Credit card number ☐☐☐☐☐☐☐☐☐☐☐☐☐☐☐☐

QUANTITY	SIZE	COLOUR	DESCRIPTION	TOTA
1	M	Blue	Jeans	£30.
1	6	Green	shoes	£59
1	m	blue	blouses	£19.99
1	m	blue	skirt	£37.49
1	m	Green	Jacket	£6000
				£256.48

4   Pronunciation: /r/

**1   📼 Listen and <u>underline</u> when you hear the
sound /r/.**

Rebecca would like to wear brown shoes, a red
dress and a green shirt to Robert's party on
Friday.

Speaking

**Talk to another student. What clothes do you
generally wear:**

- to a party?
- to work or school?
- to relax in at home at the weekend?
- to travel on holiday?
- to work in the garden?

5 Reading

Read the party invitation below. Are these sentences true (T) or false (F)?

Example: The party is on Saturday. – T

1 It doesn't start at 8 pm. T
2 It is in the afternoon. T
3 It isn't in a hotel. T
4 The person having the party hasn't got a phone. F
5 This person would like an answer to the invitation. T

6 Grammar

Negatives 2

1 Look at the invitation again and answer these questions.

1 You would like to go to the party. How do you answer?
2 It is impossible for you to go to the party. How do you answer?
3 What is the contracted form of *cannot?*

2 Look at the true or false sentences in Exercise 5 Reading. Find two negatives formed without *do*.

3 Complete this chart.

	Positive	Negative	Questions
can be have got	I can come. It is in a hotel. He has got a phone.	I can't come.	Can you come? Is it in a hotel? . . .?
start finish like	It starts at 8.00. It finishes at 12.00. They like parties.	It doesn't	Does it . . .? . . .? . . .?

There's a Party!

on Saturday, 21 March

At 8.30 p.m.

At Tony Barratt's, 78 Oxford Road, Manchester   (061) 860 5430

I hope you can come!

R.S.V.P

I'd love to come /
I'm sorry I can't come

Short answers

Question	Short answers
Is there a party on Saturday?	Yes, there *is*. No, there *isn't*.
Did you go to the party last week?	Yes, I *did*. No, I *didn't*.

1 Write short answers for the questions in the chart on page 50.

Example: Can you come? – Yes, I can./No, I can't.

2 Talk to other students. Ask and answer to complete the chart below, like this:

A: Have you got any brothers and sisters?
B: Yes, I have./No, I haven't.

Find someone who	Name
hasn't got any brothers or sisters.	. . .
isn't married.	. . .
can't see English films on TV at home.	. . .
doesn't like watching TV.	. . .
doesn't drink.	. . .
doesn't wear jeans.	. . .

7 Listening

📼 **Listen. Simon, Neesha and Rob receive the party invitation. Answer these questions.**

1 Who can't go to the party? Why not?
2 Why is there a party?
3 What does Neesha decide to wear?
4 What present do they decide to take?
5 What time do they decide to get there?

8 Grammar: *going to*

> Tony *is going to* have a party on Saturday.

1 Look at the example sentence above and answer this question.

When is the party – in the past, present or future?

2 📼 Listen to the conversation again. Complete these questions about the weekend.

ROB: What . . . do?
SIMON: What . . . wear?
NEESHA: What . . . take?

Pronunciation: /ə/

1 📼 Listen and mark the main stress on this question.

What are you going to do at the weekend?

2 Listen and repeat. Which words are pronounced with /ə/ ?

3 Ask other students this question.

What are you going to do at the weekend?

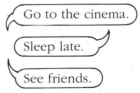

Go to the cinema.

Sleep late.

See friends.

ENGLISH IN ACTION

Touch of Class

DRY CLEANING SPECIALISTS TEL. 39777

Your class is going to have a party.

1 Work with other students. Answer these questions.

1 When are you going to have the party?
2 What are you going to eat and drink?
3 What music are you going to have?
4 Who are you going to invite?

2 Make a list of your ideas. Offer to bring things, like this:

> I'll bring pizza

> I'll bring red wine

> I'll bring Brazilian music

Food	Drink	Music
Pizza (Marcella)	Red Wine (Carlos)	Brazilian music (Suzanne)

3 Tell your teacher what everyone is going to bring.

Example: Marcella is going to bring pizza.

NB *Going to vs will*

CARLOS: I'm *going to* bring red wine.
TEACHER: OK then. *I'll* bring white wine!

Did Carlos decide:
a at the time of speaking?
b before speaking?

Did the teacher decide:
a at the time of speaking?
b before speaking?

---

4 Make a list of the clothes you are going to wear to the party.

PRICE LIST

Suit	£10.00
Jacket	£7.00
Trousers	£5.00
Shirt	£1.75
Blouse	£1.75
Dress	£5.00
Skirt	£2.50
Sweater	£2.00

You take the clothes you need to the drycleaner's. There is a customer in the shop.

5 ▣ Listen and answer these questions.

1 What clothes does the customer give the assistant?
2 How much is she going to pay?
3 When is she going to pay?

6 Listen again and complete the gaps.

CUSTOMER: Good morning. Can I have these by Friday?
ASSISTANT: Yes, of course. What have you got exactly?
CUSTOMER: Well, there's a . . .
ASSISTANT: That's fine. Is Friday afternoon OK?
CUSTOMER: Yes, about what time?
ASSISTANT: 3.30?
CUSTOMER: OK. How much is it going to be?
ASSISTANT: . . .
CUSTOMER: Fine.
ASSISTANT: Can you bring this ticket with you on Friday?
CUSTOMER: Thanks very much.

7 Practise the dialogue with another student. Talk about the clothes on your list.

Language review 8

1 Nouns: plurals for clothes

These clothes are plural in English.

jeans   trousers   shorts   pyjamas

a Describe these clothes. Use *it's* or *they're*.

Example: It's a red dress. They're blue jeans.

2 Verbs

• *going to* (future plans)

Positive

I	am	
You/we/they	are	going to watch TV tonight.
She/he/it	is	

Question

Am	I	
Are	you/we/they	going to watch TV tonight?
Is	she/he/it	

• Short answers

Question	Positive answer	Negative answer
Do you like apples?	Yes, I *do*	No, I *don't*
Did he go?	Yes, he *did*	No, he *didn't*
Can you see?	Yes, I *can*	No, I *can't*
Are they late?	Yes, they *are*	No, they *aren't*
Has she got a car?	Yes, she *has*	No, she *hasn't*

• Negative forms: Key verbs: *to be, can, have got*

Be	I	am	not late.
	You/we/they	are	
	She/he/it	is	

Can	I/you/we/they	cannot come
	She/he/it	

Have got	I/you/we/they	have	not got time
	She/he/it	has	

b Make questions from these words.

Example:
tonight what you going are do to? – What are you going to do tonight?

1 when you going homework to are do your?
2 going eat to where you are evening this?
3 watch time you going what are to TV?
4 when see going to you are mother your?
5 going you when are buy to new trousers?
6 weekend what you to going are do the at?

c Answer the questions in exercise b in complete sentences.

Example:
What are you going to do tonight? – I'm going to see friends.

d Write short answers to these questions.

Example: Can you speak English? – Yes, I can.

1 Are you a student?
2 Have you got a big family?
3 Do you like reading?
4 Can you cook?
5 Did you go to the cinema last night?
6 Have you got a red pen?
7 Do you know London?
8 Are you Dutch?

e Complete the dialogue below using these negatives.

don't   doesn't   haven't   hasn't   can't   isn't

A: Are you going to the office party tomorrow?
B: No, I can't I'm going to see Philip's parents in Cambridge for the weekend.
A: What about you, Anna?
C: I don't know. The problem is that I haven't got time.
B: Is Michelle going?
C: No, she isn't. She hasn't got time either.
B: And what about Brian?
A: No, he doesn't like office parties. I think I'm the only one going!

53

9 Move that body!

The body; prepositions of place; *every day/not often/never*

1 Revision

Talk to another student. Ask and answer these questions.

1 What did you do yesterday evening?
2 What are you going to do this evening?

2 Vocabulary: the body

1 Talk to other students. Ask and answer this question.

1 How often do you do any exercise?

   Every day   Not often   Never!

2 Look at the picture below and number the parts of the body.

hair **2**   head .**7**.   foot .**16**.   nose .**5**.   eye .**3**.
leg ..**14**.   knee ..**17**.   finger .**11**.   mouth .**6**.   hand .**1**.
toe ..**15**.   shoulder .**10**.   face ..**4**.   arm .**9**.   back .**13**.
ear .**8**.   stomach .**12**.

3 🎧 Listen and check your answers.

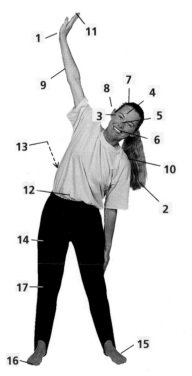

3 Grammar: prepositions 3

Put your arms straight up *next to* your ears.

Put your right leg straight out *behind* you.

Look straight *in front of* you.

Touch the floor *between* your feet.

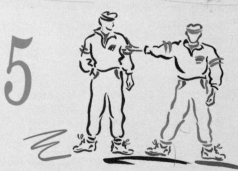

Touch the person *on your right*.

1 Look at the pictures and instructions above. Do the actions.

2 Now do these actions.

Look *behind* you.
Put your arms out *in front of* you.
Stand *next to* another student.
Put your head *between* your hands.
Touch the person *on your left*.

4 Reading

1 **Look at the keep fit exercises below and match the instructions to the diagrams.**

2 ▣ **Listen and check your answers.**

3 **Write another exercise. Give instructions to other students.**

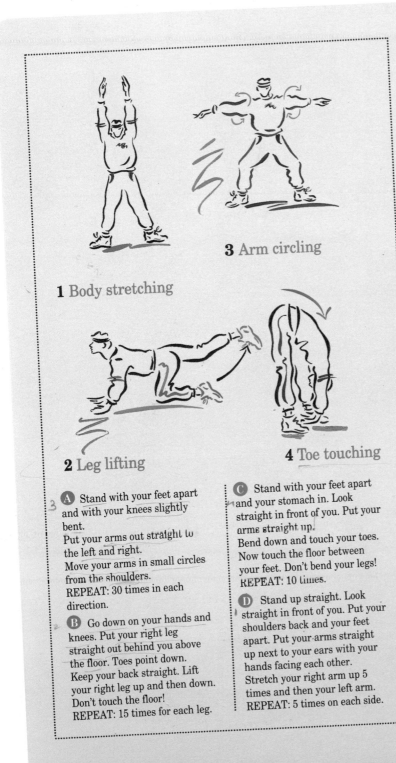

1 Body stretching

3 Arm circling

2 Leg lifting

4 Toe touching

Ⓐ Stand with your feet apart and with your knees slightly bent.
Put your arms out straight to the left and right.
Move your arms in small circles from the shoulders.
REPEAT: 30 times in each direction.

Ⓑ Go down on your hands and knees. Put your right leg straight out behind you above the floor. Toes point down. Keep your back straight. Lift your right leg up and then down. Don't touch the floor!
REPEAT: 15 times for each leg.

Ⓒ Stand with your feet apart and your stomach in. Look straight in front of you. Put your arms straight up.
Bend down and touch your toes. Now touch the floor between your feet. Don't bend your legs!
REPEAT: 10 times.

Ⓓ Stand up straight. Look straight in front of you. Put your shoulders back and your feet apart. Put your arms straight up next to your ears with your hands facing each other. Stretch your right arm up 5 times and then your left arm.
REPEAT: 5 times on each side.

5 Pronunciation

can and can't

1 ▣ **Listen and answer these questions.**

  1 Can the speaker do the keep fit exercises?
  2 Does she think exercises 1 and 2 are easy or difficult?

2 **Listen again. How does she pronounce *can* and *can't*?**

3 **Tell another student which exercises above you *can* or *can't* do.**

4 **Read the questionnaire below.**

  1 How do you ask each question?
  2 What are the short answers?
  3 How do you pronounce *can* and *can't* in short answers?

5 **Complete the questionnaire about you. Add three more questions then ask other students about their abilities.**

Who can . . .	Me	2.	E.S	M	m
speak a little English?	✓	✓	✓	✓	✓
play a musical instrument?	✗	✓	✗	✗	✓	✓
type?	✓	✓	✓	✗	✗
cook?	✓	✓	✓	✗	✗
stand on her/his head?	✗	✗	✗	✗	✗	✗
drive?	✗	✗	✓	✗	✗	✗
read book		✓	✓	✓	✓
sing		✓	✗	✗	✓	✗
speak french		✓	✗	✓	✓	✓

THE OKEY COKEY

This is a famous action song from 1941, described as 'the big dance favourite' in Britain during the Second World War. Some people still sing and do the actions in a large circle on social occasions and at parties.

6 Listening

1 🖭 **Listen to the first part of the song. What parts of the body do you hear?**

2 **Listen again and complete the gaps.**

Put . . . right . . . in,
Your right . . . out,
In, out, in, . . .
Shake it all about.
. . . the okey cokey and
turn around
. . .'s what it's all about.

CHORUS:
Oh! Oh! The okey cokey.
Oh! Oh! The okey cokey.
Oh! Oh! The okey cokey.
. . . bend, . . . stretch,
Rah, rah, rah!

3 🖭 **Now listen to the complete song. What are the changes in each verse?**

4 **Work with another student. Write at least one new verse.**

7 Grammar

Imperatives

> *Put* your right arm in.
> *Don't* touch the floor!

1 Look at the instructions above. Find other instructions like these in the keep fit exercises on page 55 and in 'The Okey Cokey'.

2 🖳 Listen to the instructions. When you hear an imperative, eg *Stand up!*, do the action. When you hear a negative imperative, eg *Don't stand up!*, don't do the action.

8 Listening

1 Look at the photograph of Martin and Rachel's wedding. Complete the sentences using the prepositions below.

Example: Rachel is . . . Martin. – Rachel is next to Martin.

on the left of   next to   behind   in front of
on the right of   between

1 Martin is *between* his wife and his brother.
2 Martin's brother is . . . Rachel's sister.
3 Rachel's sister is . . . Martin's brother.
4 Rachel is . . . her husband.
5 Martin's brother is . . . Martin.

2 🖳 The photographer took another photograph of the same people. Listen to his instructions. Which two new people were in this photograph?

3 Listen again. Name each person in the second photograph.

4 Listen again. Write the verbs he used in these instructions.

Sit down where you are.   *Look* into her eyes.
Stand behind Rachel and Martin.   *Smile* everyone.
Change places with your husband.   *Say* cheese!
Hold your left arm around your wife.

ENGLISH IN ACTION

You're going to take a photo of the students in your class, but you haven't got a film. You can buy film at the chemist's.

1 **This dialogue with the chemist is in the wrong order. Tell another student how to put it in the correct order.**

Example: Put the third sentence first, then put the sixth sentence second . . .

1 Would you like prints or slides? –3
2 Thanks very much. Goodbye. –8
3 Good morning. Can I help you? – 1
4 Prints, please. –4
5 How many – twelve, twenty-four or thirty-six? –5
6 Yes, please. I'd like to buy a colour film for this camera. –2
7 That will be £3.25 please. –7
8 Thirty-six, please. –6

2 📺 **Listen and check your answers.**

3 **Practise the dialogue together.**

You've got your new film.

Now organise the photo of your class.

1 Plan where people are going to sit or stand.
2 Tell them where to go.
3 Take the photo.

Language review 9

1 Prepositions: of place

A is *next to* B
B is *between* A and C
D is *in front* of B
E is *behind* B
C is *on the left of* B
A is *on the right of* B

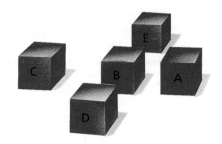

a Complete these sentences with the prepositions on the left.

Example:
The Russian is . . . the Italian and the German. – The Russian is between the Italian and the German.

1   The American is . . . the Australian.
2   The Brazilian is . . . the Italian.
3   The Italian is . . . the Russian.
4   The German is . . . the Russian.
5   The Australian is . . . the Italian.

2 Verbs

* **New verbs**

Irregular

Verb	Past Simple
put	put
stand	stood
sit	sat
say	said
drive	drove

Regular

Verb	Past Simple
play	played
type	typed
smile	smiled
move	moved

* **Imperatives: giving instructions**

Positive	Negative
Stop!	Don't stop!
Pull!	Don't pull!

* **Key verb: *can* and *can't* (ability)**

Positive

I		
You/we/they	can	swim.
She/he/it		

Negative

I		
You/we/they	cannot	swim.
She/he/it	can't	

Question

	I	
Can	you/we/they	swim?
	she/he/it	

b Put the verb in (brackets) in the correct form.

1   Where did you . . . in the theatre? (sit)
2   I . . . to London yesterday. (drive)
3   I don't understand the last thing she . . . (say)
4   Where did I . . . my pen? (put)
5   I didn't . . . the letter. (type)
6   She looked at her brother. He . . . (smile)
7   Did you . . . the car? (move)

c Put these imperatives in pairs.

Example: Come! – Go!

Come! Stop! Close! Push! Sit! Give! Eat! Run! Take! Walk! Open! Start! Drink! Pull! Stand! Go!

d Write eight sentences about what you *can* and *can't* do. Use these verbs, and three others.

swim   drive   ski   play   tennis   type

10 Consolidation

1 Thinking about learning: Grammar

Revises:
Vocabulary: Countries + nationalities/
languages; grammar words
Grammar: Key verb: *to be*; adjectives;
prepositions; *a/an;* auxiliary *do*

1 Answer these questions.

1 Where do you come from?
2 What nationality are you?
3 What language do you speak?

2 Read about the differences between English grammar and other languages. Is your language similar to English?

3 Talk to another student about the differences between your language and English.

Mohamed

In Arabic, we don't generally
use the verb *to be* in the
present.
ARABIC: I Egyptian.
ENGLISH: I *am* Egyptian.

*Is your language similar
to Arabic or English?*

In Italian, the possessive
adjective agrees with the noun
after it.
ITALIAN: Look at Maria and his
father.
ENGLISH: Look at Maria and
her father.

*Is your language similar to
Italian or English?*

Luciana

In Spanish, we use plural
adjectives with plural nouns.
SPANISH: The books are reds.
ENGLISH: The books are *red*.

*Is your language similar to
Spanish or English?*

Pilar

In Portuguese, adjectives
generally go after the noun.
PORTUGUESE: I like food French
ENGLISH: I like *French* food.

*Is your language similar to
Portuguese or English?*

In French, we don't put
a/an before jobs.
FRENCH: I am doctor.
ENGLISH: I am *a* doctor.

*Is your language similar to
French or English?*

Luis

Juliette

In Greek, we use one preposition
of place to say *to, in* or *at.*
GREEK: I put my books to my bag,
went to work and sat to the table.
ENGLISH: I put my books *in* my bag,
went to work and sat *at* the table.

In German, we haven't got the
auxiliary verb *do.*
GERMAN: I speak not English.
ENGLISH: I *do* not speak English.

*Is your language similar to
German or English?*

*Is your language similar to
Greek or English?*

Petra

Nicos

Dear Mariko,

Hi! How are you?

Thank you for your letter. I liked reading about you and your family. Now I'm going to tell you about me.

I've got a big family: my mother and father of course, and then 3 brothers and two sisters. We are very close and spend a lot of time together.

I finished school last year. I would like to go to Rome and study to be actor but I haven't got enough money at the moment. So for the moment, I work in a bank small about 2km from home. I do not like it very much but it's OK. In the evenings and in the weekend I go out with my girlfriend, Sylvana and his brother. We generally go to the cinema or to a bar with a group of goods friends. I'd like to buy a motor-bike and go to different places at the weekend but money the problem!

You wrote that you would like to come to Italy for a holiday in the summer. That's a fantastic idea! Of course you can come and stay with my family. - just write when you know the dates.

Please write soon.

Marco.

4 **Look at the penfriend letter from Marco to Mariko. Are these questions true (T) or false (F)?**

Example: Marco is Italian.– T

1 There are only boys in the family. F
2 Marco is a student. F
3 He is single. T
4 He has got a motor-bike. F
5 Marco wants Mariko to visit his family. T

5 **Work with another student. There are seven grammar mistakes in the letter. They are all in the paragraph beginning _I finished school last year._ Correct the mistakes.**

2 Across cultures: body language

Revises:
Vocabulary: The body

1 Ask another student these questions and tick (✓) a, b or c.

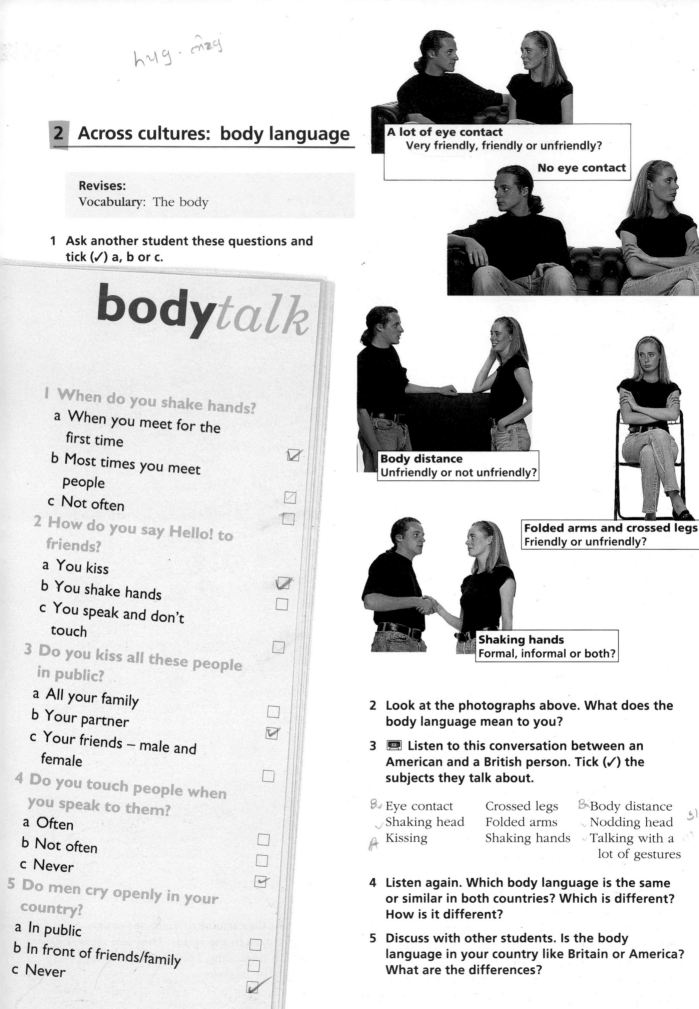

A lot of eye contact
Very friendly, friendly or unfriendly?

No eye contact

Body distance
Unfriendly or not unfriendly?

Folded arms and crossed legs
Friendly or unfriendly?

Shaking hands
Formal, informal or both?

body*talk*

1 When do you shake hands?
a When you meet for the first time
b Most times you meet people ☑
c Not often ☑

2 How do you say Hello! to friends?
a You kiss
b You shake hands ☑
c You speak and don't touch

3 Do you kiss all these people in public?
a All your family
b Your partner
c Your friends – male and female ☑

4 Do you touch people when you speak to them?
a Often
b Not often
c Never ☑

5 Do men cry openly in your country?
a In public
b In front of friends/family
c Never ☑

2 Look at the photographs above. What does the body language mean to you?

3 📺 **Listen to this conversation between an American and a British person. Tick (✓) the subjects they talk about.**

Eye contact	Crossed legs	Body distance
Shaking head	Folded arms	Nodding head
Kissing	Shaking hands	Talking with a lot of gestures

4 Listen again. Which body language is the same or similar in both countries? Which is different? How is it different?

5 Discuss with other students. Is the body language in your country like Britain or America? What are the differences?

3 Language in context: the time

Revises:
Vocabulary: Numbers
Grammar: *going to*

1 **Before you listen, what do you think the title of the song means?**

2 **Predict the missing words in the choruses.**

3 ▣ **Listen to the two choruses. Were you correct?**

4 ▣ **Now listen to the complete song.**

1 How many times do you hear the first chorus?
2 How many times do you hear the second chorus?

rock around the clock

Chorus 1
One, *two*, three o'clock, four o'clock rock,
Five, six, *seven* o'clock, *eight* o'clock rock,
Nine, *ten*, eleven o'clock, twelve o'clock *rock*,
We're gonna* *rock* around *the* clock tonight.

Chorus 2
We're gonna rock *around* the clock tonight,
We're *gonna* rock, *rock*, rock, 'til broad daylight,**
We're gonna *rock*, gonna rock, around the *clock* tonight.

Glossary
* gonna = going to (spoken English)
** 'til broad daylight = from night to late morning

Rock 'n' Roll
Rock 'n' roll first arrived on the American music scene in the 1950s. Early rock 'n' roll was predominantly white music but it was strongly influenced by black rhythm and blues. It was the first music exclusively for young people with its own folklore, heroes and even vocabulary. The singer Bill Haley and his band, The Comets, had international success and recognition with their hit 'Rock around the clock', one of the first examples of the new music.

Check what you know!
Now turn to page 129 and complete Check what you know 2.

Party!

1 You are going to a party. Look at the things you can say. Write the expressions below in the correct place on the picture.

I don't know. What about you?
To Cairo. It was fantastic!
What time is it?
Would you like to dance?
Fine, thanks. How are you?
No, sorry, I haven't.
Are you married?
Yes, goodbye, and thank you for the party.
Bill Haley, I think.
Hello!
Yes, please! What have you got?
How many children have you got?
Do you like classical music?
Hiromi, this is Danny. Danny, this is Hiromi.

2 Listen and check your answers.

3 Now have a party! Speak to lots of people. Have a good time!

1 . . . . — Hello! Come in. How nice to see you.

4 . . . . — Perhaps a little later.

8 . . . . — Two girls and a boy.

9 . . . . — No, I'm not actually. Are you?

12 . . . . — Where did you go on holiday? You're so brown!

13 . . . . — What are you going to do after the party?

11 *Just good friends!*

Very/not very; describing people

WELL, YOU'VE GOT A GOOD SENSE OF HUMOUR, YOU'RE HANDSOME AND INTELLIGENT, WE'VE GOT THE SAME INTERESTS AND LIFESTYLES... BUT I DON'T LIKE YOUR SHOES.

1 Revision

1 What do you think? Which are more important to you – friends or family?

2 Complete the questionnaire. What is important in a new friend/partner?

	Very Important	Important	Not very important
Physical appearance		✓	✗
Clothes		✓	
Job or education	✓		
Family			✓
Money and possessions	✓		
Personality or character		✓	
Religion			✓
Politics		✓	✓
Other(...)		✓	

3 Tell other students what you think.

2 Vocabulary: describing people

1 Match these characteristics to their definitions.

Characteristics

E	1 attractive	G	7 kind
F	2 tall	L	8 educated
A	3 a professional	J	9 sense of humour
H	4 intelligent	I	10 slim
K	5 affectionate	D	11 non-smoker
B	6 sincere	C	12 handsome

Definitions

A works as a doctor, a teacher, an engineer or in a similar profession

B means what she/he says

C is physically good-looking (men only)

D doesn't smoke

E is physically good-looking and/or has got a nice personality

F is not short

G is good to other people and does things for them

H is good at understanding, learning and thinking

I is not fat

J can understand when things are amusing

K shows love physically

L finished school/university with good results and understanding

2 Write the characteristics in groups of two. Tell another student why you put words together.

Example: I put *intelligent* with *non-smoker* because it's stupid to smoke!

NB Handsome vs beautiful

We generally say a *handsome* man but a *beautiful* woman.

Which word in the list of characteristics above means *handsome/beautiful* for both men and women?

SO, WHO'S SPECIAL IN YOUR LIFE AT THE MOMENT?

ME.

WELL, I HAVE A GOO RELATIONSHIP WITH M WHY CAN'T YOU?

Reading

1 Put the characteristics on page 66 in order of importance for you when choosing a partner.

2 Now read the article 'The Main Attraction'. Where is your order different?

3 Read the first part of the article again. Use these words to answer the questions below.

eyes legs face smile figure teeth

1 Which do men think are most important?
2 Which do women think are most important?
3 Do you agree?

3 Grammar: object pronouns

I like *you*	You like *me*
She likes *him*	He likes *her*
We like *them*	They like *us*

1 Look at the sentences above and complete this chart.

Subject pronoun	Object pronoun
I	me
you	you
she	her
he	him
it	it
we	us
you	you
they	them

2 Work with another student. Ask why she/he likes the people below.

Example: A: Why do you like your best friend?
 B: I like her because she's got a good sense of humour.

boyfriend/girlfriend
brothers and sisters
husband/wife/partner
friends

3 What do you think? Why do they like you?

THE MAIN ATTRACTION

Suddenly it happens. You just know he's the man for you, and you haven't even been introduced yet.

But how do you know? And how can you make sure he feels the same way? *Company* investigates ...

What first attracts men to women? Whereas women tend to notice the eyes, teeth and smile in particular, men will be more likely to assess the face in general and pay more attention to figure and legs.

According to a recent survey by *Singles* magazine, these are the top ten attributes that men and women look for in each other, in order of priority.

Men look for a woman who is:
- attractive
- sincere
- slim
- a non-smoker
- intelligent
- with a sense of humour
- affectionate
- tall
- kind

Women look for a man who is:
- tall
- professional
- with a sense of humour
- attractive (not necessarily handsome)
- sincere
- intelligent
- handsome
- kind
- educated

4 Listening

1 📼 **Listen to these people describing how they first met. Complete the chart.**

	Simon and Neesha	Trisha and Sandra	Carlos and Pat
• Where did they meet?	party	stratford ypon Avon	English Oxford
• When did they meet?	1989	sep-1992	June 1990
• Why did she like her/him?	attractive	political	very good teacher
• Why did he like her/him?	friendly		very good student
• What are their plans for the future?	children large family		Job teaching english spam.

5 Grammar: Past Simple *to be*, and *ago*

1 Complete these sentences. What did the first couple say?

We . . . at a party when we met.
I liked Simon because he . . . very attractive.
I liked Neesha because she . . . very friendly.

2 📼 **Listen again and check your answers.**

When do you say *was?* When do you say *were?*
How are they pronounced in the sentences above?

3 Complete the answer to this question.

How long ago did Simon and Neesha meet?
In 1989, . . . years ago.

4 Use the chart above to answer these questions.

1 How long ago did Trisha and Sandra meet?
2 How long ago did Carlos and Pat meet?

5 Now answer these questions about you.

How long ago did you meet your teacher/your best friend/your partner?

a long time ago   five years ago   a few weeks ago
not very long ago   recently

6 Ask other students these questions. How long ago did you:

• see a good film? What was it? yes y
• read a good book? What . . .? no
• have a good meal? What did . . .? Where . . .? yes
• buy new clothes? What . . .? yes
• go on holiday? Where . . .? no

To M.M.
The first time
we met as strangers
We parted as friends

The second time
we met as friends
We parted as lovers

The last time
we met as lovers
We parted as friends

We did not meet again
We are now
not even friends

Gerald England

6 Reading

1 What do you think? Is it possible to stay friends after a serious relationship finishes?

2 Read the poem *To MM* and answer these questions.

1 Who are the two people in the poem?
2 Did they have a serious relationship?
3 Did they stay friends?
4 Do you think the poet is happy now?

Giving opinions;
I think/I don't think;

7 Speaking

1 Look at the advertisements below and answer these questions.

1 Where can you find advertisements like this?
2 Why do people write them?

2 Read the advertisements. Who interests you most?

3 Put possible couples together. Match the numbers with the letters.

4 Tell another student what you think. Are the couples you put together the same or different? Give your opinions, like this:

> I think 4 goes with E because they both like sport.

> Oh no! I don't think 4 goes with E because their ages are very different.

1 ● ALMOST ATTRACTIVE MAN, 32, n/s, un-Tory. Sincere, fun, friendly, occasionally witty. Into media, arts, skiing, countryside. Seeks female soulmate. Photo?
● INTELLIGENT, American

2 ● GOOD LOOKING MAN, 48, company director, slim, fair hair, non-smoker, seeking slim, attractive, sophisticated lady to enjoy dining out, theatre, travel and friendship, and possible lasting relationship. Photo please, returned with mine. Box Z324.
● TALL ATTRACTIVE, humorous, travel,

3 ● LUNATIC, LOVER, POET! humorous, intelligent, athletic man, 39, London. Seeks attractive girl friend for films, theatre, travel, fun. Box Z259.

4 ● WINDSOR BASED ATHLETIC MALE, 35, tall, fit, solvent, seeks slim, intelligent, sporty female under 35, to share dinner, romance, adventure. Box Z372.
● ATTRACTIVE MAN

5 Photo? Box Z362.
● INTELLIGENT, PROFESSIONAL American man, 35, desires correspondence leading to serious, permanent relationship with woman 21-35. Photo appreciated. Box Z188.
● GOOD LOOKING MAN, 38, director,

A please. Box Z163.
● BRIGHT AND BEAUTIFUL, woman, 33. Interests art, film, music, theatre, travel. Seeks exceptional, sophisticated, caring affectionate, romantic man. Photo essential. Box Z489.
● BLONDE female

B ● FEMALE, 27, attractive, with long black hair, seeks gorgeous, educated, sporty, fun-loving, professional male (26-30), for outings and fun. Photo. Box Z311.

C ● ATTRACTIVE, SLIM, BLONDE female (long hair), intelligent, warm, fun. Seeks tall, attractive, American male (thirties), for 1:1 relationship. Photo please. Box Z424.
● BRIGHT FEMALE

D ● WOMAN late 30's, intelligent, tall, attractive, seeks caring, humorous, affectionate man for committed relationship. No smokers or Tories. Letter and photo please. Box Z143.
● BEAUTIFUL WOMAN

E ● PASSIONATE ABOUT LIFE? Me too. Attractive, vibrant, successful, separated, well-educated, sporty but feminine lady (45), Surrey area. First time advertising seeks genuine, attractive, assertive, intelligent man (fortysomething), for love, laughter, tennis, skiing, travel and good living - perhaps forever. Secret smoker, willing to stop if necessary. Photo/telephone please. Box Z071
● SPORTY WOMAN, late 30's intelligent

Pronunciation: sentence stress

1 🖥 **Listen to the first verse of the poem.**

1 Which words are stressed?
2 How is *as* pronounced?

2 Listen to the complete poem. Which words are stressed?

3 Say the poem to another student and listen to your partner's pronunciation. Is the important information clear?

From *Time Out*

69

You see these 'Wanted' advertisements in *Time Out* magazine.

You decide to write an advertisement for something you want to find or offer.

1 Work with another student. Say what you think each person wants, like this:

> I think the person in the first advertisement wants a flat.

2 Look at this form from *Time Out*. How much will your advertisement cost?

3 Look at other students' advertisements. Can you answer any of them?

CLASSIFIED

25 WANTED

- **Wanted** small, self-contained flat in North London. One bedroom. Will pay up to £50 per week. Urgent. Ring 081 340 9668.
- **Have you got** a washing machine you no longer need? I will pay up to £40 and collect it. 071 492 1297.
- **Graduate**, 29, seeks job with advertising company. Any job/salary considered, but must be central London. Write to Box 343.
- **Wanted** old Ford Escorts (1985-89). Good cash prices paid for cars in good condition. Write to Box 1017.
- **French and Spanish** teachers wanted for private lessons. Good rates. No experience necessary. Apply Box 1171.
- **Au Pair** wanted. Tel: 081 802 7942 after 7 pm.

33 DISCOS

- **LAs Discotheque**/Equipment hire. 071 811 8011.

34 THEATREBOARD

- **Drama school entry.** Coaching by Professional Drama School Teacher. Ring Dorinda Davis 081 443 4568.
- **Set designers** and actors wanted for shows in London. April to August. Ring 081 771 8769.
- **Drama student.** Irish. 35 London-based. Versatile, seeks some acting experience as soon as possible. Please help. Telephone James 071 892 2572.
- **Theatre workshops.** Classical/modern techniques. South London. One day or one week workshops. For more details, phone 081 556 7867.
- **Actor seeks work.** Any role considered. Vast experience. Phone Ali on 071 334 7796.

35 TUITION

- **German lessons** in your own home. Beginners—advanced. Ring 071 556 1243.
- **Portuguese lessons** by native speaker. Vacancies in July/August. Central London. 071 326 4528.
- **Guitar tuition.** All styles and levels. Tom 081 802 7959.
- **French tuition** classes, conversational, exam tuition, business. 071 836 4835.

CLASSIFIED AD FORM

Name Mylini.

Address 25 whitehook Lame London.

Telephone: Day _____ **Evening** 081 80635788

Please insert my ad in the following number of issues:

Classification (see ad rates) [ ]

Number of words: [13]

Cost for one issue: [23.40]

Cost for two or more issues: [ ]

Tick if semi-display required: [ ]
(min 20 words)

Tick if box number required: [ ]
(obligatory in Lonely Hearts)

ACCESS/VISA CARD NO [ ][ ][ ][ ][ ][ ][ ][ ][ ][ ][ ][ ][ ][ ][ ][ ]

EXPIRY DATE [ ][ ][ ][ ]

SIGNATURE _____

Cardholder's Address (if not as above)

Lineage
£1.80 per word

PAYMENT METHODS
All advertisements must be pre-paid. We accept Postal Orders, Cheques (with your name and address on the reverse, payable to Time Out Ltd), Access or Visa. If paying by credit card complete the information below.

Print your ad below in BLOCK CAPITALS, one word in each box (telephone number equals one word). Underline any words you require in Capital letters and send your ad to: **Classified Ad Dept, Time Out, Tower House, Southampton Street, London WC2E 7HD.** 01-836 5131. VAT 233 109402.

wanted	an	electric
hoover	about	£75
secondhead	max	2
years	old	081 80635887

Language review 11

1 Pronouns: as objects and after prepositions

Subject pronoun	Object pronoun
I	me
you	you
she	her
he	him
it	it
we	us
you	you
they	them

a Complete these sentences with subject or object pronouns.

1 If you don't like Hugh and Craig, why did *you* go to the restaurant with *them*?
2 It was my birthday yesterday. Antonio gave *me* a new camera.
3 I loved Annie from the first moment *I* saw *her*.
4 They bought *us* six beautiful champagne glasses for our wedding anniversary.
5 When I asked *him* to go, he was very angry.
6 I haven't got your address. Can you write *it* in my address book?

2 Verbs

• **Past Simple key verb: *to be***

Positive

I/she/he/it	was	late.
You/we/they	were	

Negative

I/she/he/it	wasn't	late.
You/we/they	weren't	

Question

Was	I/she/he/it	late?
Were	you/we/they	

• **Past Simple + *ago***

Question words	Question form	Answers
How long *ago*	did you go?	Six years *ago*.
How long *ago*	were you there?	Two hours *ago*.

b Complete the account of this witness, using *was* or *were*.

POLICEMAN: And where *were* you when the accident happened?
WITNESS: I *was* in front of the bank.
POLICEMAN: Where *was* the cyclist when the motorist hit her?
WITNESS: She *was* just next to that telephone box.
POLICEMAN: How many people *were* in the car?
WITNESS: There *were* three, I think.
POLICEMAN: What time *was* the accident?
WITNESS: 5 pm.

c Write complete answers to these questions, using *ago*.

Example: A: When was the last time you went abroad?
B: I went abroad six months ago.

When was the last time you:
• read a good book?
• wrote a letter?
• saw a good film?
• met an interesting new person?

3 Adjectives with *very/not very*

***Very* + adjective intensifies the adjective.**
She's *very* tall. She's 1.82 m.
She's *not very* tall. She's 1.52 m.

d Look at the picture below and write sentences using these words.

Example: She's very tall. He's not very rich.

tall rich happy hot big

12 I love fast food!

Love/hate; meals

1 Revision

1 Work with another student. Which countries are famous for this food?

paella   fish and chips
tacos   hamburgers
pizza   doughnuts
sukiyaki   moussaka

2 Put the food in the correct column for your partner. Ask and answer, like this:

> Do you like paella?

> Yes, I love it.

> Do you like tacos?

> No, I hate them.

+ + love	+ like	– don't like	– – hate
paella			tacos

3 Tell the class what your partner likes and dislikes.

2 Reading

1 Read the cartoon below. Why is Snoopy holding up flags? What does Snoopy think of food?

2 Read the cartoon again and complete this chart.

Flag	Meal	Time
	breakfast	8.00 am
	~~mid morning~~ ~~lunch~~ *midmorning*	11.00 am
	~~Afternoon~~ *Lynch*	1.00 pm
	~~bedtime~~ *afternoon (tea)*	4.00 pm
	. . . * *sypper (Dinner)*	7.00 pm
	. . . *bedtime*	10.00 pm

* also called dinner

3 Ask other students these questions.

How many meals a day do you have? What are they? What time do you have them?

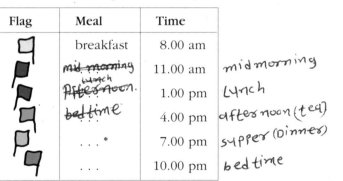

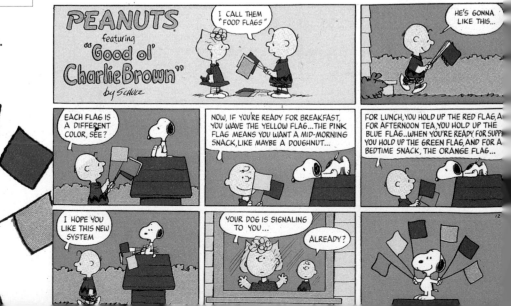

CHICKEN & PEPPER TACOS

8 taco shells
taco sauce
1½ oz of butter
2 small onions
2 chicken breasts
1 green pepper
7 fl oz water
2 tomatoes
1 avocado
4 oz grated cheese
natural yoghurt
shredded lettuce
sour cream

12

Method

1 Melt butte
lowish hea
Mix. Mix we
about 1-2 r

2 Add choppe
again until a
moving the
around to p

3 Add tomatoe

4 Add the wate
cook until th
thickish saud

5 Add cheese a
Keep stirring

13

Food; *some/any*; countable + uncountable
nouns; *often/never*; need + nouns

---

3 Vocabulary: food

**1 Work with another student. Find this food in
the picture above.**

salt and pepper   chicken   onions   yoghurt
green peppers   cream   lettuce   water
avocado   meat

2 ⌨ Listen to the words and mark the stress.

**3 Talk to other students about eating habits in
your country or family. Which food do you
often have for breakfast/lunch/a bedtime
snack? Which food do you never have?**

4 Listening

**1 Look at the recipe for tacos at the top of the
page. Neesha and Simon want to make tacos
for dinner. What food do they need?**

**2 ⌨ Listen and write the food in the correct
column.**

They've got some	They haven't got any
taco shells taco sauce	green peppers

3 Check your answers with another student.

A: Have they got any . . .?
B: Yes, they have./No, they haven't.

5 Grammar: *a/some/any*

**1 Look at the sentences in Exercise 4 Listening.
Which is correct, a or b?**

1a They use *some* in the positive sentence.
 b They use *any* in the positive sentence.
2a They use *some* in the negative sentence.
 b They use *any* in the negative sentence.
3a They use *some* in the question.
 b They use *any* in the question.

**2 Work with another student. Prepare to make
tacos for supper. Have you got enough food in
your fridge?**

STUDENT A: Look in the fridge on page 127.
Answer Student B's questions.
STUDENT B: Look at the recipe for tacos again. Ask
Student A if she/he has got the food
you need. Make a shopping list of
things to buy.

NB Countable/uncountable nouns	
Countable nouns	**Uncountable nouns**
Singular an onion	(some) water
Plural (some) onions	

Which food in the picture is countable,
uncountable or both?

Adjectives, *once/twice a week,
three/four times a week*

BIG MAC MEAL

McCHICKEN SANDWICH MEAL

ONLY
2·88

6 Listening

1 Answer these questions.

1 Which fast food chain can you see above?
2 Which fast food chains are there in your
   country?
3 How often do you eat fast food? – once/twice
   a week, three/four times a week?

**2 🖳 Listen and decide which of these three
people likes fast food most, Ivan, Rose or
Rohana.**

**3 Listen again. Look at these adjectives and
answer the questions below.**

cheap   hot   slow   friendly
clean   tasty   nice   crowded

1 Which of these adjectives can you see in the
   picture above?
2 Which adjectives does Ivan use to describe the
   meals, the people and the restaurant?
3 Which adjectives does Rose use to describe
   the food, the restaurant and the service?
4 Which adjectives does Rohana use to describe
   the chips and fast food generally.

**4 Write one sentence about each person above.
Say if they like or don't like fast food
restaurants and why.**

Example: Rose doesn't like them because the
food is always cold and the service is slow.

7 Vocabulary: adjectives

**1 Look at the words below. Which can you use
with the words in the box?**

Example: Cheap/expensive can go with food,
clothes and places.

food   clothes   people   places   service

fast/slow   cheap/expensive
hot/cold   friendly/unfriendly
tasty/tasteless   crowded/uncrowded
clean/dirty   nice/nasty

**2 Talk to other students about where you live
and work. What do you think of:**

• the public transport?
• the local shops?
• the people you work/study with?
• the place you work/study in?

Example: The public transport is cheap but very
crowded.

74

8 Grammar: prepositions 4

1 Look at the advertisement for McDonald's. Does it say McDonald's is:

a *next to* the tourist attractions?
b *far from* the tourist attractions?
c *near* the tourist attractions?
d *opposite* the tourist attractions?

2 Answer these questions.

1 How far is McDonald's:
• from Westminster Cathedral?
• from Oxford Circus?

2 How long does it take to get from McDonald's:
• to Piccadilly Circus?
• to The British Museum?
• to The Commonwealth Institute?

3 Ask and answer with another student.

Where do you live? How far is it from here?
How long does it take to get to work/school
/the shops/the bank/the nearest public transport?

9 Vocabulary: transport

1 Look at the McDonald's advertisement again. Which of these forms of transport can you see?

a plane   a taxi   a motor bike
a bicycle a car   the underground
a boat   a train   a bus

2 Tell another student when you last travelled by each of the forms of transport above. Say where you went.

Example: I last travelled by boat three years ago. I went to Greece.

NB *Far* vs *a long way*

How *far* is McDonald's from here?
It's *a long way.*/ It isn't *far.*

When do you use *far*?
a in questions?   b in positive sentences?
c in negative sentences?

SO WHAT'S THE BIG ATTRACTION?

Westminster Cathedral
Only 50 metres from McDonald's
155 Victoria Street

Oxford Circus
Only 150 metres from McDonald's
185 Oxford Street

Piccadilly Circus
Only 2 minutes walk from McDonald's
57 Haymarket

The British Museum
Only 3 minutes walk from McDonald's
112 High Holborn

The Commonwealth Institute
Only 5 minutes walk from McDonald's
108 Kensington High Street

Have a quick look
at some
of London's sights,
then take in a
McDonald's restaurant.

A VISIT TO McDONALD'S MAKES YOUR DAY.

ENGLISH IN ACTION

1 Read this letter to McDonald's from a Greek student who wants a job. Answer the questions.

1 Where did Dimitra live when she wrote the letter?
2 How did she know there was a possible job?
3 When are her English classes? Are they in the morning or in the afternoon?
4 When is she going to return to Greece?

2 Write a letter to apply for the job that you would like.

1 Where do you put your address and the date?
2 How do you begin and end a formal letter?

---

53 Fulham Rd.
London W2 6 4T

7. 2. 92

Dear Sir/Madam,
    I saw your notice asking for part-time and full-time assistants in your Fulham Road branch. I would like to apply for a full-time job. I am available from 9 - 1 p.m. every day. I study English at the International English Centre every day and am going to be in London until the end of June.

    Yours faithfully
    Dimitra Leonidas

**Situations **

ROYAL THEATRE
LEATHERHEAD

requires
BOX OFFICE ASSISTANT
Training given.
Friendly atmosphere, flexible 3 hours duties, rota system to su occasional Saturdays.
Please write to:
Elaine Thirlby, Royal Theatre, Church Str Leatherhead, Surrey KT22 8DF.

Queen's Arms
45 Cheam Road, Ewell
requires
PART TIME BAR STAF
Experience not necessary.
Top rates paid.
Phone Barry or Dick
081-393 1647.

MORLEYS
Department Store, High Street, S

Part Time Staff Requir
2-5 days. No Saturdays.
Contact: 071-643 500

WEEKEND STAI

Language Review 12

1 Nouns: with *some* and *any*

	Positive	Negative	Question
Uncountable	some	not any	any
Countable plural	some	not any	any

I've got *some* sugar but I haven't got *any* milk.
Have you got *any*?
I've got *some* apples but I haven't got *any* oranges.
Have you got *any*?

a Complete the sentences with *some* or *any*.

1 I haven't got . . . money. Have you?
  Yes, I've got . . . but not a lot.
2 We know . . . good restaurants but I don't know if
  . . . of them open at 7.00.
3 Did you go to . . . pubs when you were in Ireland?
  Yes, . . . but I don't think they were very typical.

2 Prepositions

- ***next to, near, far from, a long way from, opposite***

Folkestone is the town next to Dover. It is near
Sandgate. It isn't far from Ashford but it's a long way
from Margate. Folkestone is opposite Calais in France.

- ***by + transport***

I go to work
  by bus
  by taxi
  by car
  by train
  by underground
or, I walk.

b Write sentences about the places on the map, using the prepositions below.

Example: San Francisco is opposite Oakland.

next to   near   far from   a long way from   opposite

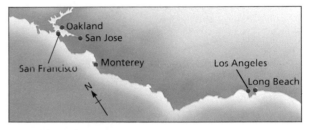

c Read Antonia Smith's diary and answer in complete sentences.

How did Antonia Smith go:
1 to the theatre?   3 to Leeds?
2 to Amsterdam?   4 to her mother's?

December

Thursday
339–26 Week 49
5
Fly to Amsterdam - Flight BA 703 - 9 p.m.
Taxi here at 7 p.m.

Friday
340–25 Week 49
● New Moon
6
Meeting at 10 a.m. Canal trip 2 p.m.
Flight home - Flight BA 704 9 p.m.

Saturday
341–24 Week 49 PAYE week 36
sr 7.51, ss 15.53
7
10 a.m. Walkers' Club Outing N.B! Good shoes
Theatre with Helen - 7.30 p.m. Book Taxi for 7.00 p.m.

Sunday
342–23 Week 49 Week 36
2nd in Advent
8
Mum's for lunch - 11 a.m. bus
Leeds Sunday p.m. Trains at 17.10 (18.30) 19.50

13 *Raining in my heart*

Weather and temperature;
adjective + verb forms

EUROPEAN WEATHER AND TRAVEL

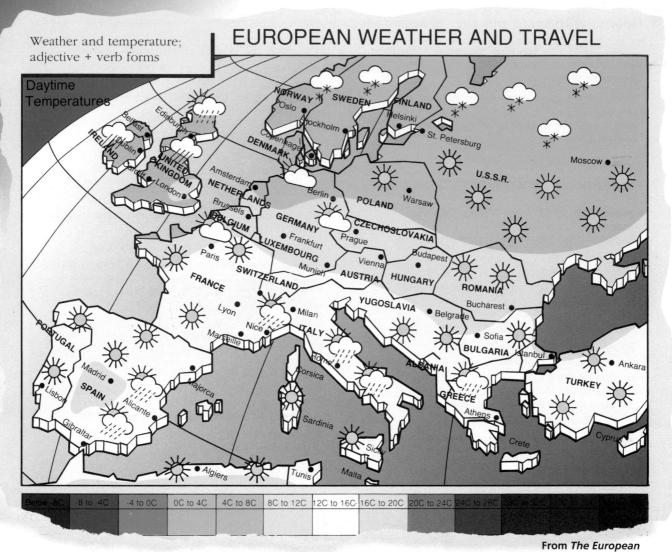

Daytime
Temperatures

Below -8C	-8 to -4C	-4 to 0C	0C to 4C	4C to 8C	8C to 12C	12C to 16C	16C to 20C	20C to 24C	24C to 28C	28C to 32C	

From *The European*

1 Revision

Work with another student.

1 What do you eat and
drink when
a the weather is hot?
b the weather is cold?

2 Vocabulary: the weather

1 Look at this weather map of Europe and name three countries
where:

it's raining   it's very cold and snowing   it's sunny

2 Complete the chart below.

Symbol	Noun	Adjective	Verb form	Temperature
☔	rain	xxxxxxx	It is *raining*	
❄	snow	xxxxxxx	It is *snowing*	hot
▒	fog	*foggy*	xxxxxxxx	warm
☁	cloud	*cloudy*	xxxxxxxx	cool
☀	sun	*sunny*	xxxxxxxx	cold
➔	wind	*windy*	xxxxxxxx	

Pronunciation: /ɒ/ vs /əʊ/

1 🔊 Listen. Write *fog* and *snow* in the correct column.

/ɒ/	/əʊ/
hot	cold
. . .	. . .

2 🔊 Listen. Which one of these towns and countries has the sound /ɒ/?

Poland   Scotland
Barcelona   Copenhagen
Cairo   Rome

3 Talk to another student.

STUDENT A: Look at the weather chart below. Ask your partner for the missing information and complete the chart.

STUDENT B: Look at the weather chart on page 126. Ask your partner for the missing information and complete the chart.

Example: A: What's the weather like in Stockholm?
B: It's sunny.

rises . . . . .y-gate prices co..
uffer-   *Comment - Page SIX*

AROUND THE WORLD
Lunchtime Reports

	C	F
Barcelona ....S	16	61
Bonn ....–	9	48
Cairo ....S	17	63
Copenhagen ....–	7	45
Glasgow C	7	45
Moscow ....–	0	32
Osaka ....R	9	48
Rio de Janeiro ...–	25	77
Rome ....Sn	0	32
Stockholm ....–	5	41
Tokyo ....R	7	45

S = Sun, R = Rain, Sn = Snow, C = Cloud

FRANCE: 178 Fr GERMANY:176M

3 Grammar

What's it like?

1 Look at this example and answer the questions below.

A: What's the weather like? *to be*
B: It's sunny and hot.

1 What is the verb in the question and answer?
2 In the answer, what does *it* mean?
3 In the question, which word/s can you change to *it*?

2 Put the words in the questions (a-c) in order and match them to the answers (1-3) below.

a your like what best friend is?
b country capital what the like is your of?
c like house what your is?

1 It's dirty and very crowded.
2 She/he's got a good sense of humour.
3 It's big. It's got three bedrooms.

3 Now ask other students the questions.

Adjectives

1 Match these adjectives to their opposites.

1 comfortable   1 good
2 cheap   6   2 unattractive
3 friendly 7   3 quiet
4 easy   8   4 unkind
5 loud   3   5 unhappy
6 attractive 2   6 expensive
7 kind   4   7 unfriendly
8 bad   1   8 difficult
9 happy   5   9 uncomfortable

2 Ask other students about people and things they know, eg family, job, home, school. Answer using the adjectives above.

Example: A: What's your brother like?
B: He's friendly.

4 Reading

1 Before you read, discuss these questions with another student.

1 What famous pop stars do you know?
2 What are they like?
3 Do pop stars have any characteristics in common?

2 Read the text and answer these questions.

1 Who is this pop star?
2 What was he like? How was he different from other pop stars?
3 Why do you think he is a legend?

buddy holly

At 1.50 am on 3rd February 1959 the American pop star Buddy Holly died in a plane crash along with Richie Valens and the Big Bopper. Holly was 22 years old. His name became a legend; songs like 'Raining in my Heart', first released after his death, were immediate hits in both America and Britain. Unlike Elvis Presley and other pop stars of his time, Holly was not handsome or loud. He was modest, sensitive and easy to understand. He was tall and slim and wore black horn-rimmed glasses. He was more like a school-boy than a pop star. His music style was unique and continued to in-fluence pop music well into the mid-sixties. In the song American Pie, Don Mclean sang about the death of Buddy Holly as 'The day the music died'.

5 Listening

1 Read the title of the song below. What do you think?

1 Is it going to be a happy song? Why/Why not?
2 Is it going to be about love, the weather or the body?
3 Is the music going to be fast or slow?

2 Listen. Were you correct?

3 Listen again and answer these questions.

1 What's the weather like in the song? _Sunny_
2 How does the singer feel? Why? _Unhappy_
3 Does he think the future is going to be good or bad? _bad_

4 Listen again. Put the lines of the song in the correct order.

Raining in my Heart

7 Oh misery, misery! What's going to become of me?

2 The weatherman says 'Clear today',
He doesn't know you've gone away,
and it's raining, raining in my heart.

6 And it's raining, raining in my heart.

1 The sun is out, the sky is blue,
there's not a cloud to spoil the view,
but it's raining, raining in my heart.

8 Oh misery, misery! What's going to become of me?

4 I tell my blues they mustn't show,
but soon these tears are bound to flow,
'cos it's raining, raining in my heart,
raining in my heart, raining in my heart.

5 But it's raining, raining in my heart.

3 I tell my blues they mustn't show,
but soon these tears are bound to flow,
'cos it's raining, raining in my heart.

5 Look at the words of the song and find:

a two words that mean unhappiness (one is also a colour!)
b a question about the singer's future life.
c the words which say why the singer is unhappy.
d the abbreviation for *because*.
e the name of a job.

80

6 Grammar: Present Continuous

It *is* It's	rain*ing*	=	now

1 Answer these questions.

1 Is it raining where you are?
2 If it isn't raining, what's the weather like?

2 Look at the examples of the Present Continuous above and answer:

1 How do you make the question?
2 How do you make the negative?

3 Look at these people. What are they wearing? Why? What's the weather like?

scarf

strip

4 Ask about other student's clothes.

Example: What is this/that?
What are these/those?

5 Stand back to back with another student. Try to remember what they are wearing, like this:

A: You're wearing jeans.
B: No, I'm not.
A: Are you wearing a blue skirt?

7 Writing

Read the rules before you play this game.

Rules
1 Work in pairs. Write four sentences describing another person in the class.
2 Don't write the person's name. Write *she* or *he*.
3 Write about their appearance, colour of eyes and hair, clothes, job, etc.
4 Say where she/he is sitting in the class.
5 Number the sentences 1-4. Begin with the most difficult sentence for other people to guess.
6 Now read your description, sentence by sentence. How soon can the class guess who you are describing?

8 Listening

Pyrple

1  Listen to a phone call from Britain to Australia. Answer these questions.

1 Who is making the phone call? Jam. happy And
2 Who is he phoning?
3 Who else would he like to speak to?

2 Listen again and answer these questions.

1 Why is the caller phoning?
2 What is the person in Australia doing? gardning 30
3 What is she wearing? Jean
4 What is she going to wear tonight? dress
5 What's the weather like in Sydney and London? nice, sunny
6 What's the new woman in the cinema like? nice
7 What's happening in her home life? Problem

3 Look at the questions above. Which are in the Present Continuous? Why?

Happy Anniversary!

Merry Christmas
and
Happy New Year

Congratulations
on the birth of
your first baby

HAPPY BIRTHDAY

Many happy
returns
I hope you enjoy your
birthday.

GOOD LUCK

You'd like to exchange greetings cards with English-speaking friends.

1 Look at the cards above. Which one did Jon send? When do we send the different cards?

2 Work with another student. Match the celebrations to the dates, then answer the questions below.

25th December — New Year's Eve
14th February — Labour Day
31st October — Christmas Day
1st May — Halloween
31st December — St Valentine's Day

1 What date is Christmas Eve?
2 What date is New Year's Day?

3 Write the celebrations in the correct column.

Spring Mar. Apr. May.	Summer Jun. Jul. Aug.	Autumn Sept. Oct. Nov.	Winter Dec. Jan. Feb.
Labour day		Halloween	Christmas day, st. valentine day, new year's eve

4 Discuss with other students.

1 Which of these occasions do you celebrate in your country? Are they in the same season?
2 What other celebrations are there in your country? What season are they in?

5 Send three cards to English-speaking friends to celebrate different occasions. Write a greeting in each card.

Language review 13

1 Adjectives

• Opposites with *un*

Adjective	Negative adjective
happy	unhappy
intelligent	unintelligent
attractive	unattractive
friendly	unfriendly
comfortable	uncomfortable

• Other opposites

Adjective	Negative adjective
clean	dirty
good	bad
cheap	expensive
fast	slow

• Weather

Weather	Adjective
fog	foggy
cloud	cloudy
wind	windy
sun	sunny

NB It is raining.
It is snowing.

a Complete the sentences below with these adjectives.

unattractive   unhappy   unfriendly
unkind   unintelligent   unimportant

1 He's very . . . He never says hello.
2 It was very . . . to kick the cat. Don't do it again.
3 She is very . . . Her grandfather died last week.
4 He isn't . . ., he just doesn't work very hard.
5 Don't cry about something so . . .
6 He thinks he's . . . but actually, he's very handsome.

2 Verbs: Key verbs *to be* + *like*

What	is	the weather	like?
		she/he/it	
	are	you/we/they	

what does he look like?
what is the book real like?
what is paris like?
what was the meal like?

b Read the answers then complete the questions.

Example: What . . .? It's windy. – What's the weather like? It's windy.

1 What . . .? He's tall and slim, with brown hair – not like me or our parents.
2 What . . .? It's good. It's about a family in the 18th century. Would you like to read it?
3 What . . .? It's beautiful. There are lots of interesting things to do, including a visit to the Eiffel Tower, of course.
4 What . . .? It was delicious. The mushroom soup was particularly good.

3 Present Continuous

Positive	She	is	working.
Negative	She	isn't	working.
Question	Is	she	working?

Short answers
Yes, she is.
No, she isn't.

c Write the questions.

Example: What/you/eat? – What are you eating?

1 What/you/do? – what are you doing?
2 What/you/wear? – what are you wearing?
3 Where/you/sit? – where are you sitting?
4 Who/sit/next/you? – who is sitting to next to you?
5 Why/you/learn English? – why are you learning english?

d Answer the questions in exercise c in complete sentences.

4 Pronouns: *it* for weather, time and distances

It is used as an empty subject (with no real meaning).

It is foggy and *it* is raining.
It is winter/spring/summer/autumn.
It is three o'clock.
It is Tuesday.
How long does *it* take?
It is 250 metres to the bank.

e Answer these questions in complete sentences.

1 What season is it?
2 What's the weather like?
3 What time is it?
4 What day of the week is it?
5 How far is it from here to your home?
6 How long does it take to get there?

14 For better, for worse

Adjectives for health and feelings

1 Revision

1 🖼 **Listen to this conversation between Jon and Neesha, at work in the cinema.**

How is Jon?
How is Neesha?

2 Listen again. Where is the stress on the first question? Where is the stress on the returned question?

NEESHA: How are you?
JON: Fine. How are you?
N : not to good.

3 Work with another student. Take it in turns to begin dialogues with the questions below.

Example: A: Where do you come from?
           B: Brazil. Where do you come from?

Where do you come from?
What languages do you speak?
Where do you live?
What do you do?
What did you do yesterday?
What are you going to do at the weekend?

2 Vocabulary: adjectives

1 Put these adjectives into two groups, positive and negative.

H very well   F happy   angry Fill
F depressed   awful B   great Both
H not very well fine B   tired Health
H not too good not bad   ill H
                      B

2 Work with another student.

Which adjectives describe health and which describe feelings? Which can you use for both?

3 Ask other students how they are, using the words above.

Example: A: How are you?
           B: Not bad. How are you?

SOLOMON GRUNDY

Solomon Grundy,
B Born on Monday,
C Christened on Tuesday,
D Married on Wednesday,
E Got ill on Thursday,
G Worse on Friday,
A Died on Saturday,
F Buried on Sunday,
This was the end
Of Solomon Grundy.

Traditional

3 Pronunciation: /ɒ/ vs /ɔː/

1 🖼 **Read and listen to the traditional verse above. Match the days to the pictures.**

Example: Monday – B

Monday – B
Tuesday – C
Wednesday – D
Thursday – E
Friday – G
Saturday – A
Sunday – F

2 Listen again and repeat the verse.

To be + born; comparatives
(1)

Grammar: *to be + born*

/ɒ/	/ɔː/
Solomon Grundy *was born* on Monday.	

1 Ask other students. When/Where were you born?

1 How many were born in the same town or country?
2 How many were born in the same year?

2 Write the infinitive of these Past Simple forms.

taught   lost   bought   washed
caught   watched   got   fought
thought   was   wore

3 💻 Listen. Do you pronounce each Past Simple form with /ɒ/ or /ɔː/?

4 Tell your partner three things you did last week. Use verbs from the list above.

4 Grammar: comparatives 1

1 Read the extract from the Church of England Marriage Ceremony below and complete the chart.

Adjective	Comparative
bad	worse
good	better
rich	richer
poor	poorer

Which adjectives are regular? Which are irregular?

> To have and to hold from this day forward, for better for worse, for richer for poorer, in sickness and in health, to love and to cherish, till death us do part.

2 Work with other students. What do you think – which is better, a or b?

1a To get married early in life.
 b To get married late in life.

2a To have no children.
 b To have a very large family.

3a To have a boring job but a good social life.
 b To have an interesting job but no social life.

4a To be OK all the time.
 b To be very happy some of the time and very depressed some of the time.

Comparatives (2)

5 Listening

1 Before you listen, think of one advantage of:

1 an arranged marriage.
2 a love marriage.

2 📟 Listen to these two British Indian women, Neesha and Menira, discussing marriage.

1 What type of marriage does each one have, an arranged or a love marriage?
2 Was Menira happy with the type of marriage she had?
3 Was Neesha happy with the type of marriage she had?

6 Grammar: comparatives 2

1 📟 Listen to the two women again and complete these sentences. How do they pronounce *than*?

a I prefer the idea of an arranged marriage; the man is generally older and the age difference makes marriage more interesting.

b I'm sure Simon's more attractive to me because I chose him, even though he's younger than me!

c Simon's got a good sense of humour. He is definitely funnier and less serious than the men in my family.

d I'm happier this way because he is more understanding than other men I know.

2 From the sentences (a-d), find comparatives of:

• one-syllable adjectives.
• two-syllable adjectives ending in y.
• adjectives of two, three (or more) syllables.

3 Make rules for comparatives from these examples.

4 Write three sentences. Compare yourself to another member of your family.

7 Speaking

1 Work with another student. Read about Simon and Neesha's life a year ago. Then look at the photo of them now. Make comparisons about:

their home   their financial situation
their car   their feelings
his job

A year ago Neesha and Simon lived in a small house and drove an old 2CV car which cost £600. Simon didn't have a very good job and they didn't have much money but they were happy. Then Simon got a new job and everything changed . . .

8 Reading

1 Before you read, match these words from the letter to words with similar meanings.

2 -	resent	be responsible for
1 -	look after	be angry about
4 -	give up	start
5 -	enjoy	stop
3 -	take on	like

2 Read this letter to a 'problem page' from Mrs X. Is her problem about:

a her children?   b her work?   c her husband?

dear gill

He expects too much

When my children were born, I gave up work to look after them. Now they're both at work, I've taken on a full time job which I thoroughly enjoy.

The problem is my husband. He seems to think that even though I'm working full time I should still do everything I did before, have his dinner on the table when he comes in (even though he gets home before me!), and do all the housework. I think he not only resents me working, but that I now earn as much as him.

I feel really put out, as I've devoted nearly 20 years of my life to the home and family, and now I want something for myself he doesn't like it. What should I do?

Mrs X, Eastleigh

You seem to have gained   your previous marriages of   **though I'm**
confidence from your new job   how thin

From *Woman's Realm*

3 Read the letter again. Are these statements true (T) or false (F)?

1 She stayed at home when her children were young. **F**
2 She has got two children. **T**
3 She doesn't like her work. **F**
4 Her husband arrives home later than her. **F**
5 He prepares dinner for her. **F**
6 They earn the same money. **T**
7 She began this job twenty years ago. **F**
8 Her husband doesn't like her working. **T**

9 Grammar: *should*

> /ʊ/   /uː/
> What   should I do?

1 Look at the question above from Mrs X's letter, asking for advice.

1 Find another example of *should* in the letter.
2 What advice would you give Mrs X? What should/ shouldn't she do?

2 Work with another student. Write a reply to Mrs X's letter. Give her advice.

Dear Mrs X,
We think you should

NB **Formal letters**

Begin your letters:
Dear Mrs X,

End your letters:
Yours sincerely
+ your name

How do you end a more formal letter which begins *Dear Sir/Madam*?

ENGLISH IN ACTION

You are not very well. What's the matter?

1 Match the words to the picture above.

a headache   a backache   a toothache
a stomachache   an earache   a cold

2 Ask and answer with another student.

Example: A: What's the matter?
          B: I've got a cold.

3 Use the ideas below to give advice, using
should/shouldn't.

Example: A: I've got a headache.
          B: You should take an aspirin

go to bed   go to work
drink hot lemon   go to the dentist's
eat anything   have lots of hot drinks
go to a party   take an aspirin
go to the doctor's

4 Have a complete conversation with another
student.

A: How are you?
B: Not very well.
A: Oh dear! What's the matter?
B: I've got . . .
A: I am sorry. You should . . .
B: I know. You're right.

You feel worse. Phone the doctor's (or

dentist's) surgery and make an appointment.

5 🖭 **Listen to the receptionist's side of the**
conversation. When can you have an
appointment?

6 Listen again and answer the receptionist's
questions.

You are in the surgery waiting room with

some other patients. You see the doctor

one by one.

7 While you are waiting, ask the other
patients – *What's the matter?*

8 When you see the doctor, say what the
matter is. What advice does she/he give?

Language review 14

1 Adjectives: comparatives

• Adjectives

Adjective	Comparative
old	older
happy	happier
expensive	more expensive
good	better
bad	worse

• + than

Helen is *older than* Kate.
Ramon is *happier than* Enrique.
Champagne is *more expensive than* wine.

a Write eight sentences to compare José and Manuel.

Example: José is older than Manuel.

José	Manuel
He is thirty.	He is twenty-six.
He is 1m 65 tall.	He is 1m 60 tall.
He is not very hungry.	He is very hungry.
He is very cold.	He is not very cold.
He doesn't feel very well.	He feels OK.
He goes to bed at 1.00 am.	He goes to bed at 12.30 am.
He is a good student.	He is a very good student.
He is modest.	He is not very modest.

2 Verbs

• Key verb: *to be + born*
Positive

I/she/he/it	was	born in 1952.
You/we/they	were	

Negative

I/she/he/it	wasn't	born in 1952.
You/we/they	weren't	

Question

Was	I/she/he/it	born in 1952?
Were	you/we/they	

• Key verb: *have got + illness.*

I/you/we/they	have got	a headache an earache a backache
She/he/it	has got	a stomachache a toothache a cold

What is the matter?   I'm not very well.
                     I've got a headache.

b Write sentences. Say when and where you and your family were born.

c Complete this dialogue with the correct form of *to be* or *have got.*

MAREK: Hello, Joanna. How *are* you?
JOANNA: Fine. How *are* you?
M: Not too good, actually.
J: Why? What *is* the matter?
M: I don't know. I *am* just depressed and I *have* a very bad headache.
J: How awful!
M: And I *am* hungry all the time. The problem *is*. I can't stop eating. That's why I *am* so depressed. This time last year I *was* slim. Now I *am* thirty-five and look at me!
J: Oh is that all! I thought it *was* something serious! Listen, why don't you come and see us this evening. I *am* going to make a special meal for Sue's birthday. Come for dinner.
M: Joanna, you *are* wonderful. I feel better already! What *are* you going to make?

3 *Should* (advice)

Positive

I/you/we/they She/he/it	should	phone. come.

Negative

I/you/we/they She/he/it	shouldn't	phone. come.

Question

Should	I/you/we/they she/he/it	phone? come?

d Give this man advice using *should* or *shouldn't*.

Example: He should stop smoking.

1 Thinking about learning: Listening and reading

> **Revises:**
> Vocabulary: Feelings; weather; transport; distance
> Grammar: Key verb: *to be*

Predicting from titles

1 **Work with another student. You are going to listen to a song by Dire Straits. Look at the title below and answer the questions.**

   1 What do you think the song is about? *Romantic.*
   2 What or who is *So far away?*
   3 How is the singer feeling?

2 📻 **Now listen to the song. Were you correct?**

Predicting from context

1 📖 **Listen and write the chorus.**

2 **Look at the verses below and predict the missing words.**

3 **Listen to the song and check your answers.**

4 **Talk to another student. What do you miss most when you are away from home?**

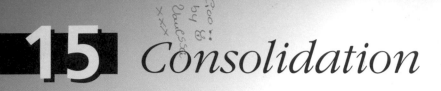

so far away

Here ... (1) am again in ... (2) mean old town
And you're so far away from ... (3)
Now ... (4) are you when the sun goes ... (5)
You're so far ... (6) from me.

CHORUS

I'm tired of being in ... (7) and being all alone
... (8) you're so far away from me
I'm tired of making out on the ... (9)
'Cos you're so far away ... (10) me

CHORUS

I get so ... (11) when I have to explain
When you're so far away from me
See you've been in the sun and I've been
in the ... (12)
And you're so far away from ... (13)

CHORUS

Dire Straits 1980

Predicting from pictures

You are going to read a poem. Look at the picture above. What is the poem about?

Predicting the meaning of new words

Work with another student. Look at the poem and list the words you don't know. Can you guess what any of them mean?

Commuter

Commuter - one who spends his life
In riding to and from his wife;
A man who shaves and takes a train
And then rides back to shave again.

E.B. White

Using a dictionary

1 Read this dictionary definition of the word *commuter* and answer the questions below.

*word   pronunciation   grammar word
                                      e.g. noun*
commuter /kəˈmjuːtə/ *(n)* a person who
lives in one town and works in another.
definition/meaning

1 Who is the commuter in these sentences, Joao or Rose?
  a Joao lives in London and works in London.
  b Rose lives in Canterbury and works in London.
2 Where is the stress on the word *commuter*?
3 How is it marked in the dictionary?

2 Check the meaning and pronunciation of new words in the poem. Use a dictionary or the wordlist on page 136.

3 Listen to the poem. Is your pronunciation correct?

4 Say the poem to another student.

Traditional Celebrations

Halloween

In Medieval times, 31st October was considered to be the last day of summer. It was a time to remember the souls of the dead who were supposed to come and revisit their homes. Nowadays, children go from house to house dressed up as witches, ghosts and monsters, asking for sweets or money and saying 'Trick or treat'. They mean that if people don't give them anything, they will play a trick on them.

35

Guy Fawkes Night

In Britain, 5th November commemorates the day that Guy Fawkes was executed in 1605 for trying to blow up the Houses of Parliament and kill James I of England. Before Guy Fawkes Night itself, children make 'guys', figures of Guy Fawkes, and collect money in the street for fireworks. On 5th November, they put their Guys on top of large bonfires. Families light fireworks as they stand around the bonfire and eat sausages and potatoes cooked on the fire.

Christmas Day

The birth of Christ is remembered on 25th December. Grandparents, aunts, uncles and cousins all meet for a big Christmas dinner of roast turkey and vegetables and then Christmas pudding. People put decorations on Christmas trees and give presents and cards. Children traditionally put up stockings on Christmas Eve for Father Christmas to fill with presents. .

---

2 Across cultures: celebrations

> **Revises:**
> **Vocabulary:** Food; special occasions; families; countries; clothes
> **Grammar:** Present Simple

1 Work in three groups, A, B and C. Each group, read about a different celebration and complete that part of the chart.

	Halloween	Christmas Day	Guy Fawkes Night
Date of celebration Reason for celebration Special food Special activities	31st oct	25th Dec. crist birth	5th novemob gary frwkes was executed saysayes&potatoes. firework.

2 Work in different groups of three, with one student from group A, one student from group B and one student from group C. Tell the two other students about the text you read. Listen to the other students and complete the chart.

3 Talk to other students about the traditions in your country or family. Tell them about:

- marriages, religious festivals, funerals and birthdays
- special food, clothes or presents
- what you say on each occasion

3 Language in context: puzzle page

Revises:
Vocabulary: Weather; clothes; body; meals; food; places
Grammar: Adjectives; comparatives; prepositions; verbs;
Present Continuous

1 Spot the difference

Find the 8 differences between picture A and picture B.

2 Solve the problem

Eleni is 23. She has got 2 brothers and
1 sister, aged 28, 26 and 17.
Katerina is taller than Costas.
Spiros is shorter than Eleni.
No one is shorter than Spiros.
Katerina is younger than Costas.
Eleni is older than Spiros.

**Name each person. How old are
they?**

3 Eye check / Word search

**Can you read all these letters?
Do you need glasses?**

```
H E A D E G G
R O P I O A S
B L U N C H   L
A   O B N G O   I
N   C L E A N   M
K   E L R H A M
```

Find the words hidden in the chart.
There are two for each of the
categories below.
Food/Places/Prepositions/Meals/
Body/Adjectives/Verbs

Check what you know!

Now turn to page 130 and
complete Check what you
know 3.

16 The biggest and the best

Adjectives of size and weight

PARKING IS SUCH SWEET SORROW

Where do you go for a real stretch limo? No, not America, not Japan. Finland. For Heikki Reijonen has just driven his 21m 94cm (72ft) car – and his little country – into *The Guinness Book of Records*. The 7.14 ton 1982 Cadillac Eldorado, with its V8 motor, cost half a million dollars and is better equipped than many homes – a 20-seater TV room, three telephones, bar with fridge, sundeck and jacuzzi. Now Reijonen plans to take the world's largest car on a tour of Europe, Australia and America.

From The Mail on Sunday

1 Revision

Read the article above and answer these questions.

1 Whose car is it?
2 Where does he come from?
3 How long is his car?
4 How many tons does it weigh?
5 How much did it cost?
6 What special features has it got?
7 Where is the owner going to take the car?

2 Vocabulary: adjectives

1 What do you think?

1 How cheap or expensive is petrol in your country at the moment?
2 Is the car above economical or uneconomical on petrol?

2 Work with another student. Which of these words and phrases describe Heikki Reijonen's car?

easy to park/difficult to park
comfortable/uncomfortable   fast/slow

3 Write the opposites of these adjectives. Use a dictionary or your wordlist if necessary.

large *small*   high *low*   heavy *light*
wide *narrow*   long *short*

4 Ask another student these questions.

Can you drive?
Have you or your family got a car?
What's it like?
Would you like a (new) car?
What kind of car would you like? Why?

> **NB Tall and short**
>
> The opposite of *tall* is *short*.
>
> What's the opposite of *long*?
> What's the difference between *long* and *tall*?

Superlatives

16

3 Grammar: superlatives

> It is the largest car in the world.

1 Look at the sentence above and answer these questions

1 Are there any cars larger than this car?
2 Which word tells you this?

2 Look at the advertisements below.

1 Find the superlatives of one-syllable adjectives.
2 Find the superlative of important.
3 Find the irregular superlatives of *good* and *bad*.

3 Complete the chart.

Adjective	Comparative	Superlative
1 long	longer (than)	the longest
2 large	larger (than)	the largest
3 big	bigger (than)	the biggest
4 heavy	heavier (than)	the heaviest
5 economical	more economical (than)	most economical
6 good	better (than)	the best
7 bad	worse (than)	the worst

4 Look at the adjectives in the chart with another student. Can you see any rules for types 1–5?

5 Write three sentences about Heikki Reijonen's car. Use superlatives.

Example: It's the largest car in the world.

Visit the
GUINNESS WORLD OF RECORDS
The Greatest Exhibition in Europe

GUINNESS WORLD OF RECORDS

FASTEST
TALLEST
DEEPEST
LONGEST
WEAKEST
LOUDEST
LIGHTEST
SMALLEST
HEAVIEST
GREATEST
YOUNGEST
BRIGHTEST
STRONGEST
AT THE
TROCADE
PICCADILLY CI

SPECIAL ISSUE   FALL 1990/$8.95
THE **LIFE** 100
MOST IMPORTANT AMERICANS OF THE 20TH CENTURY

LONDON'S BIGGEST SELLING GUIDE TO FILM·THEATRE·MUSIC·NIGHTLI
August 25-31 1983
No. 679 60p
Time Ou
The Best...

Best hamburgers. Best-dressed novelists. Best gym for women bodybuilders. Best opening night parties. Best value restaurant. Best kept radio secret. Best fish and chips.

the Worst.

Worst coffee. Worst drag pub. Worst party policy. Worst bookshop. Worst cricket team. Worst rubbish collecting. Worst poet. Worst...

A totally biased guide to London.

Which . . .?; Superlatives; agreeing and disagreeing: I agree/I don't agree

4 Pronunciation: superlatives

1 Say this sentence.

/ɪ/ /ɪ/ /e/
It's the biggest and the best.

2 Look at the chart below about British weather. Say the superlatives at the top of the chart.

Heat is on, maybe

	Coldest	Hottest	Wettest	Driest	Sunniest	Dullest
JAN		1916		1766	1959	1917
FEB	1947	1779	1833		1949	1940
MAR	1674		1947	1742	1929	1964
APR	1837	1865	1756	1938		1920
MAY	1698	1833	1773	1844	1989	
JUN	1675		1860	1925	1957	1987
JUL	1816	1983		1825	1911	1944
AUG		1975	1737	1747	1947	1912
SEP	1694	1729		1754	1911	1945
OCT	1740	1969	1903	1781		1968
NOV	1782	1818	1852	1945	1989	
DEC		1934	1914	1799	1962	1956
Year	1740	1989	1872	1731	1989	1932

YOU may have turned a beautiful shade of tomato red by sitti... join Friends of the Earth? The Eighties did include

Adapted from *Today*

3 Talk to another student.

STUDENT A: Look at the weather chart on this page. Ask your partner for the missing information to complete your chart.

STUDENT B: Look at the weather chart on page 127. Ask your partner for the missing information to complete your chart.

Example: A: When was the coldest January?
B: In 1795.

This month's Bes

Citroën 2CV • Length: 3.92m
• Top Speed: 71.5 m.p.h. • 55.0 M.P.G.
• Price: £4,322

Porsche 944 • Length: 4.29m
• Top Speed: 163.0 m.p.h. • 39.8 M.P.G.
• Price: £43,648

Volvo Estate • Length: 4.99m
• Top Speed: 123.0 m.p.h. • 38.2 M.P.G.
• Price: £27,670

5 Speaking

1 Read the information above about cars and discuss these questions with other students.

1 Which is the largest/smallest?
2 Which is the fastest/slowest?
3 Which is the most expensive/the least expensive?
4 Which is the most economical/the least economical?

2 Discuss these questions with other students.

1 Which car do you like best? Why?
2 Which is the best car for the town and which is best for the country?

3 Look at these sentences. Which two people think the same?

A: I think the Citroën is the best for the town.
B: I agree. It's the most economical on petrol.
C: I don't agree. I don't think it's comfortable enough.

erformers

Range Rover • Length: 4.57m
Top Speed: 111.8 m.p.h. • 26.9 M.P.G
Price: £27,175

da Riva • Length: 4.23m
op Speed: 96.3 m.p.h. • 40.9 M.P.G.
rice: £4,999

Escort • Length: 4.03m
Speed: 96.0 m.p.h. • 53.3 M.P.G.
ce: £9,185

SPECIFI

TOYO'
LAY(
Front
drive
ENGIN
capacit
Bore 8'
Stroke
Comp
Head,
Valve
cylina
Fuel a
injectio
Max p
Max to
GEAR
4-spe
Rat'
Fir,
SU
Fro
strut
damp.
Rear
stru'
arms
damp
STEE
Rack
2.7 t
BRA
Fron
Rear
Antilo
WHE'
TYF

4 **Talk to other students. Decide which car is the most suitable for the people below. You can only choose each car once.**

A A young professional couple who are going to buy a house in the country. They like exciting holidays abroad.

B An unmarried doctor who likes the good life but has got very little money in the bank.

C A family. The father is a teacher and the mother works at home. They have got three young children and a dog.

D A farmer whose younger brother also needs the car but is nervous about driving.

E A rich retired couple who would like a car mainly for shopping in town and taking their four grandchildren out at weekends.

F A busy accountant who works in London and uses her car for business and to go windsurfing at the weekends.

6 Listening

1 🖭 **Listen to Jon and Neesha talking on the telephone and answer these questions.**

1 Why is she phoning him?
2 When is she going to his house?

2 **Mark the route from Neesha's house to Jon's house on the map.**

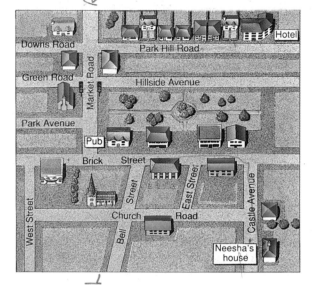

7 Vocabulary: street directions

1 🖭 **Listen again and complete the sentences.**
Go out of Castle Avenue.
Turn Left into Brick Street.
Go straight on past the pub.
Turn right
Go down Market Road to the traffic lights.
Go past the traffic lights.
Take the second road on the right.

2 **Work with another student. Write the directions from Jon's house to Neesha's house.**

8 Speaking

1 **Draw a map showing how to get from the nearest underground/station/bus-stop to your house.**

2 **Use your map and tell another student how to get to your house.**

> Go out of the station and turn right . . .

Dear

I'd love to stay with you when I visit your country next week. I'm going to arrive at the airport at about 7.30pm on Saturday evening. I've got your address but I need to know the best way to get to your house. Can you write or phone and let me know?

I'm really looking forward to seeing you again and meeting all your family.

See you soon,

All the best,

Last week you invited an English-speaking

friend to come and stay with you.

1 Read her/his reply and answer these questions.

1 Can your friend come?
2 What information does she/he need?
3 What does she/he want you to do?

2 Where do these details go in the letter above?

Your name
Your friend's name
Your friend's address
The date

3 Reply to the letter. Tell your friend how to get to your house from the airport.

4 Your friend is arriving tomorrow. Telephone her/him to find out the time of her/his arrival and to explain the directions. Begin and end the conversation like this:

YOUR FRIEND:	Hello.
YOU:	Hello. This is (your name).
YOUR FRIEND:	Oh, hello! How are you?
YOU:	. . .
YOUR FRIEND:	. . .
YOUR FRIEND:	OK. Fine. Thanks for phoning. Bye.
YOU:	Bye. See you tomorrow.

NB Finishing letters

Letters to friends and family finish with:
Love (from) + name.

More formal letters or letters from a man to another man finish with:
Best wishes from + name.

Find a similar ending in the letter above.

Language review 16

1 Superlatives

• Regular

Adjective	Comparative	Superlative
old	older	the oldest
heavy	heavier	the heaviest
expensive	more expensive	the most expensive

• Irregular

Adjective	Comparative	Superlative
good	better	the best
bad	worse	the worst

a Write about these things in order of importance.

Example:
Rome, Petra, London. (old) – Petra is the oldest. Rome is older than London.

1 House, castle, room. (big)
2 Lead, paper, wood. (heavy)
3 Horse, cheetah, cow. (fast)
4 Bicycle, car, motorbike. (economical)
5 Leather, cotton, plastic. (expensive)
6 The Beatles, Madonna, Pavarotti. (good)

2 Verbs: imperatives for street directions

Use these verbs for giving directions

go + straight on/past/across/out of/into/down/up
turn + left/right
take + the first/second/on the left/right

b Look at this map and write directions from the station to the Tourist Information Centre.

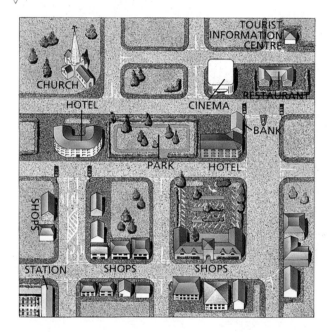

3 Think/don't think/agree/don't agree

• Giving opinions

I think it's nice/expensive/cheap.
I don't think it's nice/expensive/cheap.

• Agreeing and disagreeing

I agree (with you).
I don't agree (with you).

c Complete this dialogue using *think, don't think, agree* or *don't agree*.

A: I think children should work for their pocket money.
B: Oh no! I . . . They work at school. They shouldn't work at home too.
A: I . . . they should. They can do small jobs around the house. But I . . . they should work outside the home.
B: Oh, I . . . with you about that. I . . . it's terrible that some children work on Saturdays or after school. I . . . the government should stop that.
A: Oh no! I . . . it's the parents' responsibility not the government's. I . . . politicians should tell parents what is good for their children.

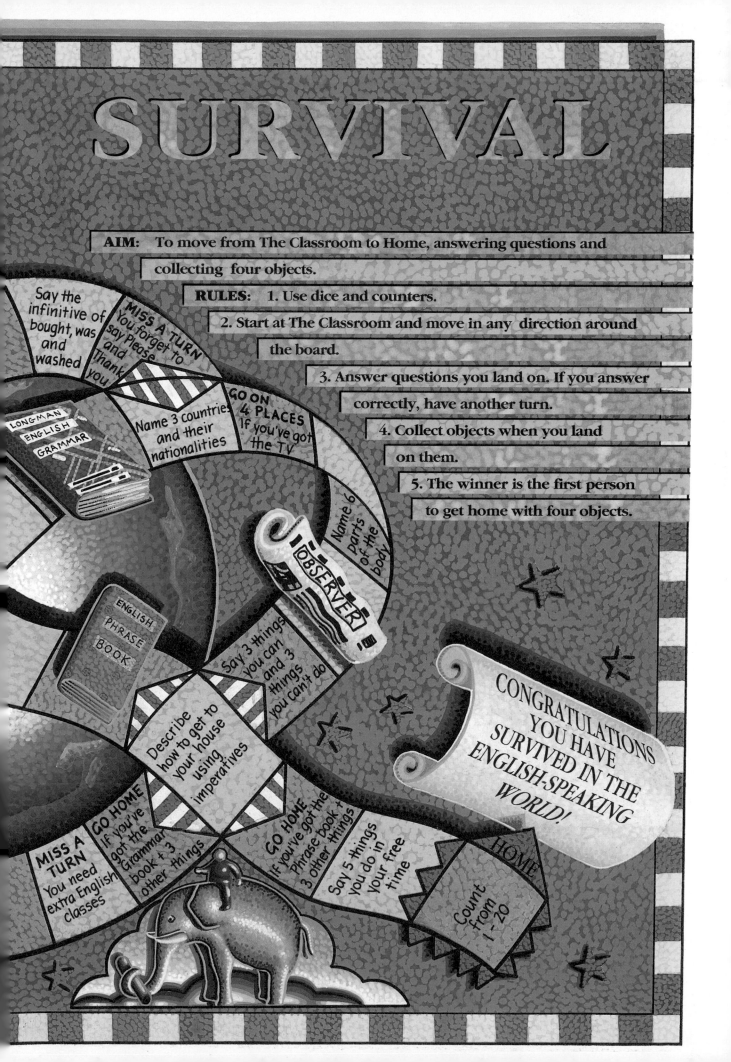

SURVIVAL

AIM: To move from The Classroom to Home, answering questions and collecting four objects.

RULES:
1. Use dice and counters.
2. Start at The Classroom and move in any direction around the board.
3. Answer questions you land on. If you answer correctly, have another turn.
4. Collect objects when you land on them.
5. The winner is the first person to get home with four objects.

Say the infinitive of bought, was and washed

MISS A TURN You forget to say Please and Thank you

LONGMAN ENGLISH GRAMMAR

Name 3 countries and their nationalities

GO ON 4 PLACES If you've got the TV

Name 6 parts of the body

OBSERVER

ENGLISH PHRASE BOOK

Say 3 things you can and 3 things you can't do

Describe how to get to your house using imperatives

CONGRATULATIONS YOU HAVE SURVIVED IN THE ENGLISH-SPEAKING WORLD!

MISS A TURN You need extra English classes

GO HOME If you've got the Grammar book + 3 other things

GO HOME If you've got the Phrase book + 3 other things

Say 5 things you do in your free time

HOME

Count from 1 - 20

17 The English-speaking world

North, south, east, west; a/an,
the + places

1 Revision

**1 Say the names of the
continents. Where's the
stress?**

Africa	North America
Asia	South America
Europe	Oceania

**2 Match these English-speaking
countries to the correct part
of the world.**

Australia	North America
England	The West Indies
Singapore	Oceania
India	South-East Asia
Jamaica	Europe
The USA	Africa
Zimbabwe	Asia

1 What is the capital of each
country?
2 Where is the capital? In the
north, south, east or west of
each country?

Example: Harare is the capital
of Zimbabwe. It's in the north
of the country.

2 Grammar: *a/an, the* or (–)

1 Complete the chart. Which is correct, *a/an, the* or (–)?

	a/an	the	(–)
Continents eg *Africa*			✓
Countries eg *Argentina*			
A group of states eg *UAE*			
A group of islands eg *British Isles*			
A city or town eg *Lisbon*			
Points of the compass eg *north, south, east, west*			
A place of which many examples exist eg *town, village*			
A place of which one unique example exists eg *capital*			

2 Complete these sentences with *a/an, the* or (–).

1 . . . Lyons is . . . city in . . . east of . . . France.
2 . . . Washington is . . . capital of . . . USA.
3 . . . Venezuela is . . . country in . . . north of . . . South America.

3 Write a sentence like this about where you live.

3 Reading

**1 What do you think? What have the three countries on page 103
got in common?**

**2 Work in three groups, A, B and C. Each group, read about a
different country and complete the chart for that country only.**

**3 Work in different groups of three, with one student from group
A, one student from group B and one student from group C. Tell
the two other students about the text you read. Listen to the
other students and complete the chart.**

4 Answer these questions.

1 Which country has got the largest population? *India.*
2 Which country has got the most languages? *English. Zimbabwe*
3 Where do people live the longest? *Jamaica.*

India

India has a large population, some 818 million in all. The large population, and a generally hot, dry climate, have caused problems with the supply of food. But India can now produce enough food for its own people and exports grain too. Life expectancy is at present around fifty-eight years. Most people are Hindus, and Muslims are the largest minority.

India became independent of Britain in 1947. The country has fifteen official national languages (225 main languages) but English, spoken by a minority, is the only language used in all parts of the country.

India now produces enough food to feed its own people.

The government follows policies of 'democratic socialism' and is right of centre.

POPULATION	818 million
LANGUAGES	225
RELIGIONS	Hindu
POLITICS	democratic
CLIMATE	1food dry
LIFE EXPECTANCY	58

Zimbabwe

Zimbabwe became independent in 1979 and changed its name from Rhodesia. It is a socialist country. Its policies are generally left of centre but, for economic reasons, there haven't been many radical changes. Thousands of clinics and hospitals have been built and more children now have the chance of education.

The dry, hot climate brings problems of food and water, but in good years farmers grow large quantities of food to use in bad years. People can expect to live for approximately fifty-nine years.

The national language of the nine million Zimbabweans is English. There are also two local languages: Shona and Sindebele.

Shona sculpture is among the finest in the world. Zimbabwean music sings of work, liberation, love and religion. Traditional religions co-exist with Christianity.

POPULATION	
LANGUAGES	9 million
RELIGIONS	
POLITICS	
CLIMATE	
LIFE EXPECTANCY	59

School children in Harare

Jamaica

The history of Jamaica is one of colonialism. English is the official language, but there is also a Jamaican patois.

The weather is generally sunny and warm, the temperature varies by only three or four degrees whatever the season.

Reggae music is everywhere and nearly always has a political and/or religious message. Different Christian religions exist, but Rastafarianism is particularly popular with young people. It stresses the spiritual unity of Africa and looks for political change.

There is parliamentary democracy in Jamaica but the country is right of centre due to economic pressures. The main export is sugar and tourism is important, but very little money reaches the poor.

However, more than 55% of the 2.5 million Jamaicans now live in towns and, on average, people live until they are seventy-three.

POPULATION	
LANGUAGES	
RELIGIONS	
POLITICS	
CLIMATE	
LIFE EXPECTANCY	

Harvesting sugar cane

Adapted from *New Internationalist*

4 Grammar: Present Perfect

> a I *have been* to Jamaica.
> b I *went* to Jamaica in 1990.

Look at the example sentences above and answer these questions.

1 Is specific time/detail more important in sentence a or b? - b
2 Is general experience more important in sentence a or b? - A

Pronunciation

1 🖳 **Listen and write the sentences in the Present Perfect. <u>Underline</u> the contracted forms. What are the full forms?**

2 **Listen again and mark the main stress in each sentence. How do you pronounce the unstressed form of *been*?**

3 **Talk to another student. Ask and answer about countries you have been to, like this:**

> Have you ever been to Argentina?

> Yes, I have.   No, never.

> When did you go?   Would you like to go?

> In 1991, I went to Buenos Aires and . . .   Yes, I . . .

5 Speaking

1 **Work in groups of three students, A, B and C.**

STUDENT A: Look at Jon's suitcase on this page.
STUDENT B: Look at Neesha's passport on page 126.
STUDENT C: Look at Simon's CV on page 127.

2 **Answer these questions together. Who has:**

1 been to America, Germany and Yugoslavia?
2 never been to Asia?
3 been to the most places in Europe?
4 been to the same place more than once?
5 been to the most countries?
6 Which two people have been to the same place in North Africa?

3 **Tell other students about places you have visited.**

1 Which was the friendliest/the cleanest/the cheapest/the coldest?
2 Which was the most exciting/attractive interesting?
3 Which places would you like to go back to?
4 Which would you like to live in for a year or more?

6 Listening

1 🖷 **Listen to the first part of an interview with two people who left their own countries to live abroad. Complete the chart.**

	Bob McDonald	Sharon Gordon
Where did they come from originally?		
Where did they go to?		
When did they change countries?		
Are they generally pleased with the change, or not?		

2 🖷 **Listen to the complete interview. Note one thing each person says about:**

the people   the weather   the food   the entertainment

7 Grammar: past participles

1 Put these past participles from the interview in the correct sentence.

eaten   seen   lived   met   gone   done

I've . . . in lots of countries.
I've . . . a lot of really interesting things.
I've . . . snails and frogs' legs!
I've . . . some fantastic Egyptian belly dancing.
I've . . . a lot of very nice people.
She's . . . to England.

2 🖷 **Listen and check your answers.**

> **NB** *Been vs gone*
>
> a He's *been* to the pyramids lots of times.
>
> b She's *gone* to England. She's going to stay there for six months.
>
> Which means to go and come back, a or b?
> Which means to go and still be there now, a or b?

3 Complete this chart.

Present	Past Simple	Past participle
go	went	been/. . .
see	saw	. . .
eat	ate	. . .
live	lived	. . .
meet	met	. . .
do	did	. . .

4 Find the regular verb in the chart. What do you notice about its past participle?

8 Speaking

1 Work with another student. Ask about these things.

- jobs/done
- tourist sights/visited
- exotic food/eaten
- museums/been to

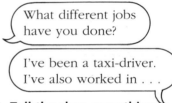

What different jobs have you done?

I've been a taxi-driver. I've also worked in . . .

2 Tell the class something interesting you have learned about your partner's experiences.

George has been a taxi-driver. He's also worked in . . .

ENGLISH IN ACTION

You have seen this advertisement for a part-time job in your home town.

The company is interested in your application.

They want you to come for an interview.

Weekend Work

Our English Company is looking for people to work at weekends this summer.

• *Do you speak a little English?*
• *Have you got time to help English-speaking tourists enjoy your country?*
• *No special qualifications necessary, just lots of enthusiasm.*

If you are interested, send a short CV in English to show relevant experience and your general qualifications, to:

London Tourist Information,
76 Burgoyne Road, London EC1 7WA.

3 Some of you are candidates and some of you are interviewers. Read your card and prepare for the interview.

INTERVIEWERS
You need to ask about:
• the candidate's experience
• their knowledge of their town
• their knowledge of local attractions for tourists
• their knowledge of local history

You need to answer questions about:
• what the candidate has to do
• the hours of work
• the places she/he has to go to
• their pay

CANDIDATES
You need to ask about:
• what you have to do
• the hours of work
• the places you have to go to
• your pay

You need to answer questions about:
• your experience
• your town
• local attractions for tourists
• local history

4 Work in pairs of interviewers and candidates. Hold the interview. Good Luck!

Congratulations! You have got the job.

5 Now make a poster to advertise your work. The British company have given you this poster on Britain as an example. Make a similar poster to advertise where you live.

1 Read the advertisement above and answer these questions.

1 What sort of job is it?
2 When is it for?
3 How much English do you need?
4 What qualifications do you need?
5 What should you do if you are interested in the job?

2 Write notes on your experience and/or qualifications for the job.

HAVE YOU VISITED BRITAIN?

■ HAVE YOU BEEN TO CARDIFF, EDINBURGH, BELFAST OR LONDON?
■ HAVE YOU SEEN THE ROYAL FAMILY, THE LOCH NESS MONSTER OR THE LITTLE GREEN PEOPLE?
■ HAVE YOU EATEN HAGGIS, LEEKS AND YORKSHIRE PUDDING?
■ HAVE YOU DRUNK SCOTCH WHISKY AND GUINNESS?
■ IF THE ANSWER TO ANY OF THESE QUESTIONS IS 'NO' THEN YOU HAVEN'T LIVED! COME TO BRITAIN THIS HOLIDAY. WE'D LOVE TO WELCOME YOU!

Language review 17

1 Articles: *a/an*, *the* or (–)

- **(–)**

Used with continents, countries or towns.
I live in (–) Africa.
I live in (–) Zambia.
I live in (–) Lusaka.

- ***a/an***

Used to describe a place where more than one exists.
Paris is *a* city in France. (There are lots of cities in France).
Zambia is *a* country in Africa. (There are lots of countries in Africa).

- ***the***

Used to describe a place where only one exists.
Lusaka is *the* capital of Zambia. (There is only one capital).
***The* is also used with north, south, east and west.**
Hiroshima is in *the* south of Japan.

a Complete the dialogue with *a/an*, *the* or (–).

A: Have you travelled a lot?
B: Well, in . . . Europe, I've been to . . . France, . . . United Kingdom, . . . Germany, . . . Italy and . . . Greece.
A: How about other parts of the world?
B: I've spent some time in . . . USA.
A: Where exactly?
B: Over in . . . west, in . . . Sacramento.
A: Where's that?
B: In . . . California. It's quite . . . large town about 100 km from San Francisco which is *the* capital of . . . state.

2 Verbs

- **Present Perfect (experience)**

Positive

I/you/we/they	have	been to Spain.
She/he/it	has	

Negative

I/you/we/they	have not	been to Spain.
She/he/it	has not	

Question

Have	I/you/we/they	been to Spain?
Has	she/he/it	

- **Present Perfect and Past Simple.**

Present Perfect General experience	Past Simple Definite time/detail
I've been to the USA .	I went to the USA last year.
She's been to Australia.	She went there by plane.

b Put the verbs into the Present Perfect or the Past Simple.

Example: you (live) abroad? – Have you lived abroad?

1 I (not see) Ivan on Wednesday.
2 he (go) to Brazil. He's going to see some important clients there.
3 you (met) his father before? He's very nice.
4 you (have) a good time at Katherine's party last night?
5 we (take) a lot of photos during our holiday in July.
6 I not (go) to America but I would like to go one day.
7 I not (do) my homework yesterday. I not (have) time.
8 you (read) this book? It's really good.

c Put the words in these questions in the correct order. They come from two different conversations.

1
1 many you countries to have been different?
2 go them when you did to?
3 most which the interesting was?

2
1 jobs different what had have you?
2 like which most the did you?
3 do have what you did to?
4 work did what hours you?

d Write answers to the questions in exercise c above. Include as much information about your experiences as possible.

A 'I QUITE LIKE having two homes. Sometimes I get a bit confused. Sometimes it's all right and sometimes it isn't.'
Lucy (aged 8)

SERVER MAGAZINE

MUM SECOND DAD DADDY

beAver me Peter

'If we can handle their divorces, they can handle what we say about them'

STEPCHILDREN S

B Robin is nine. His parents were divorced in 1980, and his mother, Mary, remarried last year. Robin's elder brother, Gavin, didn't want to be interviewed: Robin talked to me on his own in the family's house in London. His father has also remarried, has a young daughter and lives in Devon. The boys visit for holidays.

'Having two homes is quite nice, because you can go away and still be with your family. I like going to my dad's, because they've got a big garden, and my sister who lives there is really nice.'

'At first, I knew I had to be well-behaved, or my step-mum might say: "That son of yours isn't well-behaved, and I don't like him coming." But I know she likes me now.

C 'Adults don't have to change parents, lose parents, get extra parents. You can talk to friends better than adults. I hate my new family.'
Kaye (aged 15)

D 'I used to blame my stepdad for my parents getting divorced and I used to hate him so much. Now I really like him.'
Annie (aged 14)

From *The Observer*

Robin with Gavin (right) and their mother.

1 Revision

1 Find someone who has done these things:

- met a famous person.
- written a book.
- learned to speak another language.
- seen a crime.
- worked with children.

2 Choose one person and find out more information. Ask questions beginning with when, where, what, who.

Example: Who did you meet?

2 Reading

1 Look at the cover of the Observer magazine on page 108.

1 How many people are there in this child's family? Who are they?
2 What is a *stepchild*?
3 What relationship is the 'Second Dad' to the child?

2 Read the magazine article. Which child seems:

a the most positive?
b the most negative?
c the most unsure?

3 Read the article again. Find words and expressions which mean the following:

Text A
1 to like a little
2 to become a little unsure
3 OK

Text B
1 to marry again
2 older
3 to act correctly (especially children)

Text C
1 the opposite of *find*
2 to have more

Text D
1 to feel another person is responsible for something negative
2 to dislike very much
3 to change status from married to single again
4 to like very much

3 Grammar: *have to* (obligation)

1 Look at Text C. Kaye says it isn't necessary for adults to do certain things.

1 How does she say this?
2 Rephrase her first sentence. Begin:
Stepchildren . . .

2 Find an example of the past form of *have to* in the last paragraph of Text B.

3 Complete this chart.

Positive	I/you/we/they	*have to*	+ verb
	She/he/it	. . .	
Negative	I/you/we/they	*don't have to*	+ verb
	She/he/it	. . . *have to*	
Question	*Do*	I/you/we/they	*have to*	+ verb
	. . .	She/he/it	. . .	

4 Write five sentences about what you have to/ had to do at school. What things don't/didn't you have to do?

- wear a uniform
- do homework
- do lots of sport
- eat school dinners

5 Talk to another student about your schooldays. Do/did you like school? Why/why not?

NB *Quite* vs *really*

Robin says,
'Having two homes is *quite* nice.'

'My sister who lives there is *really* nice.'

Which is he more positive about, his homes or his sister?

4 Listening

1 Look at the pictures. Do you know the story?

Why are the pumpkin and the slipper important? What happened at the ball?

2 Find these people in the pictures.

Cinderella	Her fairy godmother
Her father	The ugly sisters
Her stepmother	The Prince

3 Talk to other students. Put the pictures in the correct order and tell the story.

4 ▣ Now, listen to the story of *Cinderella*. Is it the same as your story?

5 Listen to the story again and answer these questions.

What did Cinderella have to:
a do for the ugly sisters in the house?
b do for the ugly sisters before the ball?
c get from the garden for the fairy godmother?
d remember to do at the ball?

Pronunciation: /ʃ/ vs /tʃ/

1 ▣ Listen and repeat.

> /ʃ/ /ʃ/ /tʃ/
> Cinderella had to wash the dishes, choose their
> /tʃ/ /ʃ/
> dresses, go by coach, and try on the shoe.

2 Say the sentence above quickly three times.

5 Grammar: adverbs of manner

1 ▣ Listen to these extracts from the story and complete the sentences with adverbs.

1 The ugly sisters treated Cinderella very . . .
2 Cinderella had to help them choose their dresses . . .
3 Her fairy godmother smiled . . .
4 The Prince and Cinderella danced so . . . together that everyone looked at them.
5 She ran very . . . and lost one of her glass slippers.
6 When she tried on the slipper, it fitted . . .
7 Cinderella and the Prince lived . . . ever after.

2 Look at the sentences again and answer these questions.

1 What do you add to adjectives to make the regular adverb?
2 What happens to adjectives ending in y?
3 Which adverbs are irregular? What are the adjectives?

6 Writing

Work in groups. Write a traditional tale like *Cinderella* from your country.

1 List the characters in the story.
2 List the main things that happen in order.
3 Write the story. Include adverbs where you can.
4 Show your story to a student from another group. Mark the parts of the text which your partner doesn't understand.
5 Rewrite your story and make it clearer.
6 Change groups and tell your story.

7 Grammar: *too* and *very*

> a The ugly sisters try on the glass slipper but their feet are *too* big.
> b The slipper is *very* small; it fits Cinderella perfectly.

1 Look at the example sentences above and answer these questions.

1 Can the ugly sisters wear the slipper?
2 Can Cinderella wear the slipper?
3 Which word tells you there's a problem, *too* or *very*?

2 Work with another student. Write answers to these questions, using *too* or *very*.

1 How does Cinderella feel in picture F?
2 How does she feel at the ball?
3 What is the matter with the dress in picture C?
4 Why can't Cinderella go home by coach?

You are in the shoe department of a department store. You want to buy a pair of shoes.

1 🔊 **Listen to a customer, talking to the shop assistant. Answer these questions.**

1 What colour shoes does the customer buy?
2 What size are they?
3 How does she pay?

2 Complete the gaps in these sentences from the conversation with *too, very, try on* or *fit*.

CUSTOMER: Can I . . . these shoes?
SHOP ASSISTANT: Yes, certainly.

How do they feel?
CUSTOMER: They're . . . small, I'm afraid.
SHOP ASSISTANT: How are these?
CUSTOMER: Great. They . . . perfectly.
They're . . . nice.

3 Practise this part of the conversation with another student.

4 Look at the size chart . Decide what colour and size shoes you want. Buy your shoes.

You want to buy some clothes to go with your shoes.

5 List the clothes you want to buy. Look at the clothes size chart. What size are you going to buy?

6 Practise the conversation with another student.

SIZES - CLOTHES AND SHOES

WOMEN

Dress size	Small	Medium	Large			
British	8	12	18			
Continental	40/36	44/40	50/46			

Shoe size						
British	3	4	5	6	7	8	9
Continental	36	37	38	39	40	41	42

MEN

Shirt size	Small	Medium	Large			
British	14	15 ½	17			
Continental	36	39	42			

Shoe size						
British	6	7	8	9	10	11
Continental	39	40	41	42	43	44

You are in the clothes department.

Half the class are customers and half are shop-assistants.

CUSTOMERS: Ask to try on different clothes. Some are too small, some are too big and some are just right.
SHOP ASSISTANTS: Try to persuade the customers to buy. Tell them how good they look!

Language review 18

1 Adjectives

- **too** and **very** + adjectives

To intensify the adjective, use very.
This coffee is very hot. It's delicious!
To suggest there is a problem, use too.
This coffee is too hot. I can't drink it!

- **quite** and **really** + adjectives

+	++	+++
It's *quite* big	It's big	It's *really* big

a Write sentences about this picture, using **too** and **very**.

b Complete these sentences with **quite** or **very**.

1 This is great! I'm . . . happy to see you.
2 I don't think he'll pass the exam. He's . . . intelligent but not very.
3 She's . . . ill but she can go to school tomorrow.
4 I like your dress very much. It's . . . nice.
5 He's . . . tall. Beds are always too short for him.

2 Verbs: *have to* (obligation)

Positive

I/you/we/they	have to	go.
She/he/it	has to	

Negative

I/you/we/they	don't	have to go.
She/he/it	doesn't	

Question

Do	I/you/we/they	have to go?
Does	she/he/it	

c Write sentences saying what these people **have to** or **don't have to** do.

Example:
Teacher – A teacher has to be good with people. She doesn't have to work irregular hours.

Job	Duties
Nurse	Work irregular hours
Police officer	Work outside
Pilot	Be good with people
Waiter	Wear a uniform
	Travel a lot
	Speak foreign languages

3 Adverbs

Adverbs answer the question – How?

A: How does she work?
B: She works quickly/carefully/fast/well, etc.

- **Regular**

Adjective	Adverb
bad	badly
quick	quickly
easy	easily

- **Irregular**

Adjective	Adverb
good	well
fast	fast

d Read this text. Are the underlined words in the correct form? If not, correct them.

Yesterday wasn't a very good day. It started bad when my alarm clock didn't work and I woke up at 10 am. I had a headache and felt terrible but, because my English class starts at 10 am, I ran fastly to catch the bus. I missed it and waited impatiently for the next one to come. I finally got to school at 10.45. I went quickly into my class, and apologised polite for being late. It was strange because the teacher wasn't my usual teacher. She asked me what class I was in and then explained quiet that I didn't have a class. It was Tuesday and I don't have classes on Tuesday.

19 *Will you still need me?*

1 Revision

1 Think of an older person you
have known. Which of these
things have they done?
Number them in the order
they did them.

.6. get married
.9. retire
.7. have a baby
.10. go out with someone
.11. die
.8. get divorced
.2. leave school
.5. fall in love
.4. meet her/his partner
.1. be born
.3. go to work

2 Tell another student about
this person's life. Is the order
for her/his person's life
different?

knit

2 Vocabulary: everyday activities

1 Look at the pictures above. Match the verbs and nouns from the
list below.

Example: to lose – hair

to lose	to mend	a door	a postcard
to lock	to dig up	a fuse	someone
to rent	to go for	weeds	a cottage
to knit	to send	hair	a sweater
to feed		a ride	

2 Talk to another student. What is happening in the pictures?

Example: He's losing his hair.

114

3 Listening

1 You are going to listen to 'When I'm sixty-four' written by The Beatles. Before you listen, do the Beatles Quiz.

2 ▣ Listen to 'When I'm sixty-four', sung by Kenny Ball, a famous jazz singer. Number the verbs on page 114 in the order you first hear them.

4 Grammar: *will* (prediction)

1 ▣ Listen to 'When I'm sixty-four' again and write the chorus.

2 Look at the words in the chorus and answer these questions.

1 Is the singer singing about his present or future life?
2 Is it planned or is he imagining it?

3 Write these sentences without contractions.

I'll need you.
I won't need you.

NB *When* + Present Simple for future time

Will you still need me when *I'm* sixty-four?

Is the singer sixty-four in
a the present?
b the future?

Is the verb after *when* in
a the present?
b the future?

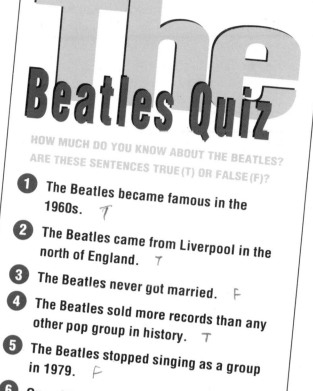

The
Beatles Quiz

HOW MUCH DO YOU KNOW ABOUT THE BEATLES?
ARE THESE SENTENCES TRUE (T) OR FALSE (F)?

1 The Beatles became famous in the 1960s. T

2 The Beatles came from Liverpool in the north of England. T

3 The Beatles never got married. F

4 The Beatles sold more records than any other pop group in history. T

5 The Beatles stopped singing as a group in 1979. F

6 One of The Beatles was killed. T

5 Pronunciation: *will/won't*

1 📟 **Listen. Which sentence do you hear, a or b?**

1 a I phone him after seven o'clock.
  b I'll phone him after seven o'clock

2 a We have lunch early.
  b We'll have lunch early.

3 a They like him very much.
  b They'll like him very much.

2 Take it in turns to test another student in the same way.

3 📟 **Listen to the difference in pronunciation between wo*n't* and *want*. Write the sentences you hear.**

4 Tell another student what you heard. Listen again if you don't agree.

5 What do you think? Discuss these questions with another student.

What is your perfect picture of old age?
Which things in the song will you do?
Which things won't you do?

6 Vocabulary: accommodation

1 Ask another student these questions.

1 When you grow old would you like to live in:
  a a cottage by the sea?
  b a big house in the country?
  c a flat in the middle of town?
2 Where do you live now?

2 Look at this magazine page. What is a housing exchange? Match the photographs of the homes to their descriptions.

3 Now answer these questions.

1 How did you choose the photograph to go with each description?
2 Which of these places would you most like to live in? Why?

HOUSING EXCHANGES

The holiday with a difference!

Do you long for a holiday complete with all the comforts of home, in the location you want? Do you live in a major city, or in unspoiled countryside? If so, maybe you should consider our Housing Exchange scheme. Simply decide where you'd like to spend your holiday, decide the time and duration of the holiday and send these details, along with a description of your home and its location, to us. We'll do the rest!

A

He _____ of the many
hc _____ register.

Describing houses; usually

● **Australia** for your holidays? We want to exchange our 2 bedroom house (1 double and 1 single) for something similar in Europe. C

● **Christmas in Hong Kong.** Luxury downtown apartment. 3 bedrooms and 3 large adjoining bathrooms. Separate toilet. Large lounge with cable TV, hifi, video and bar. Consider anything in exchange but not big city. D

● **London.** 3 bedroom centrally-heated flat in central London for exchange, 2 minutes from Piccadilly Circus. Large kitchen – dining room complete with washing-machine, dishwasher, fridge and microwave. Separate bathroom/WC. A

● **San Francisco.** Attractive apartment to trade. Renovated, all new. Beautifully furnished living-room leading to patio and garden. Any time August thru' October. E

● **Sunny Barbados!** Small, attractive house with character. Balcony overlooking the sea. Music and sun. What more do you want? We need something larger for family holiday. Any suggestions? B

D

B

C

E

7 Speaking

1 Talk to other students. Find out in which room they usually do these things.

eat   watch TV
study   talk to friends
read   do the washing   *in the kitchen*
cook   write letters
sleep   listen to music

Example: A: Which room do you usually eat in?
B: The dining room.

2 Work with another student. Describe your house or flat. Take it in turns to ask and answer these questions.

- How many bedrooms are there?
- What's the kitchen like?
- Have you got a shower or a bath, or both?
- Is there a separate toilet?
- Is there a garden or garage?
- How near is it to public transport?
- Which is your favourite room? Why?

where do you usually study.
- my bedroom

ENGLISH IN ACTION

You want to exchange your home and have a holiday in an English-speaking country.

1 Read this advertisement from *Time Out*. Phone for further information.

44 TEMP ACCOMMODATION

• **WORLDWIDE HOME EXCHANGE**
Long established company offers wide range exchanges. Personally arranged to suit all requirements. For more details and an application form, telephone 071-701 1762

• **N16**, furnished family house, available 8 weeks...

fessionals
287 6315.
lats, all
Street.

, non

'04.
'se

• **FUI**
flat. Su
3 mon
Wk:836
• **N15,**
housesha
inclusive.
• **EAST**
luxury

You receive this form through the post.

2 Read the form and complete it.

Worldwide Home Exchange

14, Leinster Gardens, Bayswater, London W2

Application for home exchange

Please complete the following details in BLOCK CAPITALS and return to the address above.

1. Name ..... Nylimi

2. Address ..... 25 white hrst lane
..... Tottenham N.17 8DU

3. Occupation ..... student

4. Intended date of exchange ..... 12 - 10 - 93

5. Briefly describe your present accommodation .....
three bed room flat Tottenham
one living room / kitchen
one Bathroom
garden
The house is beautiful

6. Preferred location ..... san francisco

7. Preferred accommodation required ..... three bedrooms
aparstments.

You arrive at your holiday home and find this note from the person you are exchanging homes with. Some words are missing.

Welcome to my home!
I hope you are going to enjoy your stay. Please help yourself to food and drink in the fridge The switch for the hot water and the central heating is in the cupboard under the stairs. The shops are a five-minute walk from the house. Turn left out of the house. The underground is opposite the shops. If there is a problem, contact my parents. Their phone number is 775 8961. Have a good time.

3 Complete the note, using the words below.

problem	to	home	fridge
central	food	good	my
walk	under	number	is

4 Now write a similar note for the visitors in your home.

You are at your holiday home.

What will you do first?

5 Tell another student what order you will do these things in.

Example: *First*, I'll unpack my case.
Then, I'll have a bath.
Then, . . .

- go into town/to the beach/for a walk
- have a shower/a bath/a snack
- go swimming/shopping
- buy a map of the area

Language review 19

1 Verbs

• New verbs

1 Regular		**2 Irregular**	
Verb	**Past Simple**	**Verb**	**Past Simple**
lock	locked	lose	lost
rent	rented	feed	fed
mend	mended	dig	dug
knit	knitted	send	sent

(handwritten numbers beside Regular: 4, 6, 2, 1; beside Irregular: 8, 3, 7, 5)

• Key verb: *will* (future predictions)

Positive

I/you/we/they She/he/it	will	visit the USA

Negative

I/you/we/they She/he/it	will not won't	visit the USA

Question

Will	I/you/we/they she/he/it	visit the USA?

a Use one of the verbs from the left-hand side of the page to complete each of these sentences. Use each verb once only.

1 My grandmother *knitted* me a beautiful sweater for Christmas. She often makes clothes for the family.
2 Can you try and *mend* the television. It's not working. There's sound but no picture.
3 Don't *feed* the cat again. I gave him some food a few minutes ago.
4 I didn't *lock* the back door because I haven't got a key.
5 They *sent* me some forms by post to complete, but not the ones I wanted.
6 We *rented* a cottage on the west coast of Portugal for two weeks. It was wonderful.
7 I'd like you to *dig* up everything in this part of the garden.
8 My grandfather *lost* his glasses yesterday.

b Write one sentence, giving your predictions about the future, about each of these subjects.

Example: Europe – I think Europe will be more powerful than America.

1 Travel
2 Work and leisure
3 War
4 Developing countries
5 World languages
6 Medicine
7 Accommodation

2 Question words

Question	Answer
What is this?	A photograph.
Who is this man?	Mr Smith.
Whose father is he?	Thomas and Kate's.
When was he born?	1952.
Where does he work?	In an office.
Which office does he work in?	The school office.
Why does he like his job?	Because it's very interesting.
How much does he earn?	£25,000 a year.
How many children has he got?	Two.
How old are they?	Six and eleven years old.

c Complete each of these questions with one of the question words/phrases on the left.

1 *Which* room do you have breakfast in?
2 *How many* weeks holiday do you have?
3 *How old* is your father? He looks very young.
4 *When* did you come to London?
5 *How much* did your bag cost?
6 *Who* is that boy near the window?
7 *What* does your wife do?
8 *Where* did you go for your last holiday?
9 *Whose* book is this?
10 *Why* don't you like Rita?

d Now match an appropriate answer to each question in exercise c above.

5 A About £30, I think.
8 B Mexico.
3 C Forty-five.
1 D The kitchen.
7 E She's a computer programmer.
6 F Jeff, my son.
4 G In January.
2 H Four a year.
10 I Because she's unfriendly.
9 J Mike's.

Photo Finish

1 Look at these photographs. What do you remember about these people?

1 What is their relationship to each other?
2 Which country do they live in?
3 What nationality are they?
4 How many children have they got?
5 Where do they work?
6 What problems do they have?

2 Now look again. Do you remember these situations from the book?

3 Work with other students and tell the story for each picture.

4 📼 **Listen to the story as it happened. How is your story different?**

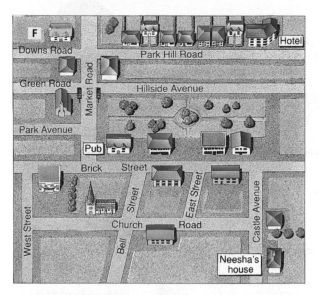

5 Read this note from Neesha to Simon. How has she decided to solve their problems? Do you think she is right? Why/why not?

Dear Simon,

After our conversation last night, I realise how bad I feel at the moment. You were very understanding and you are right, I do need a break. I tried to phone you but you weren't in the office. I've decided to go and stay with a friend from work for a while; I'm not sure for how long. I haven't got the telephone number on me but I'll phone and let you know. Don't think too badly of me.

love,

Neesha.

6 Talk to another student. What's going to happen next?

1 What do you think Simon will do when he sees Neesha's note?
2 What is Neesha going to do now?

7 ▣ Listen to the final part of the story. What news has Jon got for Simon? Who is Barbara? Were your predictions right?

20 Consolidation

1 Thinking about learning: speaking and writing

Revises:
Vocabulary: Activities; clothes; families; letter writing
Grammar: Present Perfect; *going to* future; *-ing* form; comparatives; Present Simple; imperatives

Speaking

1 What do you think? Complete the questionnaire below.

	Important	Quite Important	Not Important
• having a good English accent is . . .	✓		
• being sure my grammar is correct is . . .		✓	
• knowing people are not going to laugh at me is . . .		✓	
• having the exact words I need is . . .		✓	
• not being treated like a foreigner is . . .	✓	✓	
• having lots of possible occasions to speak is . . .	✓		
• speaking to native English speakers is . . .	✓		
• communicating what I want to say, correctly or not, is . . .	✓		

2 Compare your answers with another student.

3 Discuss with other students. Which of these ideas will help you speak better English? Put them in order of importance, (1–7).

   . . . repeating new words and expressions lots of times.

   . . . going to an English-speaking country.

   . . . learning a lot of vocabulary.

   . . . watching TV/films in English.

   . . . going to English classes.

   . . . reading in English.

   . . . being corrected a lot.

What other ideas have you got?

4 Tell another student. Which of these things have you already done? Which are you going to do in the future?

Durham Enterprises ❧ Fax

To: Ms Jill Barnes
From: Dick Clayton
Date: 23rd July 1991
Subject: Outstanding invoices

Your Fax No: (0737) 244117
Our Fax No: (0737) 243024
No. of pages (incl. this sheet): 1

Message:

I am sending the information you asked for in your letter last week.

opping
nions
potatoes
lettuce
green and red
peppers
milk
orange juice

Dear Hugh,
Yesterday was the most exciting day of my life. I don't understand what is happening but I feel great. I can't wait to see you again. I want

Writing

1 Look at the texts above.

1 What are they?
2 In your own language, which of them do you write?
3 Which do you write quickly? Which take time and probably need more than one try?

2 Complete the chart. Fill in the empty boxes with the instructions at the bottom.

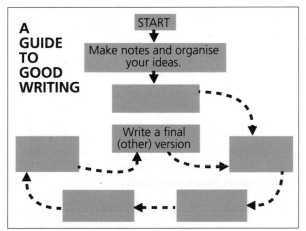

A GUIDE TO GOOD WRITING

START

Make notes and organise your ideas.

Write a final (other) version

- Have a break • Show another person
- Write first version • Check grammar and spelling
- Read text and make changes

3 Look at your completed chart. Do you write important things like this in your own language? Do you think it is more or less necessary in a foreign language?

4 Work with another student. Look at this English child's writing about her family and answer these questions.

1 How many people does she write about?
2 Who are they?

Justine Strachan.
7 yrs old. My
Grandmother is my
mammys mother
She is verey old and
nice as well and she
brings me nice things
My Grandfather is my
mammys father a
Grandmother is a
verey old lady
my mammy is my
Grandmother dauter
and my Grandfather
dauter as well
She lives at 79 Chirton
Rd

From Grandmas and Grandpas

5 Correct the spelling and punctuation.

6 Write a short text. Say what you think can help students write and speak well in English. Use your completed chart to help you organise your writing.

THE NATIONAL CURRICULUM • A GUIDE FOR PARENTS

What is the National Curriculum?

All children in England and Wales have to study:

- English
- Mathematics
- Science
- Technology (and design)
- History
- Geography
- Music
- Art
- Physical education
- A modern foreign language (for 11-16 year olds).
- Religious Education but children don't have to study it, if their parents prefer them not to.

What examinations do children have to take?

There will be four stages for different ages, known as 'Key stages'. These will help parents to know what their child should be l...

How does it fit into the education system?

			Work			
			Polytechnic	University	College of Education	Age
Work	College of further education		'A' level examinations			18
						17
			GCSE examinations			16
						15
		C O M P U L S O R Y				14
			Secondary school			13
						12
						11
						10
						9
			Primary school			8
						7
						6
						5
			Nursery school (voluntary)			

Adapted from *National Curriculum: A Guide for Parents*

---

2 Across cultures: education

> **Revises:**
> **Vocabulary:** School subjects and systems
> **Grammar:** superlatives; *have to*

1 Read the information above about the National Curriculum. Do any of the subject words look the same or similar in your language?

2 🖳 Listen and mark the stress on the subject words.

Which of these subjects have you studied?
What are you studying now?

> **NB Maths**
>
> In British English mathematics = *maths*.
> In American English mathematics = *math*.
>
> Is there a similar abbreviation in your language?

3 Talk to another student. Say which school subjects:

- you like/liked the most.
- you like/liked the least.
- you find/found the easiest/the most difficult.
- you think are the most important.

4 Work with other students. Look at the chart of the British education system above. Is it the same as the education system in your country? Think about these questions.

At what age do children have to start school?
When can they leave?
Can parents choose their child's school?
What subjects do school children have to study?
Do they often need private teachers too?
Do they have to do school years again if they are not very good students?
At what age/s do they have to take important exams?
What do they have to do to get to university?
What other forms of higher education are there?

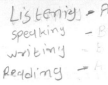
3 Language in context: school

> **Revises:**
> **Vocabulary:** Schools, education
> **Grammar:** Present Simple; superlatives; *going to* future

1 ▣ **Listen to this song about education. Is the song for or against school?**

2 **Look at these examples of informal language from the song.**

> We *don't* need *no* education
> Teachers leave *them* kids alone

1 What do you think *kids* means?
2 How do you say these sentences using correct grammar?

3 **Use a dictionary to find the meaning of other new words in the song.**

4 ▣ **Listen to three children saying what they think about school.**

1 Who likes school most? – History Simon
2 Who likes school least?

5 **Listen again and answer these questions for each child.**

1 What do they like about school?
2 What do they dislike?
3 What are they going to do when they leave school?

6 **Talk to another student about your future plans.**

1 What are you going to do after this course?
2 How are you going to use your English?

> We don't need no education *(any)*
> We don't need no thought control
> No dark sarcasm in the classroom
> Teachers leave them kids alone *(those)*
> Hey, teachers, leave them kids alone.
> **Chorus:** All in all, you're just another brick in the wall.
> All in all, you're just another brick in the wall.

Pink Floyd

The group began in 1965. They have always been very different and controversial. In their early days, they were famous for their 'psychedelic' music and later on, for their incredible stage shows. Perhaps their most famous album is 'The Wall' which they produced in 1980. The film *Pink Floyd – The Wall* came out two years later and Bob Geldof played the lead role of 'Pink'. It looks at what happens when people build barriers between each other. The song 'Another Brick in the Wall' from the album was released as a single on November 16 1980, selling 340,000 copies in five days and taking only one week to become Number One in the British charts.

> **Check what you know!**
> Now turn to page 131 and complete
> Check what you know 4.

125

Communication activities

Unit 1 Exercise 6

Student B

Hear	Say
673 9327	839 7118
267 7029	end
993 8630	204 6419
601 3788	223 3927
734 7455	566 7890

Unit 3 Exercise 4

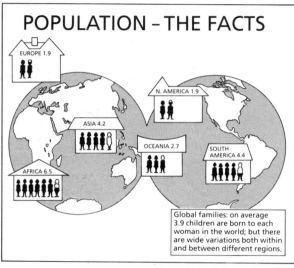

POPULATION – THE FACTS

EUROPE 1.9

N. AMERICA 1.9

ASIA 4.2

OCEANIA 2.7

SOUTH AMERICA 4.4

AFRICA 6.5

Global families: on average 3.9 children are born to each woman in the world; but there are wide variations both within and between different regions.

From *New Internationalist*

Unit 4 Exercise 4

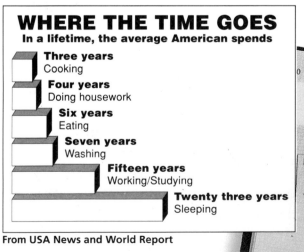

WHERE THE TIME GOES
In a lifetime, the average American spends

Three years
Cooking

Four years
Doing housework

Six years
Eating

Seven years
Washing

Fifteen years
Working/Studying

Twenty three years
Sleeping

From USA News and World Report

Unit 13 Exercise 2

AROUND THE WORLD
Lunchtime Reports

		C	F
Barcelona	S	16	61
Bonn	C	9	48
Cairo	S	17	63
Copenhagen	R	7	45
Glasgow	S	7	45
Moscow	Sn	0	32
Osaka	R	9	48
Rio de Janeiro	S	25	77
Rome	Sn	0	32
Stockholm	S	5	41
Tokyo	R	7	45

S = Sun, R = Rain, Sn = Snow, C = Cloud

Unit 17 Exercise 5

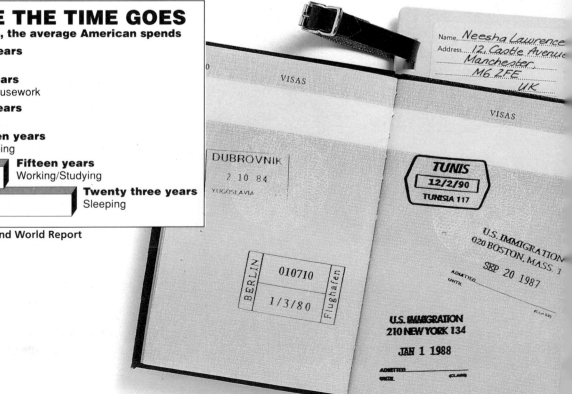

Unit 1 Exercise 6

Student C

Hear	Say
839 7118	491 2598
249 3491	673 9327
566 7890	453 6419
735 5566	267 7029
234 8122	734 7455

Unit 16 Exercise 4

Heat is on, maybe

	Coldest	Hottest	Wettest	Driest	Sunniest	Dullest
JAN	1795	1916	1948	1766	1959	1917
FEB	1947	1779	1833	1891	1949	1940
MAR	1674	1957	1947	1742	1929	1964
APR	1837	1865	1756	1938	1914	1920
MAY	1698	1833	1773	1844	1989	1932
JUN	1675	1989	1860	1925	1957	1987
JUL	1816	1983	1758	1825	1911	1944
AUG	1912	1975	1737	1747	1947	1912
SEP	1694	1729	1918	1756	1911	1945
OCT	1740	1969	1903	1781	1959	1968
NOV	1782	1818	1852	1945	1989	1934
DEC	1890	1934	1914	1799	1962	1956
Year	1740	1989	1872	1731	1989	1932

Unit 12 Exercise 5

Unit 17 Exercise 5

```
                 CURRICULUM VITAE

    NAME:           Simon Lawrence

    ADDRESS:        12 Castle Avenue,
                    Manchester, M6 2FE
                    (061 688 9710)


    DATE OF BIRTH:  30/10/58

    PLACE OF BIRTH: Manchester, England

    QUALIFICATIONS: 7 GCE 'O' Levels - Maths
                    History, Geography,
                    Biology,
                    French, Spanish, English
                    3 'A' Levels - Spanish (B),
                    French (B), History (D)
                    BA Hons. French 2(2)
                    (Exeter University)


    WORK EXPERIENCE:
    Summers 1979-82 Tourist guide in Majorca,
                    Crete and Yugoslavia
            1981    Assistant in French lycée
                    (Paris)
            1983    Joined Barclays Bank
```

Check what you know 1

1 Listening

1 Listen to José Gonzales and write short answers to these questions.

1 Where does he come from?
2 How old is he?
3 What time does he go to school?
4 What days does he have English at school.
5 What does he have for lunch, at 12 o'clock?
6 What time does he get home?

2 Grammar

Write five sentences about José.

3 Pronunciation

1 Listen and mark the stress on these words.

Example: sugar

seven   mother   Saturday   o'clock
breakfast   cigarette   chocolate

4 Vocabulary

1 Write three words in each of these groups.

- Food
- Drink
- Places
- Nationalities
- Activities and interests

2 Complete this dialogue, ordering breakfast.

WAITER: good morning, Madam.
CUSTOMER: Good morning. I have a . English breakfast, please
WAITER: Of course. Tea or coffee?
CUSTOMER: Coffee, please. And can I have a . croissant too?
WAITER: Yes, certainly. With or syup jam ?
CUSTOMER: Without, thank you

5 Reading

1 Read the text and complete the family tree with the correct names.

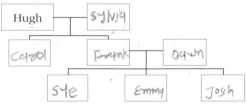

Hugh and Sylvia are married. They have got two children, a son and a daughter. The son's name is Frank and he's married to Dawn. Carol is Frank's sister and she is not married. Frank and Dawn have got three children, a boy and two girls. Josh is the baby of the three. Sue and Emma are his sisters.

2 Complete these sentences about the family.

1 Josh is Frank son.
2 Hugh is Sue grandfather.
3 Dawn is Emma mother.
4 Frank is Josh father.
5 Emma is Sue sister.

6 Writing

1 Complete this form about you.

Name: Nalini - A . Patel.
Address: 25 white first lane
Tel. No.: 808 5749
Country of origin: London
Age: 23
Marital status: married
No. of children: -

2 Write the questions.

Example: Name - What's your name?

7 Speaking

Talk about you, your family and interests. Give all the information in the form and other information, in complete sentences.

Check what you know 2

1 ▣ Listening

1 Listen to the dictation. Do not write or draw.
2 Listen again and complete the picture below.

3 Write seven sentences about the picture. Use each of these prepositions only once.

Example: The chair is on the left of the table.

on   next to   between   behind
in front of   on the left of   on the right of

2 Grammar

There are ten grammar mistakes in this text. Find and correct them.

A: Would you like come to a disco, Pilar?
B: No, I can't. I haven't got a money and I don't like going to discos. I don't like pop music.
A: These disco is different. It only has rock n' roll. I went there last weekend. It was fantastic! We dance from 11 pm to 4 am and then have a hamburger at a fast food restaurant.
B: Who did you went with?
A: My sister, her two friend from school and they brothers.

3 Pronunciation

1 Put these Past Simple verbs in the correct column.

lived   watched   started   opened   waited   asked

/t/	/d/	/ɪd/

2 ▣ Listen and write the questions and sentences you hear using *can* or *can't*.

4 Reading

1 Put these paragraphs about Margaret Thatcher's life in a logical order.

A She married her husband, Denis, in December 1951 and had her two children, Mark and Carol, in 1953.

B Margaret worked hard at school and went to Oxford University in 1943 where she studied chemistry.

C She became a Member of Parliament in 1959. On 4 May 1979 she became Prime Minister and worked in this position until December 1990.

D Margaret Thatcher was born on 13 October 1925 in Grantham in the middle of England.

E Her father had a small shop and they did not have a lot of money.

F She went from Oxford to work in industry for three years and she then practised law for about five years.

2 Answer these questions in complete sentences.

1 Where does Margaret Thatcher come from?
2 When is her birthday?
3 Which university did she go to?
4 When did she go to university?
5 Did she study arts or science?
6 Did she work before she got married?
7 When did she get married?
8 How many children has she got?
9 What are their names?
10 When did she become Prime Minister of Britain?

5 Writing

Write a text like the one about Margaret Thatcher, describing your life.

6 Vocabulary

Write three words in each of these groups.

- clothes
- colours
- hotel facilities
- jobs
- parts of the body

7 Speaking

Talk about what you did last weekend and what you are going to do this weekend. Think about:

- what?
- where?
- who with?
- when exactly?

Check what you know 3

1 Listening

1 Listen to Mirella talking about where she lives and works. Complete the information below.

1 Home town: *Rome*
2 Job: . . .
3 Place of work: . . .
4 Distance from home: . . .
5 Method of transport: . . .
6 Journey time: . . .

2 Write the questions.

Example: 1 - Where do you live?

2 Vocabulary

Read the clues and complete the crossword.

ACROSS →
1 Opposite of *hot* (4)
4 Someone who works for a newspaper (8)
6 Not fast (4)
9 I go to work by . . . every day. It's fast and I can read on it (5)
10 *Am/is/are* = verb to . . . (2)
11 Would you like some tea? . . ., thank you (2)
12 It's very . . . today. No boats are going between England and France (5)

DOWN
1 Opposite of *expensive* (5)
2 I felt very tired . . . the weekend, but I feel better now (2)
3 I don't like going to work by bus. It's always . . . and I can't find a seat (7)
5 I had a bad stomachache . . . Friday night, so I didn't go to the party (2)
6 If it's . . . tomorrow, we can go to the beach (5)
7 . . . isn't very warm today, is it? (2)
8 If we don't have some . . . soon, the flowers and plants are going to die (4)
13 I've got . . . terrible headache (1)

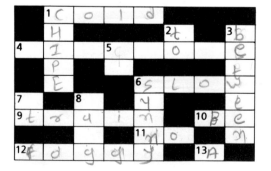

3 Reading

There are two letters in this text. Separate the two letters and put them in order, like this:

Letter 1: e, j . . .
Letter 2: i, k . . .

a Please write and tell me about the differences between life in this country and life in your country.

b I look forward to hearing from you soon.

c I would like to know how the new models are better than the old and what the different prices are.

d As I told you then, I'm a newspaper reporter.

e Dear Mr Stone,

f At the moment I have an old TX model and am interested in buying a new machine.

g Yours faithfully, J.A. Brown (Mr)

h I hope you are going to have a good time here and that we can meet again soon.

i Dear Sir/Madam,

j It was very nice to meet you in the train last week.

k I am writing to ask for information about your latest line in washing machines.

l Yours sincerely, James Blake

m I would like to write an article based on a visitor's view of this country.

4 Writing

Write a reply to one of the letters in exercise 3. Use three or more comparatives. Put your name, address and the date in the letter.

5 Grammar

1 Complete the sentences with *a, an, some,* or *any.*

1 I'm very unhappy. I haven't got . . . friends.
2 She's got . . . money in the bank but not much.
3 I've got . . . headache. Have you got . . . aspirins?
4 They can't get to the party. They haven't got . . . car
5 He hasn't got . . . milk in the fridge.
6 I'd like . . . apple with my lunch.

2 Give advice. Write two sentences using *should* or *shouldn't* for each of the following people:

1 I'm working very hard. I feel tired all the time.
2 I would like to speak English well.
3 I've got a terrible toothache.
4 I would love to be slim.
5 I'd like to stop smoking.

6 Pronunciation

Put the words below in the correct column.

/ɒ/	/əʊ/
not	go

hot   cold   not   foggy   know   Scotland   body
Rome   phone   go   watch   job   home

7 Speaking

Phone an English speaking friend in another town/country. Ask and answer about:

• health.   • family.   • the weather.
• what you are both doing at the moment.
• what you are both going to do this evening.

Check what you know 4

1 Vocabulary

1 Complete these sentences.

1 The most important city in a country is its c . . .
2 He worked f . . . and finished the report in half an hour.
3 You usually use a key to l . . . a door.
4 The smallest room in the house is usually the t . . .
5 I've got a large car and it's difficult to p . . .
6 H . . . is the school subject where you learn about the past.
7 The place where you eat at home is the d . . . r . . .
8 If you marry someone who has children from an earlier marriage, these are your s . . .-children.
9 In Britain, men generally r . . . at sixty-five.

2 Reading

1 Read the text below and answer these questions.

1 This person has travelled a lot for
a her job
b enjoyment
c her job and enjoyment

2 Her first job as a teacher of English was in
a France
b The Lebanon
c Libya

3 She has mainly travelled to
a European countries
b Arabic–speaking countries
c South America and Japan

4 She likes her job because
a she likes sport
b she gets to know different people
c she doesn't have to travel

5 In the future she'd like to
a stay in her own country
b go back to places she knows
c travel to new countries

I have travelled abroad a great deal in my life, mainly for work but also on holiday. I studied French at school and at university and so I often visited France.

When I first started my career as a teacher of English as a foreign language I went to the Lebanon. It was a really beautiful country; you could ski in the morning and swim in the afternoon.

Then I went to Libya. What I liked most about Libya was the people.

After a short time back in Britain I went to Egypt. The pyramids and ancient ruins were fantastic. So was the number of people. The streets and markets were terribly crowded but this is part of the charm of life in Cairo.

I'm back in London again now but not for long I hope. My work gives me the chance to travel and meet new people which I love. Where next? I don't know. I'd love to go to South America or the Far East. We'll have to wait and see.

3 Writing

Write about your country. Include information on these things:

- geographical location
- major cities
- population
- climate
- tourist attractions

4 Grammar

1 Complete the sentences with *too, very, quite, really* or *not very*. Use each word once only.

James . . . didn't like Shaun. His parents liked him of course. He was . . . polite. But for James he was . . . cold to be a real friend. He was . . . friendly and he didn't like working with other people. The other boys didn't like him at all. He was . . . good at school work, but not that good. The teachers didn't seem to like him either.

2 Complete with *a/an, the* or (–).

Stavros is . . . small village in . . . west of . . . Crete. It is famous on . . . island because of . . . film, Zorba . . . Greek. It is only . . . quarter of . . . hour away from . . . Chania, . . . nearest town.

5 Pronunciation

1 Put the words below in the correct column.

/e/	/ɪ/

any   English   friend   women   egg   says
kitchen   fit   men   biggest

6 Listening

1 🖭 Listen to Ursula talking about her new job and answer these questions.

1 What is her new job?
2 What does she like best about it?
3 What does she like least?
4 How does it compare to her last job?

2 Listen again and complete her conditions of work.

Number of days a week: . . .
Number of people in the office: . . .
Number of weeks holiday: . . .
Number of hours a week: . . .
Amount of time for lunch: . . .
Pay: . . .

7 Speaking

Talk about your work or school life.

What is it like?
What work do you have to do on a typical day?
What do you like best about it?
What do you like least about it?
What are you going to do next (when you finish school or change jobs)?

Tapescript

UNIT 1

Exercise 4 Listening: 1

Conversation 1
WAITER: Good morning, Madam.
WOMAN: Good morning. An English Breakfast, please.
WAITER: Tea or coffee?
WOMAN: Tea, please.

Conversation 2
WOMAN: Cup of coffee?
CLIENT: Oh yes, please. That'd be lovely.
WOMAN: Sugar?
CLIENT: Just one, please.

Conversation 3
CUSTOMER: A tea, 2 black coffees and an orange juice, please.
WAITER: Anything else?
CUSTOMER: No, thank you.

Exercise 8 Listening: 1

RECEPTIONIST: Hello, the Grosvenor Hotel.
WOMAN: Hello. Can I speak to Mark Andrews, please?
RECEPTIONIST: No, I'm sorry, he's not here at the moment.
WOMAN: Well, I'm phoning from France and it's quite important.
RECEPTIONIST: Can I have your name and phone number, please.
WOMAN: Yes, it's Mrs Mary Bryant and my number is Paris 45 67 88 99.
RECEPTIONIST: 45 67 88 99. And, how do you spell your surname?
WOMAN: Bryant, B-R-Y-A-N-T.
RECEPTIONIST: Thank you Mrs Bryant, I'll tell him.
WOMAN: Thank you. Goodbye.
RECEPTIONIST: Goodbye.

UNIT 2

Exercise 7 Listening: 1

ROB: . . . So, what time do you go to work in the morning?
JON: Well, it depends . . . generally, at about 3.30.
ROB: What about breakfast?
JON: I don't have time for a big breakfast but I have a coffee at about 3.15 before I go.
ROB: So, what time do you get to the post-office?
JON: At about 4.00.
ROB: That's early!
JON: Yes, but I go home early too, at about 7.15. I usually get home by about 7.45, in time to make Alex and Alison's breakfast before they go to school.
ROB: What a day!
JON: And then I work at home all morning. I go to the cinema from 12-3.
ROB: The cinema! I'm not surprised!
JON: No, no. You don't understand. I work there!

English in action: 3

CUSTOMER: Can I have seven stamps for Brazil, please.
CLERK: Yes, here you are. Anything else?
CUSTOMER: No, thank you.
CLERK: That'll be £2.45, please.
CUSTOMER: Thank you.

UNIT 3

Exercise 5 Listening: 2

He's got the whole world in His hands
He's got the whole world in His hands
He's got the whole world in His hands
He's got the whole world in His hands

He's got you and me, sister, in His hands
He's got you and me, brother, in His hands
He's got you and me, sister, in His hands
He's got the whole world in His hands

He's got the little tiny baby in His hands
He's got the little tiny baby in His hands
He's got the little tiny baby in His hands
He's got the whole world in His hands

He's got all of us here in His hands
He's got all of us here in His hands
He's got all of us here in His hands
He's got the whole world in His hands

English in action: 3

MOTHER: Hello. How nice to meet you. Come and meet the family. Tell me about your home. Have you got a big family ?
STUDENT: . . .
MOTHER: I see. This is Jane, my daughter. Say hello, Jane.
JANE: Hello. What's your name?
STUDENT: . . .
MOTHER: What a nice name! And this is my son.
STEVE: Hello. I'm Steve. You won't see much of me: I'm at school all day. Are you a student too?
STUDENT: . . .
STEVE: Where do you go to school?
STUDENT: . . .
MOTHER: It's not like your school, Steve. This is my mother. Mum, this is our guest from. . .Oh I'm sorry, where do you come from?
STUDENT: . . .
GRANDMOTHER: What a lovely place! I hope you'll enjoy your stay with us. Now dear, I'm in charge of breakfast. Do you have tea or coffee for breakfast?
STUDENT: . . .
GRANDFATHER: Good. That's just like me. And what time do you go to your English classes?
STUDENT: . . .
JANE: And when do you get home?
STUDENT: . . .

UNIT 4

Exercise 7 Listening: 2

ASSISTANT: Oh yes, most of the perfume comes from France. French perfume is very popular but very expensive.
INTERVIEWER: Yes, of course. Now, what about food? Do the oranges you sell come from the States or Spain?
ASSISTANT: They are mostly American. Oranges from Europe are too expensive. We also sell a lot of Indian tea. And Brazilian coffee, of course.
INTERVIEWER: So tea from India and coffee from Brazil. Now, how about chocolate? Is that Swiss or British?
ASSISTANT: A lot is Swiss. We also import fresh flowers from Holland. Dutch tulips from Amsterdam, for example. Very popular but expensive, of course.
INTERVIEWER: And what about drink? Do you sell more wine from Italy or Portugal?
ASSISTANT: We sell a lot of Italian wine, no Portuguese wine at all in fact.
INTERVIEWER: Oh I am surprised! I thought. . .

English in action: 4

BBC English Magazine
PO Box 76
Bush House
London
WC2B 4PH

UNIT 5

3 Language in context: 1, 4

2, 4, 6, 8
Who do we appreciate?
S.C.O.T.L.A.N.D
Scotland!

Dialogue 1
JULIE: Hi Tony! Come in.
TONY: Thanks.
JULIE: Tony, this is Ian, my youngest son.
TONY: Hello Ian. And how old are you?
BOY: I'm 4.
TONY: My, aren't you big! How old are your other children, Julie?
JULIE: Well, Mark is 12 and Suzanne is 16.
TONY: Quite a big family then. What time do Mark and Suzanne get home from school?
JULIE: At about 5.15. They should get here any minute now . . .

Dialogue 2
RECEPTIONIST: Hello. BHP Incorporated. Can I help you?

BILL NORMAN: Yes. Can I speak to Roy Jones, please?
RECEPTIONIST: I'm sorry. He's not here until 6.45 this evening.
BILL NORMAN: Can I leave a message, please?
RECEPTIONIST: Yes, of course.
BILL NORMAN: My name's Bill Norman. Please ask Roy to phone me back this evening, if possible.
RECEPTIONIST: Certainly. What's your telephone number Mr Norman?
BILL NORMAN: 371 93 56
RECEPTIONIST: 371 93 56
BILL NORMAN: That's right. Thanks very much.
RECEPTIONIST: You're welcome. Goodbye.

Dialogue 3
TOURIST: Good morning. Can you help me please?
ASSISTANT: Yeah! That's what I'm here for.
TOURIST: Right. Well, what time are the banks open?
ASSISTANT: Let me see . . . from 8.30 to 5.30, Monday to Friday.
TOURIST: Good. Oh and . . . can I have a map of Palm Springs?
ASSISTANT: Yeah. This one OK?
TOURIST: Fine. How much is it?
ASSISTANT: It says here . . . 1 dollar 99.
TOURIST: That's fine. Here you are.
ASSISTANT: Thanks. Have a nice day!

UNIT 6

Exercise 1 Revision: 2
WOMAN: I like my job but I have to go early in the morning. I get to work at about 8 o'clock. I open up the place. Customers start arriving from about 8.45 so I open the shop early most mornings. I like serving the customers. They ask me about the books before they buy them. I like reading the sports magazines when they arrive on Monday morning. But I don't like having to answer the phone. It's part of my job but I don't like speaking on the phone.

Exercise 7 Reading: Grammar 2
Happy birthday to you
Happy birthday to you
Happy birthday dear Alison
Happy birthday to you

Exercise 8 Listening: 1
JOURNALIST: Well, as you know, I'd like some information about Richard Branson. I'm writing an article about famous British businessmen.
SECRETARY: Well, where shall I start?
JOURNALIST: How about school? He finished early, didn't he?
SECRETARY: Yes, he finished school in 1967, when he was seventeen.
JOURNALIST: So, when did he start work?
SECRETARY: He started work straight after school, in 1967. He worked on a magazine called *Student*. It wasn't until a few years later that he opened his famous Virgin shops.
JOURNALIST: When did he open his first shop?
SECRETARY: In 1971. It was near Oxford Street, in the centre of London. It was very popular from the minute it opened. In fact, he made his first £1 000 000 in 1973, when he was twenty-three.
JOURNALIST: That was quick!

UNIT 7

Exercise 6 Listening: 1
ROB: So, how was your holiday in Istanbul?
SIMON: Fantastic! Well, after the first night.
ROB: Why? What happened?
NEESHA: Well, we got to the hotel very late on Saturday evening,
SIMON: About one o'clock in the morning, actually.
NEESHA: We went to reception and gave our names but the hotel didn't have a double room.
ROB: Oh no! Didn't you reserve a room before you went?
SIMON: Yes, of course. But they gave it to someone else because we were late.
NEESHA: Yes . . . and they wanted to put us in a twin-bedded room.
ROB: What, you mean with two single beds!
NEESHA: Yes, and it was very small. So we went back to reception . . .
ROB: And what did they say?
NEESHA: Well, the receptionist was very friendly but they didn't have a double room.
SIMON: Anyway, he spoke to the manager.
NEESHA: And the manager spoke to his wife and the result was we slept in their room!

SIMON: And it was fantastic! There was an enormous colour TV and a bar with lots of drinks.
NEESHA: We even had a bathroom with a bath, a shower and our own jacuzzi. Oh yes, and the bed was very comfortable!

UNIT 8

Exercise 7 Listening
ROB: So, what are you going to do at the weekend?
NEESHA: Well, actually, we've got an invitation to a party at Tony Barratt's.
ROB: Oh good! Me too.
SIMON: The problem is I can't go.
NEESHA: Oh Simon. Why not? It's his birthday.
SIMON: I can't, honestly. I've got important work to do. But you go.
NEESHA: Yes, OK, I will. It is his 21st birthday on Saturday, so it's important too.
SIMON: Alright. Alright. So, anyway, what are you going to wear?
NEESHA: Oh, I don't know. Perhaps my black dress.
SIMON: Not jeans then?
NEESHA: No, I don't think so. Listen, Rob . . . what present are you going to take, have you thought?
ROB: No, why don't we buy one good present from all of us?
SIMON: That's a good idea! What about some compact discs?
ROB: Yes, great! What time does the party start?
NEESHA: It says half past eight. Let's go at nine and get there for nine thirty. I hate being the first to arrive . . .

English in action: 5
CUSTOMER: Good morning. Can I have these by Friday?
ASSISTANT: Yes, of course. What have you got exactly?
CUSTOMER: Well, there's a skirt, three blouses and a sweater.
ASSISTANT: That's fine. Is Friday afternoon OK?
CUSTOMER: Yes, about what time?
ASSISTANT: 3.30?
CUSTOMER: OK. How much is it going to be?
ASSISTANT: Um . . . £2.50 for the skirt, 3 blouses at £1.75 each, that's £5.25 and the sweater is £2. That makes £9.75 in all.
CUSTOMER: Fine.
ASSISTANT: Can you bring this ticket with you on Friday?
CUSTOMER: Thanks very much.

UNIT 9

Exercise 4 Reading: 2
INSTRUCTOR: OK everybody. Are you ready? Exercise 1 is for your arms and back. So, stand up straight. Look straight in front of you. Put your shoulders back and your feet apart. Good! Now, put your arms straight up next to your ears with your hands facing each other. That's right. Now, stretch your right arm up five times and then your left arm. Ready? 1, 2, 3, 4, 5. Now the other arm. 1, 2 , 3, 4, 5. Good!
Now, exercise 2. This exercise is for your legs. Go down on your hands and knees. Put your right leg straight out behind you, above the floor. Toes point down. Keep your back straight. Lift your right leg up and then down. But don't touch the floor! Good – well done! And now the other leg.
Exercise 3 is for the top of your body. Stand with your feet apart and your knees slightly bent. Put your arms out straight to the left and right. Now, move your arms in small circles from the shoulders. Good!
Right. The last one now, everyone.
OK, exercise 4 is for the top of your body and legs. Now stand with your feet apart and your stomach in. Look straight in front of you. Put your arms straight up. Right up, that's it. And bend down and touch your toes. Now touch the floor between your feet. But don't bend your legs! Good!
OK, everyone, relax . . .

Exercise 6 Listening: 3
The Okey Cokey
Put your right arm in,
Your right arm out,
In, out, in, out,
Shake it all about.
Do the okey cokey and turn around,
That's what it's all about.

Chorus

Oh! Oh! The okey cokey.
Oh! Oh! The okey cokey.
Oh! Oh! The okey cokey.
Knees bend, arms stretch
Rah, rah, rah!

Put your left arm in,
Your left arm out,
In, out, in, out,
Shake it all about.
Do the okey cokey and turn around,
That's what it's all about.

(Chorus)

Put your right leg in,
Your right leg out,
In, out, in, out,
Shake it all about.
Do the okey cokey and turn around,
That's what it's all about.

(Chorus)

Put your left leg in,
Your left leg out,
In, out, in, out,
Shake it all about.
Do the okey cokey and turn around,
That's what it's all about.

(Chorus)

Put your whole self in,
Your whole self out,
In, out, in, out,
Shake it all about.
Do the okey cokey and turn around,
That's what it's all about.

Exercise 8 Listening: 2

PHOTOGRAPHER: That's lovely. Now just one more of the family. Could you bring those two chairs over please. That's right, thank you. Now Rachel and Martin, sit down where you are, please. Fine. Now Rachel's mother and father, I'd like you in this photo. Yes, Rachel's mother and father? Hello. Can you come in this photo please? Yes, now stand behind Rachel and Martin, that's right. No, Rachel's mum, please change places with your husband so you're behind your daughter. Yes, and Rachel's father is behind Martin. Good! Now then, Rachel's sister, Gillian isn't it? Could you stand next to your mother, on her left and Martin's brother, could you stand next to Rachel's father, on his right. Fine! Good! Now, Martin, put your left arm around your wife. Good. Look into her eyes. Lovely. Smile everyone. Say cheese! Great. That's it. Well, now we'll have a full group photo. Could everyone . . .

English in action: 2

CHEMIST: Good morning. Can I help you?
CUSTOMER: Yes. I'd like to buy a colour film for this camera.
CHEMIST: Prints or slides.
CUSTOMER: Prints, please.
CHEMIST: How many – 12, 24 or 36?
CUSTOMER: 36, please.
CHEMIST: That'll be £3.25 please.
CUSTOMER: Thanks very much. Goodbye.

UNIT 10

2 Across cultures: 3

MAN: . . . And do you like living in Britain, Melissa?
MELISSA: Oh yes, very much.
MAN: Even the weather?
MELISSA: Well . . . umm . . . the weather is the one problem.
MAN: Have you noticed many differences between the Americans and the British?
MELISSA: Oh yes, lots of things.
MAN: Oh what, for example?
MELISSA: Well, Americans are more direct. They say what they think and, I know what it is – they have a lot of eye contact when they speak.
MAN: The British do too.
MELISSA: No, not so much. We generally want more eye contact than

the British.
MAN: I see. And what about body distance? Do you generally feel comfortable about how near British people stand to you?
MELISSA: Yes, it's fine. I think it is the same as in America. But we generally use gestures more when we speak.
MAN: You mean you move your hands and arms all the time!
MELISSA: Not all the time!
MAN: Well, is anything the same? Shaking your head in the States means 'No' and nodding means 'Yes', doesn't it?
MELISSA: Of course! It is the same language!
MAN: And what about kissing? That's always an important one. Britain is different to a lot of countries. What about America?
MELISSA: Well, yes, there are differences. It's quite common, for example, to kiss people in your family, on the lips.
MAN: On the lips! You kiss your brothers and sisters on the lips?
MELISSA: Yes, even my parents!
MAN: Well, that certainly is different to Britain!

3 Language in context: 4

Rock around the clock

Chorus 1

One, two, three 'o clock, four 'o clock rock,
Five, six, seven 'o clock, eight 'o clock rock,
Nine, ten, eleven 'o clock, twelve 'o clock rock,
We're gonna rock around the clock tonight.

Put your glad rags on, and join me hon'
We'll have some fun when the clock strikes one,

Chorus 2

We're gonna rock around the clock tonight,
We're gonna rock, rock, rock, 'til broad daylight,
We're gonna rock, gonna rock around the clock tonight.

When the clock strikes two, and three and four,
If the band slows down we'll yell for more,

(Chorus 2)

When the chimes ring five and six and seven,
We'll be right in seventh heaven,

(Chorus 2)

When it's eight, nine, ten, eleven, too,
I'll be going strong and so will you,

(Chorus 2)

When the clock strikes twelve, we'll cool off then,
Start a rockin' 'round the clock again,

(Chorus 2)

UNIT 11

Exercise 4 Listening: 1

Neesha and Simon

INTERVIEWER: So, Neesha and Simon, how did you two first meet?
NEESHA: We were at a party when we met, weren't we Simon?
SIMON: Yes, we were. Quite a dull party if I remember correctly.
NEESHA: I liked Simon because he was very attractive.
SIMON: And I liked Neesha because she was very friendly.
INTERVIEWER: Good. And when was that?
NEESHA: In 1989.
SIMON: Yes, 1989.
INTERVIEWER: And what about the future? What are your plans for the future? Have you any?
NEESHA: Well, I'd like to have a really large family.
SIMON: Yes, I know Neesha would like to have a lot of children.
INTERVIEWER: Good. Good.

Sandra and Trisha

INTERVIEWER: Now, Sandra and Trisha, hello.
SANDRA: Hi.
TRISHA: Hi.
INTERVIEWER: How did you two first meet?
TRISHA: Well, you won't believe this, we were both over on a trip to London, England, and were on a tour to . . . what was the name again?
SANDRA: Stratford-Upon-Avon.
TRISHA: Stratford-Upon-Avon.
INTERVIEWER: Oh, yes?
SANDRA: And we met in a pub, a pub and we got talking and she's got a great sense of humour, this girl. I was laughing . . . oh my . . .

TRISHA:	Yeah, that was, when was that – about September last year?
SANDRA:	I reckon that was about September.
INTERVIEWER:	Oh, last year? Only last year?
SANDRA:	Yeah, uh huh, and, er, any, anyway we got talking and we had the same kind of political ideas.
TRISHA:	Well, I liked Sandra's ideas, she liked mine and we just got on so well.
SANDRA:	And she's a great cook! She is the greatest cook so I said how about we open . . . some kind of a restaurant here.
TRISHA:	Hey, listen . . .
INTERVIEWER:	Ah.
SANDRA:	We're gonna open a business together.
INTERVIEWER:	Really?
TRISHA:	Well, that's what we thought. We thought we'd do that, as she's such a great, terrific cook . . .

Carlos and Pat

INTERVIEWER:	And how did you two meet, Carlos and Pat?
PAT:	Well . . . you say.
CARLOS:	Well, um, er, I came over to England to study English in a language school in Oxford.
INTERVIEWER:	Yeah? And when was this?
CARLOS:	And Pat, she was the teacher there.
INTERVIEWER:	Oh, yes?
CARLOS:	This was . . .
PAT:	May, May?
CARLOS:	No, no, it was June, June 1990.
INTERVIEWER:	Oh, yeah?
PAT:	That's right. How could I forget?
CARLOS:	I was really nervous about coming over from Spain to learn English but Pat was a really good teacher and . . .
INTERVIEWER:	Oh, good.
CARLOS:	. . . she made it all so easy.
PAT:	Oh, no.
INTERVIEWER:	Was he a good student?
PAT:	A very good student. He was very good at English. Still is.
CARLOS:	No, no.
INTERVIEWER:	You are! You speak perfect English.
PAT:	And I thought Carlos was really handsome.
INTERVIEWER:	Uh huh.
CARLOS:	And now we're going back to Spain together, and, to Barcelona, where I live and . . .
PAT:	And I've got a job out there, teaching English.
INTERVIEWER:	Oh, smashing. Well, really good luck for the future, both of you.
CARLOS:	Thank you.
PAT:	Thank you.
INTERVIEWER:	Thanks for talking to me.

UNIT 12

Exercise 4 Listening: 2

SIMON:	Yes, tacos. That's a good idea. We've got the box of shells and the taco sauce. What else do we need? I'll make a list.
NEESHA:	OK. It says we need a green pepper.
SIMON:	Well, we haven't got any peppers so I'll buy one.
NEESHA:	Have we got any onions? We need two in fact.
SIMON:	Two onions! That's fine. We've got the onions.
NEESHA:	Oh, I know, we haven't got any chicken. We need two chicken breasts.
SIMON:	Right. I'll buy a complete roasted chicken. What else?
NEESHA:	Well, that's it really. Now we need some toppings. Have we got any lettuce?
SIMON:	Yes. There's some in the fridge. There are some tomatoes too.
NEESHA:	Good! We've got the two tomatoes then. Have we got any grated cheese? That really makes a difference.
SIMON:	No, no cheese. I'll buy some.
NEESHA:	We need an avocado as well.
SIMON:	Oh right, well, we haven't got any. So, I'll buy an avocado.
NEESHA:	What about cream and yoghurt?
SIMON:	We haven't got any cream but we've got some yoghurt.
NEESHA:	Oh, buy some cream. I love it.
SIMON:	OK. Now, let's just check . . . this is what we need to buy – a chicken, some cheese, some . . .

Exercise 6 Listening: 2

INTERVIEWER:	So what do you think Ivan?
IVAN:	Er, you can get some pretty good, tasty meals in fast food places – I like them OK but I do prefer real restaurants. The people in fast food places are generally

very nice and friendly. They do get crowded though, especially on Saturdays when families are out doing their shopping.

INTERVIEWER:	Do you agree, Rose?
ROSE:	No, not really. We don't often eat fast food. I don't like it and Justin, my boyfriend, hates hamburgers. Although the restaurants are very clean, the food is always cold and the service is so slow.
INTERVIEWER:	What about you Rohana? What do you think?
ROHANA:	I love fast food! I often go after the cinema with my friends. The hamburgers with cheese are my favourite, and the chips are always nice and hot too. I always have the vanilla milkshake. The best thing about fast food is it's cheap! As I'm a student, I haven't got much money, so that's really important.

UNIT 13

Exercise 5 Listening: 2

Raining in my heart

The sun is out, the sky is blue, there's not a cloud to spoil the view,
but it's raining, raining in my heart.
The weatherman says 'Clear today'. He doesn't know, you've gone
away, and it's raining, raining in my heart.
Oh misery, misery! What's going to become of me?
I tell my blues they mustn't show, but soon these tears are bound to
flow, 'cos it's raining, raining in my heart.
But it's raining, raining in my heart.
And it's raining, raining in my heart.
Oh misery, misery! What's going to become of me?
I tell my blues they mustn't show, but soon these tears are bound to
flow, 'cos it's raining, raining in my heart, raining in my heart,
raining in my heart.

Exercise 8 Listening: 1

JON:	Hi Mum! It's me.
MAUREEN:	Jon. How nice to hear from you. How are you?
JON:	Fine, fine. I'm just calling to say Happy 30th Anniversary!
MAUREEN:	Oh, that is kind of you. Imagine being married 30 years! I got your card this morning.
JON:	Oh good. Are you doing anything special today?
MAUREEN:	Well, at the moment, I'm in my jeans, cleaning up the garden. We're going to have a barbecue in the garden this evening with some friends. And I'm going to wear a new dress your father gave me.
JON:	Great! What's the weather like?
MAUREEN:	It's nice and sunny, not a cloud in sight.
JON:	It's raining here, as usual. Typical!
MAUREEN:	How's work? What's that new woman like – you know, the woman working with you in the cinema?
JON:	Oh Neesha?
MAUREEN:	Yes, that's right.
JON:	Oh she's nice. In fact, she's very nice. She's got one or two problems at home . . . it's all rather difficult. I'll tell you about it another time. Listen, is Dad there? I'd like to speak to him.
MAUREEN:	Yes, of course dear. Thanks for calling, it was nice of you. Bye! Harry! It's Jon on the phone . . .

UNIT 14

Exercise 1 Revision: 1

NEESHA:	Hi Jon! How are you?
JON:	Fine! How are you?
NEESHA:	Not too good.
JON:	Oh dear. I'm sorry. Listen. I'm going to a cafe for lunch, why . . . .

Exercise 5 Listening: 2

MENIRA:	Neesha, you didn't have an arranged marriage, did you?
NEESHA:	No. I wanted to marry Simon and my family liked him. What about you?
MENIRA:	My family chose my husband but I was very happy. I prefer the idea of an arranged marriage; the man is generally older and the age difference makes marriage more interesting, I think.
NEESHA:	I can understand that. There are advantages.
MENIRA:	Yes. My family knows his family very well so there are no nasty surprises.
NEESHA:	True, but I like to make my own decisions. I'm sure Simon's more attractive to me because I chose him, even though he's

MENIRA: younger than me!
MENIRA: But attraction can change.
NEESHA: I know, but if I made a mistake it is my mistake not my family's mistake. I prefer that. My family usually like such serious people. Simon's got a good sense of humour, he is definitely funnier and less serious than the men in my family.
MENIRA: My husband has got a good sense of humour too but for me kindness is the most important thing. I'm happier this way because he is more understanding than other men I know.
NEESHA: Do you think . . .

English in action: 5

RECEPTIONIST: Hello. Dr. Barker's surgery. Can I help you?
STUDENT: . . .
RECEPTIONIST: Fine. Which day would you like to come?
STUDENT: . . .
RECEPTIONIST: Yes that's OK. Can you come at 10 o'clock?
STUDENT: . . .
RECEPTIONIST: Well, in that case, what about 4.15?
STUDENT: . . .
RECEPTIONIST: Good. Now, can you give me your name, please?
STUDENT: . . .
RECEPTIONIST: How do you spell your surname?
STUDENT: . . .
RECEPTIONIST: Fine, so we'll see you at 4.15 on . . .

UNIT 15

1 Thinking about learning: 2

So far away

Here I am again in this mean old town
And you're so far away from me
Now where are you when the sun goes down
You're so far away from me

Chorus

You're so far away from me
You're so far I just can't see
You're so far away from me
You're so far away from me

I'm tired of being in love and being all alone
When you're so far away from me
I'm tired of making out on the telephone
Cos' you're so far away from me

(Chorus)

I get so tired when I have to explain
When you're so far away from me
See you've been in the sun and I've been in the rain
And you're so far away from me

(Chorus)

UNIT 16

Exercise 6 Listening: 1

NEESHA: Hi, is that Jon?
JON: Yes, speaking.
NEESHA: Hi. This is Neesha.
JON: Oh hi, Neesha. How are you? Is everything OK? You can still babysit, can't you?
NEESHA: Yes. Don't worry, but you forgot to tell me how to get to your house.
JON: Oh no. How stupid of me! Where do you live exactly?
NEESHA: Castle Avenue.
JON: Oh yeah, I know. That's fine, not far at all. Probably the quickest and the easiest way is to go out of Castle Avenue and turn left into Brick Street. Go straight on, past the pub and then turn right.
NEESHA: Past the pub and then right. Yes, I know where you mean. Into Market Road.
JON: That's it. Then go down Market Road to the traffic lights, go past the traffic lights and then take the second road on the right. That's Park Hill Road where I live. It's number 76, next to the hotel and there's a large garden in front. You can't miss it.
NEESHA: 76 Park Hill Road? OK. No problem.
JON: Right, well, once again, thanks a lot for agreeing to look after the children.
NEESHA: That's OK.
JON: I'll see you later this evening, then.

NEESHA: Fine. I'll be there by six.
JON: Thanks. See you then.
NEESHA: Bye.
JON: Bye.

UNIT 17

Exercise 6 Listening: 2

Interview 1

INTERVIEWER: Now, you're from Scotland, aren't you Bob?
BOB: Yes, that's right. From Edinburgh, in fact.
INTERVIEWER: When did you come to Egypt exactly?
BOB: About a year ago.
INTERVIEWER: And what's it like?
BOB: Well, basically, it's great. I've lived in lots of countries and this is certainly the best! I mean, everyone is incredibly friendly. People are always ready to help and they often invite you into their homes.
INTERVIEWER: That must be very interesting. And how about the food? Have you had much Egyptian food?
BOB: Yes. And I love it. It's really different but very tasty.
INTERVIEWER: And what about the weather? Is it difficult living in such a hot climate?
BOB: I have a lot of showers! In fact, I prefer hot weather to cold so I like it really.
INTERVIEWER: And what about your free time? There must be lots to do.
BOB: Yes . . . I've been to the Pyramids lots of times of course and to the bazaar at Khan el Khalili. You can buy wonderful things. And I've seen some fantastic Egyptian belly-dancing.
INTERVIEWER: Oh really, where do you go to . . .

Interview 2

INTERVIEWER: So what do you think of France, Sharon?
SHARON: Well, I don't know France very well – only Paris really. It's certainly different from New Zealand.
INTERVIEWER: When did you come here?
SHARON: About six months ago. My sister came here with me originally, but now she's gone to England.
INTERVIEWER: And do you miss New Zealand?
SHARON: Yes, sometimes, especially family and friends, but I'm really pleased I came.
INTERVIEWER: Is it difficult to meet people here?
SHARON: No, not really. I've met a lot of very nice people, so that's been OK.
INTERVIEWER: And what do you think of Paris?
SHARON: It's beautiful, I just love walking around the city. And, of course, the food is fantastic. I can't believe it but I've eaten snails and frogs' legs and loved them.
INTERVIEWER: And what about the weather?
SHARON: That's better in New Zealand. It hasn't been very good here, but you can't have everything!
INTERVIEWER: But there's plenty to do?
SHARON: Oh yes. I've done lots of really interesting things. I've been to so many museums and art galleries . . .

UNIT 18

Exercise 4 Listening: 4

Once upon a time there was a kind and beautiful girl called Cinderella. When her mother died her father remarried. Her new stepmother was proud and cruel and had two daughters from her first marriage. They were extremely ugly and treated Cinderella very badly. Poor Cinderella had to do all the housework: wash the dishes, sweep the floors, clean the rooms and do all the cooking.
One day the ugly sisters received an invitation from the palace. The prince was giving a ball and everybody was invited. The two ugly sisters were very excited. They spent a long time getting ready. Cinderella had to help them choose their dresses carefully and do their hair in the latest styles. But she was not invited to the ball.
Sadly, Cinderella watched her sisters go. She started to cry she was so unhappy. However, Cinderella did have one good friend and that was her fairy godmother. Cinderella told her everything. Her fairy godmother smiled kindly and said 'But you can go to the ball, Cinderella'. She told Cinderella to get her a large pumpkin, six white mice, a rat and four lizards from the garden.
Then she waved her magic wand and they changed into a magnificent coach, with six white horses, a coachman and four handsome footmen. Next, Cinderella's fairy godmother touched her old clothes and they changed immediately into the most beautiful dress she had ever seen. On her feet were a pair of beautiful glass

slippers. As Cinderella got into the coach her fairy godmother said 'Don't forget to leave the ball before midnight because at twelve o'clock everything will change back to normal again'.

When Cinderella got to the palace everyone looked at her in wonder. They thought she was a Princess, she looked so beautiful. The Prince saw her and immediately asked her to dance. He danced with her and no-one else for the entire evening. They danced so well together that everyone looked at them. Cinderella was very happy and forgot the time. But then she heard the clock strike twelve 'ONE-TWO-THREE . . .'

She ran out of the palace. She ran very fast and as she ran she lost one of her glass slippers. The Prince ran after her but he didn't manage to stop her. Instead he found the glass slipper which could only belong to the smallest foot in the land. 'I'll marry the owner of the glass slipper', he promised.

The next day the Prince went to every house in the land to see if he could find his beautiful princess. When he arrived at Cinderella's house, the two ugly sisters tried on the glass slipper but their feet were much too big. The slipper was very small. To their horror, when Cinderella tried on the slipper, it fitted perfectly. At that moment Cinderella's fairy godmother appeared and changed her back into a Princess.

The Prince asked Cinderella to marry him and they invited everyone to the wedding – even the ugly sisters. Cinderella and the Prince lived happily ever after.

English in action: 1

ASSISTANT: Can I help you?
CUSTOMER: Yes, please. Can I try on these shoes?
ASSISTANT: Yes, certainly. What size are you?
CUSTOMER: 38, I think. Have you got them in green?
ASSISTANT: I don't think we have them in green.
CUSTOMER: Never mind. This colour is fine.
ASSISTANT: Here you are then. 38s in brown. Try them on. How do they feel?
CUSTOMER: They're too small, I'm afraid. Can I try the 39s on?
ASSISTANT: Of course. Here you are. How are these?
CUSTOMER: Great. They fit perfectly. They're very nice. Can I pay by cheque?
ASSISTANT: Yes, of course.

UNIT 19

Exercise 3 Listening: 2

When I'm sixty-four

When I get older, losing my hair
many years from now,
Will you still be sending me a Valentine,
birthday greetings, bottle of wine?
If I'd been out till quarter to three,
would you lock the door?
Will you still need me, will you still
feed me, when I'm sixty-four?

You'll be older too,
And if you say the word, I could stay with you.
I could be handy, mending a fuse
when your lights have gone.
You can knit a sweater by the fireside.
Sunday mornings go for a ride.
Doin' the garden, diggin' the weeds.
Who could ask for more?
Will you still need me, will you still
feed me, when I'm sixty-four?

Every summer we can rent a cottage
in the Isle of Wight, if it's not too dear.
We shall scrimp and save, grandchildren on your knee
Harry, Bert and Dave.
Send me a postcard, drop me a line,
stating point of view.
Indicate precisely what you mean to say,
yours sincerely wasting away.
Give me an answer, fill in a form.
Mine for evermore.
Will you still need me, will you still
feed me, when I'm sixty-four?

PHOTO FINISH

Unit 2, Exercise 7: 1
Unit 7, Exercise 6: 1

Unit 8, Exercise 7: 1
Unit 11, Exercise 4: 1
Unit 13, Exercise 8: 1
Unit 14, Exercise 1: 1
Unit 16, Exercise 6: 1

7 The final part of the story.

SIMON: Oh, hello Jon
JON: Hi, Simon. I'm pleased you're at home. I've got something important to say.
SIMON: I thought you'd come. Oh, you'd better come in.
JON: Simon, I don't know how to tell you this, but, well, I'm going to get married again. But, um . . . I need to talk to you . . .
SIMON: Well, I hardly think I'm the person . . .
JON: You see, she has been married before and well, I didn't think after my wife died I'd get married again, but things change. The children need a mother. What do you think? What should I do?
SIMON: Are you really sure? Are you sure it isn't just a passing thing?
JON: No, I know it's what I want to do. Barbara says she's sure too.
SIMON: Well, then . . . Barbara? Barbara who?
JON: You know, she works in the cinema. She's a friend of Neesha too. We all work in the cinema together. Don't you know her?
SIMON: No!
JON: How strange! In fact, Neesha is at her house at the moment. Didn't Neesha say anything about me and Barbara?
SIMON: No, no she didn't. But I thought . . .
JON: Well, Neesha said she is coming here at 8 o'clock with Barbara to meet us. The idea is to go out for a celebration meal together.
SIMON: Is Neesha coming?
JON: Yes, but I wanted to tell you the news first. Are you OK, Simon? You look awful. Don't you want to celebrate?
SIMON: Oh yes! I feel much better now! Jon, I'm sure you're doing the right thing. Congratulations!

UNIT 20

3 Language in context: 4

1

INTERVIEWER: So, what do you think of school, Kate?
KATE: I think school's OK really. Um. I quite like history. Um. 'Cos the history teacher's really nice. Um, but the other subjects are really boring 'cos I don't really like them. I think Wednesdays is my favourite day because we have sport on Wednesdays and I'm quite good at that. Um. The worst thing about school is the dinners. The food is horrible.
INTERVIEWER: And what are you going to do when you leave school?
KATE: Um. I'm not really sure, but I love animals. I love cats, dogs, birds, and I'd just love to work with animals.

2

INTERVIEWER: Right, now then Simon, what do you think about school?
SIMON: I like school a lot. Um. I like all the teachers, except for one, the maths teacher. Um. I think my favourite subject is French, 'cos I'm quite good at that. Um. This summer I'm gonna stay with a French family in France.
INTERVIEWER: That sounds great!
SIMON: Yeah, I'm looking forward to it a lot. Um. I think the bad things about school are all the homework and the – you have to work really hard, it takes up a lot of your time. So, um, I like doing the extra things as well, like the school orchestra, and playing the violin, um, and the school football team.
INTERVIEWER: So, what do you want to do when you leave school?
SIMON: Um. I think I'd like to be a French teacher, or even a football player for England!

3

INTERVIEWER: What do you think of school, Ruth?
RUTH: I hate school. The teachers hate me and I hate them. I've got no friends. That's because we moved recently. The only thing I like about my school is that we've got a swimming pool, but it's not open all the time. I really like swimming. I can't wait to leave school.
INTERVIEWER: What are you going to do when you leave school?
RUTH: I want to be an actress and work on television.

Wordlist

This Wordlist contains the most important words in *The Beginners' Choice*. For the groups of words below, please see the following pages:
- countries and continents   9, 19, 29
- days of the week   13
- months of the year   35
- nationalities and languages   27, 28, 29
- numbers   9, 12, 21, 35, 36

The Wordlist contains definitions from the Longman *New Junior English Dictionary*.

Abbreviations: *n.* noun; *adj.* adjective; *v.* verb; *adv.* adverb; *prep.* preposition; *pl.* plural.

/'/ shows main stress.

/ʳ/ at the end of a word means that /r/ is usually pronounced when the next word begins with a vowel sound.

Phonemic chart

Consonants				Vowels			
/p/	pen	/s/	son	/iː/	eat	/eɪ/	say
/b/	bed	/z/	cheese	/ɪ/	sit	/əʊ/	no
/t/	tall	/ʃ/	shop	/e/	egg	/aɪ/	my
/d/	day	/ʒ/	television	/æ/	taxi	/aʊ/	how
/k/	car	/h/	hot	/ɑː/	far	/ɔɪ/	boy
/g/	go	/m/	man	/ɒ/	chocolate	/ɪə/	here
		/n/	finish	/ɔː/	door	/eə/	where
/tʃ/	chair	/ŋ/	sing	/ʊ/	book	/ʊə/	tourist
/dʒ/	jam	/l/	look	/uː/	shoe		
		/r/	read	/ʌ/	bus		
/f/	four	/j/	young	/ɜː/	shirt		
/v/	very	/w/	walk	/ə/	butter		
/θ/	think						
/ð/	this						

Numbers are page numbers. LR means Language Review.

about /ə'baʊt/ *prep, adv.* a little more or less than: *Come (at)* **about** *six o'clock.* p12

above /ə'bʌv/ *prep.* higher than: *The lamp is* **above** *the table.* p41

accountant /ə'kaʊntənt/ *n.* a person whose job it is to keep lists of money spent and money earned for people or companies. p97

activity /æk'tɪvətɪ/ *n. (pl.* **activities**) things we do, especially for enjoyment: *Dancing is her favourite* **activity**. p24

address /ə'dres/ *n. (pl.* **addresses**) the name of the place where you live. p20

advertisement /əd'vɜːtɪsmənt/ *n. I hate the* **advertisements** *on television.* p27

affectionate /ə'fekʃnət/ *adj.* feeling or showing love. p66

afternoon /ɑːftə'nuːn/ *n.* the time between midday and evening. p13

again /ə'gen, ə'geɪn/ *adv.* one more time; once more: *Come and see us* **again** *soon.* p69

ago /ə'gəʊ/ *adv.* in the past: *We came to live here six years* **ago**. p68

agree /ə'griː/ *to think the same as someone else: I* **agree** *with you.* p96

airmail letter /'eəmeɪl letə/ *n.* see picture. p16

angry /'æŋgrɪ/ *adj.* (**angrier, angriest**) feeling anger: *I came home late and my mother was* **angry** *(with me).* **angrily** *adv.* p84

answer /'ɑːnsəʳ/ *v.* to say or write something after you have been asked a question: *"Did you do it?" "No, I didn't,"* *she* **answered**. p8

arm /ɑːm/ *n.* part of the body - see picture. p54

assassinate /ə'sæsɪneɪt/ *v.* kill a famous person, often for political reasons. p35

astronaut /'æstrənɔːt/ *n.* a person who travels in space - see picture. p35

ask /ɑːsk/ *v.* to say a question: *"Who are you?" she* **asked**. p31

attractive /ə'træktɪv/ *adj.* pleasing, especially to look at. p66

aunt /ɑːnt/ *n.* the sister of one of your parents, or the wife of the brother of one of your parents. p18

autumn /'ɔːtəm/ *n. adj.* the season before winter in cool countries. p82

awful /'ɔːfəl/ *adj.* not pleasing; not liked: *That's an* **awful** *book.* p84

baby /'beɪbɪ/ *n. (pl.* **babies**) a very young child. p21

babysit /'beɪbɪsɪt/ *v.* to look after young children while the parents are out for a short time. p97

back /bæk/
1 *n.* a part of the body - see picture. p54
2 *adv.* to do again: *I went* **back** *to the place where I was born.* p91

backache /'bækeɪk/ *n.* a pain in the back - see picture. p88

bacon /'beɪkən/ *n.* food - see picture. p6

bad /bæd/ *adj.* (**worse** /wɜːs/, **worst** /wɜːst/) not good: *I am* **bad** *at English, but Jo is* **worse** *- he got the* **worst** *(= lowest) marks in the class.* p79

balcony /'bælkənɪ/ *n.* attached to the house - see picture. p116

bank /bæŋk/ *n.* a place where money is kept and paid out - see picture. p13

bar /bɑːʳ/ *n.* a place where drinks and sometimes food can be bought. p41

bathroom /'bɑːθruːm/ *n.* a room where you wash - see picture. p40

beautiful /'bjuːtɪfəl/ *adj.* very good-looking; very pleasing: *What a* **beautiful** *day!* p66

become /bɪ'kʌm/ *v.* to change or grow to be: *The prince* **became** *king when his father died.* p35

bed /bed/ *n.* the thing we sleep on: *What time did you go to* **bed** *last night?* p40

bedroom /'bedruːm/ *n.* a room where you sleep - see picture. p40

beer /bɪəʳ/ *n.* a drink - see picture. p16

behind /bɪ'haɪnd/ *prep.* at the back (of) - see picture. LR9

best /best/ *adj.* superlative of *good: It's the* **best** *film I have ever seen.* p95

better /'betəʳ/ *adj.* comparative of *good: His English is* **better** *than his sister's.* p85

between /bɪ'twiːn/ *prep.* in the middle (of) - see picture. p54

bicycle /'baɪsɪkl/ *or* **bike** /baɪk/ *n.* a machine with two wheels for riding on. p75

big /bɪg/ *adj.* (**bigger, biggest**) large in size, weight, number, importance, etc.: *How* **big** *is the school you go to?* p8

birthday /'bɜːθdeɪ/ *n.* the day of the year on which a person was born. p36

black /blæk/ *adj.* the darkest colour; the colour of the words in this book: *At night the sky looks* **black**. p7

blouse /blaʊz/ *n.* an item of clothing - see picture. p48

blue /bluː/ *adj., n.* the colour of the sky when there are no clouds: *The sea is* **blue**. p21

boat /bəʊt/ *n.* transport by sea. p75

body /'bɒdɪ/ *n.* see picture. p54

book /bʊk/ *n.* see picture. p22

boring /'bɔːrɪŋ/ *adj.* not interesting: *My job is very* **boring**. p85

born /bɔːn/ *adj.* given life: *The baby was* **born** *yesterday.* p85

both /bəʊθ/ this one and that one; the two: *We* **both** *want to go to the party.* p24

bottle /'bɒtl/ *n.* see picture. p47

boy /bɔɪ/ *n.* a male child: *They have five children: three* **boys** *and two girls.* p18

bread /bred/ *n.* food - see picture. p6

breakfast /'brekfəst/ *n.* the first meal of the day. p6

bring /brɪŋ/ *v.* to carry something, or go with someone, to the speaker: *Please* **bring** *a bottle of milk home with you.* p52

brother /'brʌðəʳ/ *n.* a boy or man with the same parents as another person: *Peter is Mary's* **brother**. p18

brown /braʊn/ *adj., n.* a dark colour like coffee or earth: **brown** *eyes.* p21

bus /bʌs/ *n.* transport - see picture. p75

busy /'bɪzɪ/ *adj.* (**busier, busiest**) working; not free; having a lot to do: *He is* **busy** *now. He's* **busy** *writing letters.* **busily** *adv.* p97

butter /'bʌtəʳ/ *n.* food - see picture. p6

buy /baɪ/ *v. (past* **bought** /bɔːt/) to get something by giving money for it: *I* **bought** *a new radio.* p16

café /'kæfeɪ/ *n.* a place to buy drinks and simple meals - see picture. p7

camera /'kæmrə/ *n.* an instrument for taking photographs. p58

capital /'kæpɪtl/ *n.* the chief city of a country, where the government is. p102

car /kɑːʳ/ *n.* transport - see picture. p4

car park /'kɑː pɑːk/ *n.* a place to leave cars in. p41

card /kɑːd/ *n.* you send these with greetings written inside on special occasions - see picture. p82

catch /kætʃ/ *v.* (*past* **caught** /kɔːt/) to get in the hand and hold: *She threw the ball and I* **caught** *it.* p85

central heating /sentrəl 'hiːtɪŋ/ *n.* a system for warming a building - see picture. p41

cereal /'sɪərɪəl/ *n.* food - see picture. p6

chair /tʃeəʳ/ *n.* a piece of furniture you sit on, with four legs and a back. p129

change /tʃeɪndʒ/ *v.* to become or make different: *She* **changed** *the red dress for a green dress.* p35

cheap /tʃiːp/ *adj.* costing only a little money: *A bicycle is* **cheaper** *than a car.* p27

cheese /tʃiːz/ *n.* food - see picture. p6

chemist's /'kemɪsts/ *n.* a shop where they make and sell medicines - see picture. p58

cheque /tʃek/ *n.* a printed piece of paper which you write on, and which can be exchanged for money at the bank. **cheque book** *n.* see picture. p16

child /tʃaɪld/ *n.* (*pl.* **children** /'tʃɪldrən/)
1 a young person older than a baby. p18
2 a son or daughter: *They have three* **children**. p18

chocolate /'tʃɒklət/ *n.* a sweet or food made from cocoa: see picture. p22

choose /tʃuːz/ *v.* (*past* **chose**) to pick out from a number of things or people the one you want: *She* **chose** *to study chemistry.* p49

Christmas /'krɪsməs/ *n.* the day of the year when Jesus Christ is said to have been born. p82

cigarette /sɪgə'ret/ *n.* tobacco smoked in paper. p16

cinema /'sɪnəmə/ *n.* a building where you see films - see picture. p4

clean /kliːn/ *adj.* not dirty: *That shirt is dirty, here is a* **clean** *one.* p74

close /kləʊz/ *v.* to shut: **Close** *the window, please.* p37

closed /kləʊzd/ *adj.* not open: *The shop is* **closed**. p13

clothes /kləʊðz/ *pl. n.* things we wear - see pictures. p48

cloud /klaʊd/ *n.* (**cloudy** *adj.*) weather - see picture. p78

coffee /'kɒfi/ *n.* a drink - see picture. p6

cold /kəʊld/
1 *adj.* not hot: *I hate* **cold** *tea!* p78
2 *n.* an illness of the nose and throat: *I've got a bad* **cold**. p88

colour /'kʌləʳ/ *n.* the quality that makes things look green, red, yellow, etc.: *I love the* **colour** *of your eyes.* p48

come /kʌm/ *v.* to move towards the person speaking: "**Come** *here Mary, I want to speak to you!*" p50

comfortable /'kʌmftəbl/ *adj. This is a very* **comfortable** *chair* (= it is nice to sit in). p94

commuter /kə'mjuːtə/ *n.* a person who lives in one town and works in another. p91

control /kən'trəʊl/ *n.* power: *He has no* **control** *over his children.* p125

cook /kʊk/ *v.* to make food ready to eat by heating it: *I haven't* **cooked** *the dinner.* p25

cool /kuːl/ *adj.* not warm, but never very cold: *The room was* **cool** *in the evening.* p78

cost /kɒst/ *v.* (*past* **cost**) to have as a price: *How much did that bag* **cost**? *It* **cost** *five pounds!* p49

cottage /'kɒtɪdʒ/ *n.* a small house in the country - see picture. p114

country /'kʌntrɪ/ *n.*
1 (*pl.* **countries**) an area ruled by one government: *France and Germany are European* **countries**. p9
2 (*no pl.*) the land that is not a town: *He lives in the* **country**. p96

cousin /'kʌzn/ *n.* the child of an aunt or uncle. p18

croissant /'kwæsɒ/ *n.* food - see picture. p6

crowded /'kraʊdɪd/ *adj.* full of people: *I don't like the market; it is too* **crowded**. p74

customer /'kʌstəməʳ/ *n.* a person who buys from a shop or market. p8

customs /'kʌstəmz/ *pl. n.* a department of the government that controls what is brought into a country: *At the airport, the* **customs officers** *opened his case.* p47

dance /dɑːns/ *v.* to move to music, or as if to music. **dancer** *n.* p64

dark /dɑːk/ *adj.*
1 Colour nearer black than white: *He wore a* **dark** *blue suit.* p149
2 Sinister and unfriendly. p125

date /deɪt/ *n.* the day, month and year: *What is the* **date** *today?* p36

daughter /'dɔːtəʳ/ *n.* a female child: *They have three* **daughters** *and one son.* p18

day /deɪ/ *n.* a period of 24 hours. p84

decide /dɪ'saɪd/ *v.* choose what to do: *She* **decided** *to have coffee not tea.* p51

dentist /'dentɪst/ *n.* a doctor who looks after your teeth. p88

depressed /dɪ'prest/ *adj.* to feel very sad or miserable: *He was* **depressed** *because he didn't pass his exams.* p84

die /daɪ/ *v.* (past **died** /daɪd/) to stop living: *to* **die** *of an illness.* p36

different /'dɪfrənt/ *adj.* not the same: *I don't like that dress, I want a* **different** *one.* p30

difficult /'dɪfɪkəlt/ *adj.* hard to do or understand; not easy: *a* **difficult** *question.* p55

dig /dɪg/ *v.* to make a hole in the ground - see picture. p114

dining room /'daɪnɪŋruːm/ *n.* a room where people eat. p116

dinner /'dɪnəʳ/ *n.* the largest meal of the day. p72

dirty /'dɜːtɪ/ *adj.* not clean: *My shoes were* **dirty**. p74

divorce /dɪ'vɔːs/ *n.* separation of husband and wife by law so that they can marry again. p108

do /duː/ *v.*
1 to act: *What are you* **doing** *at the weekend?* p25
2 to have as a job: *What do you* **do**? *I'm an engineer.* p34
3 auxiliary verb in questions: *Where do you live?* p15

doctor /'dɒktəʳ/ *n.* a person who looks after people's health. p88

double /'dʌbl/ *adj.*
1 made for two: *a* **double** *bed.* p42

2 with two parts: *You spell 'coffee' with* **double** *f and* **double** *e.* p9

doughnut /'dəʊnʌt/ *n.* a sweet American bread/cake. p72

down /daʊn/ *prep.* in or to a lower place: *Men's clothes are* **down** *on the first floor.* p55

dress /dres/ *n.* an item of clothing for women - see picture. p48

drink /drɪŋk/
1 *n.* liquid e.g. water, milk, beer. p7
2 *v.* to take liquid into the mouth: *He* **drinks** *his coffee without milk.* p46

drive /draɪv/ *v.* to make a vehicle move in the direction you want: *Can you* **drive** *(a car)?* p55

dry /draɪ/ *adj.* not wet: *An umbrella keeps you* **dry** *in the rain.* p96

dry cleaner's /draɪ 'kliːnəz/ *n.* a shop for cleaning clothes - see picture. p52

each /iːtʃ/ every one separately: **Each** *student has got a book.* p41

ear /ɪəʳ/ *n.* a part of the head - see picture. p54

earache /'ɪəreɪk/ *n.* a pain in the ear - see picture. p88

east /iːst/ *n.* the direction from which the sun comes up in the morning. p102

easy /'iːzɪ/ *adj.* (**easier, easiest**) not difficult; done with no trouble: *It was an* **easy** *job and we did it quickly.* p55

eat /iːt/ *v.* put food in your mouth: *I eat sandwiches for lunch.* p25

economical /iːkə'nɒmɪkl/ *adj.* cheap: *Going by train is more* **economical** *than going by plane.* p94

educated /'edʒəkeɪtɪd/ *adj.* with a good education. p66

education /edʒəkeɪʃən/ *n.* teaching and learning: *Children get their formal* **education** *at school.* p125

egg /eg/ *n.* food - see picture. p6

evening /'iːvnɪŋ/ *n.* the time between the end of the afternoon and when you go to bed. p12

exciting /ɪk'saɪtɪŋ/ *adj.* not boring: *Time passed really quickly because the film was so* **exciting**. p104

expensive /ɪk'spensɪv/ *adj.* costing a lot of money: *It is* **expensive** *to travel by plane.* p27

eye /aɪ/ *n.* you see with this part of the face - see picture. p54

face /feɪs/ *n.* the front part of the head, with the eyes, nose, and mouth - see picture. p54

family /'fæmlɪ/ *n.* (*pl.* **families**) a group of relatives *eg* mother, son, daughter. p18

famous /'feɪməs/ *adj.* well-known: *This town is* **famous** *for its beautiful buildings.* p34

far /fɑːʳ/ *adj.* not near: *My house isn't* **far** *from the school.* p75

fast /fɑːst/
1 *adj.* not slow: *A Porsche is a* **fast** *car.* p74
2 *adv.* quickly: *He ran* **fast** *to catch the bus.* p111

father /'fɑːðəʳ/ *n.* a male parent. p18

favourite /'feɪvrɪt/ *adj.* that is liked best of all: *Oranges are my* **favourite** *fruit.* p117

feed /fiːd/ *v.* to give food to: *Have you* **fed** *the animals* - see picture. p114

figure /'fɪgəʳ/ *n.* the shape of the body. p67

film /fɪlm/ *n.*
1 a story shown in a cinema or on television. p24

2 a band put into a camera on which photographs are made. p58

fine /faɪn/ *adj.* nice; pleasant; very good: *I'm* **fine**. *How are you?* p21

finger /'fɪŋɡəʳ/ *n.* one of the five long parts of your hand – see picture. p54

finish /'fɪnɪʃ/ *v.* to end: *the game* **finished** *at four o'clock.* p37

first /fɜːst/ *adj.* coming before all others; earliest: *The* **first** *month of the year is January.* **First** *we'll have breakfast, then we'll walk to school.* p36

fish /fɪʃ/ *n.* a cold-blooded animal that lives in water: *A person who catches* **fish** *is a* **fisherman** /'fɪʃəmən/. p72

flag /flæɡ/ *n.* a piece of cloth with a special pattern on it, used as the sign of a country, club, etc. – see picture. p72

flat /flæt/ *n.* a number of rooms on one floor of a building where a person or family lives. p116

flight /flaɪt/ *n.* flying: *The (plane)* **flight** *took three hours.* p46

flight attendant /'flaɪt ətendənt/ *n.* person who looks after passengers in a plane. p46

floor /flɔːʳ/ all the rooms on one level: *We live on the third* **floor.** p40

flower /'flaʊəʳ/ *n.* part of a plant – see picture. p22

fly /flaɪ/ *v.* to move through the air: *The plane* **flew** *from Paris to Rome.* p.35

fog /fɒɡ/ *n.* thick cloud near the ground. p78

foggy /'fɒɡɪ/ *adj.* a type of weather: *It is so* **foggy** *that I can't see anything in front of me.* p78

food /fuːd/ *n.* (*no pl.*) what you eat: *Is there enough* **food** *for everyone?* p73

foot /fʊt/ *n.* (*pl.* **feet**) the part of the leg that you stand on – see picture. p54

football /'fʊtbɔːl/ *n.* a game where two teams try and kick a ball into a special space. p33

fridge /frɪdʒ/ *n.* the usual word for a **refrigerator**; a machine for keeping food cold and fresh. p73

friend /frend/ *n.* a person you like: *We are* **friends**. *Peter is Jane's* **boyfriend** (= special male friend) – *Jane is Peter's* **girlfriend**. p15

friendly *adj.* *He is* **friendly** (= kind and helpful) *to us all.* p66

funny /'fʌnɪ/ *adj.* (**funnier, funniest**) Making you laugh; amusing: *a* **funny** *joke.* p86

garage /'ɡærɑːʒ/ or /'ɡærɪdʒ/ *n.* a place where cars, buses, etc. are kept or repaired. p116

garden /'ɡɑːdn/ *n.* a place where trees, flowers, or vegetables are grown, round a house or in a public place. p116

get /ɡet/ *v.*
1 to arrive: *I* **get** *to work at about 9 am.* p15
2 have got: *I've* **got** *a dog.* p19
3 to become: *She* **got** *married yesterday.* p114

get up *v.* to get out of bed. p26

girl /ɡɜːl/ *n.* a female child: *She has got two children, a* **girl** *and a boy.* p18

give /ɡɪv/ *v.* to let someone have something: *I* **gave** *him my address.* p31

go /ɡəʊ/ *v.* to move: *Are you* **going** *to school today?* p15

good /ɡʊd/ *adj.* not wrong or bad: *He is a* **good** *man - he always tries to do what is right.* p79

grandfather/mother /'ɡrænfɑːðə/ *n.* male/female parent of your parents. p18

great /ɡreɪt/ *adj.* very good: *It was a* **great** *party.* p84

green /ɡriːn/ the colour of growing leaves and grass: *She wore a* **green** *dress* - see picture. p46

grey /ɡreɪ/ *adj. n.* a colour: a mixture of black and white: *She wore a* **grey** *dress* – see picture. p48

hair /heəʳ/ *n.* grows on the head – see picture. p54

hairdresser's /'heədresəz/ *n.* a shop where a hairdresser cuts your hair. p41

ham /hæm/ *n.* food – see picture. p6

hand /hænd/ *n.* the end part of your arm – see picture. p54

handsome /'hænsəm/ *adj.* nice to look at (usually used of men). p66

happen /'hæpən/ *v.* to take place; be: *The accident* **happened** *outside my house.* p47

happy /'hæpɪ/ *adj.* (**happier, happiest**) feeling very pleased: *I am* **happy** *to see you again.* p68

happily *adv: They were laughing* **happily.** p68

hate /heɪt/ *v.* not to like: *I* **hate** *the rain.* p72

have /v, əv, həv; *strong* hæv/ *v.*
1 to eat or drink: *I* **have** *breakfast at 8 am.* p6
2 to possess (**have got**): *I* **have got** *a new stereo.* p20
3 obligation (**have to**): *She* **has to** *wear a school uniform.* p109

head /hed/ *n.* the top part of the body where the eyes, nose and mouth are – see picture. p54

headache /'hedeɪk/ *n.* a pain in the head: *I've got a* **headache.** p88

heavy /'hevɪ/ *adj.* not light, weighing a lot: *The piano was too* **heavy** *to move.* p94

high /haɪ/ *adj.* tall, or far from the ground, not low: *The* **highest** *mountain in Africa is Mount Kilimanjaro. It is nearly 20,000 feet* **high.** p94

holiday /'hɒlɪdeɪ/ *n.* a time when you do not work or go to school: *When I was on* **holiday** *I visited my uncle.* p41

home /həʊm/ *n., adj, adv.* the place where someone lives: *I stayed at* **home** *to read.* p15

homework *n.* work given to you at school to be done at home. p109

honeymoon /'hʌnɪmuːn/ *n.* a holiday taken by people who have just got married. p42

hot /hɒt/ *adj.* (**hotter, hottest**) not cold: *The sun is very* **hot.** p78

hotel /həʊ'tel/ *n.* a building where visitors can sleep and eat meals if they pay – see picture. p40

hour /aʊəʳ/ *n.* sixty minutes: *He went away for an* **hour.** p25

house /haʊs/ *n.* a building that people live in – see picture. p97

housework /'haʊswɜːk/ *n.* everyday jobs in the house eg cleaning windows, washing clothes etc. p25

hungry /'hʌŋɡrɪ/ *adj.* (**hungrier, hungriest**): *Can I have a sandwich? I'm* **hungry.** p89

husband /'hʌzbənd/ *n.* the man a woman is married to. p57

ice /aɪs/ *n.* (*no pl.*) water which is so cold that it has become hard: *He put some* **ice** *in his drink to make it cold.* p46

if /ɪf/ on condition that: *You can catch the bus* **if** *you go now.* p44

ill /ɪl/ *adj.* (**worse** /wɜːs/ **worst** /wɜːst/) not feeling healthy; unwell: *She can't go*

to school because she is **ill.** p84

important /ɪm'pɔːtnt/ *adj.* having power; of great value: *The headmaster is the most* **important** *person in the school.* p66

in /ɪn/ *prep.* showing where someone or something is: *She is* **in** *the bathroom.* p7

in front of /ɪn'frʌnt əv/ *prep.* not behind – see picture. p54

intelligent /ɪn'telɪdʒənt/ *adj.* being quick at thinking. p66

interesting /'ɪntrəstɪŋ/ *adj.* not boring: *This book is very* **interesting.** p85

interests /'ɪntrəsts/ *pl. n.* things you enjoy doing in your free time: *I have a lot of different* **interests** *including politics and classical music.* p24

interview /'ɪntəvjuː/ *v.* to talk to someone to see if she/he is suitable for a job, or to ask her/his opinions. p106

invitation /ɪnvɪ'teɪʃn/ *n. We had three* **invitations** (= letters inviting us) *to parties.* p50

jacket /'dʒækɪt/ *n.* a short coat with sleeves (= covering for the arms) – see picture. p48

jam /dʒæm/ *n.* food – see picture. p6

jeans /dʒiːnz/ *pl. n.* trousers of strong cotton – see picture. p48

job /dʒɒb/ *n.* work that you are paid to do: *What is your* **job?** - *I'm a teacher.* p34

kind /kaɪnd/ *adj.* good; helpful; wanting to do things that make other people happy: *She was* **kind** *to me when I was unhappy.* p66

king /kɪŋ/ *n.* male ruler of a country, opposite of queen. p36

kiss /kɪs/ *v.* to touch someone with the lips. *He* **kissed** *his wife goodbye.* p62

knee /niː/ *n.* middle of the leg – see picture. p54

know /nəʊ/ *v.*
1 to have in the mind; have learnt: *I* **know** *how to swim.* p7
2 to have met or seen before: *I don't* **know** *that boy; who is he?* p4

language /'læŋɡwɪdʒ/ *n.* the words people use in speaking and writing: *People in different countries speak different* **languages.** p28

large /lɑːdʒ/ *adj.* (**larger, largest**) big; not small, able to hold a lot: *They need a* **large** *house because they have nine children.* p94

last /lɑːst/ *adj.* happening just before this time; the time before now: *I saw my friend* **last** *week, but I haven't seen him this week.* p37

late /leɪt/ *adj.* (**later, latest**) after the usual or agreed time; not early: *I was* **late** *for school because I got up late.* p30

learn /lɜːn/ *v.* to get knowledge of something or of how to do something: *Have you* **learnt** *to swim? I am* **learning** *English.*

leave /liːv/ *v.*
1 to go away (from): *The train* **leaves** *(the station) in five minutes.* p125
2 **leave alone** let things stay as they are: *Don't be unkind to the dog -* **leave** *it* **alone.** p125

left /left/
1 *n. sing.* opposite of right: *The school is on the* **left** *of the cinema.* p54
2 *adv.* opposite of right: *Turn* **left** *at the traffic lights.* p97

leg /leɡ/ *n.* part of the body used for walking – see picture. p54

lemon /'lemən/ n. a yellow fruit with a sour taste. p46

letter /'letə'/ n.

1 one of the signs we use to write words: *A, B, C, and D are the first four* **letters** *in the alphabet.* p9

2 a written message sent to someone by post: *to post a* **letter.** p28

life /laɪf/ n. the time that someone is alive: *He has lived in the same village all his* **life.** p38

lift /lɪft/ n. a machine that carries people or things between floors of a tall building. p41

like /laɪk/ v. to find pleasant; enjoy: *Do you* **like** *your teacher?* p24

list /lɪst/ n. a lot of names of things written down one under another: *Make a* **list** *of things to buy.* p12

listen /'lɪsn/ v. to try to hear a thing; take notice of what someone is saying: *I like* **listening** *to the radio in the morning.* p5

live /lɪv/ v. to stay in a place or at a house; have your home somewhere: *I* **live** *in a town.* p105

living room /'lɪvɪŋru:m/ n. a room where people sit, relax and watch television. p116

lock /lɒk/ v. to close a lock with a key – see picture. p114

long /lɒŋ/ adj.

1 not short: *He's got a very* **long** *nose!* p94

2 a great distance or time from one end to the other: *I take a* **long** *time to walk to school because it's a* **long** *way.* p75

look /lʊk/ v. use the eyes to see: **Look** *at those people!* p31

look after /lʊk'ɑ:ftə/ v. care for: *Can you* **look after** *the children this evening?* p87

lose /lu:z/ v. not to have something any more: *I have* **lost** *my watch. I can't find it anywhere.* p114

lot /lɒt/ n. or **lots** pl. n. a large amount or number: *He's got a* **lot** *of money. He buys* **lots** *of expensive clothes.* p105

loud /laʊd/ n. having or making a lot of noise, not quiet: *The teacher's voice is very* **loud**; *we can all hear it.* p79

love /lʌv/ v.

1 to have a very strong warm feeling for someone: *Mothers and fathers* **love** *their children.*

2 to like very much: *Maria* **loves** *reading.* p72

lover /'lʌvə'/ n. person who loves. p69

lunch /lʌntʃ/ n. meal in the middle of the day. p72

magazine /mægə'zi:n/ n. a paper-covered book containing stories, articles, and pictures: **Magazines** *are sold weekly or monthly.* p24

make /meɪk/ (past. **made** /meɪd/) v.

1 to do: *She* **made** *a list before she went shopping.* p12

2 to earn: *He* **makes** *a lot of money. He's got a very good job.* p37

man /mæn/ n. (pl. **men** /men/) a fully grown human male. p18

map /mæp/ n. a flat drawing of a large surface: *In the library there are* **maps** *of towns, countries, and the world.* p19

marmalade /'mɑ:məleɪd/ n. jam made of oranges – see picture. p6

married /'mærɪd/ adj. to be husband or wife: *They got* **married** *on Saturday.* p20

meal /mi:l/ n. the food we eat at regular times: *I always enjoy my evening* **meal.** p72

meat /mi:t/ n. (no pl.) the parts of an animal's body used as food – see picture. p73

meet /mi:t/ v. (past **met** /met/) to come together: *I* **met** *my teacher in the street today.* p66

mend /mend/ v. to repair or fix something broken or with a hole in it: *Can you* **mend** *the hole in my shirt?* p114

menu /'menju/ n. a list of food that you can choose to eat, in a hotel, etc. p8

milk /mɪlk/ n. a drink – see picture. p6

mistake /mɪ'steɪk/ n. something incorrect: *She made three* **mistakes** *in her homework.* p61

money /'mʌni/ n. (no pl.) coins and paper banknotes: *He makes a lot of* **money** *selling clothes.* p66

month /mʌnθ/ n. one of the twelve periods of time which make a year. p35

morning /'mɔ:nɪŋ/ n. the time from when the sun rises to midday. p12

mother /'mʌðə'/ n. a female parent: *the* **mother** *of three sons.* p18

motorbike /'məʊtəbaɪk/ n. a big bicycle worked by an engine. p75

mouth /maʊθ/ n. part of your face for speaking and eating – see picture. p54

move /mu:v/ v. to go or put from one place to another: **Move** *that chair into the kitchen.* p54

museum /mju:'zɪəm/ n. a building in which interesting objects are kept and shown to visitors. p43

music /'mju:zɪk/ n. (no pl.) the pleasant sounds made by voices or by instruments: *to listen to* **music.** p24

name /neɪm/ n. the word used in speaking to or about a person or thing: *My* **name** *is Jane Smith.* p10

nasty /'nɑ:sti/ adj. not nice or pleasant: *Don't be* **nasty**, *help your brother!* p74

near /nɪə'/ prep. not far: *I like living* **near** *the school.* p75

need /ni:d/ v. not have something that is necessary: *I* **need** *more time to finish this work.* p73

never /'nevə'/ adv. not at any time; not ever: *I* **never** *go to the theatre. I don't have time.* p54

next to /'neks tə/ prep. on one side of: *He is standing* **next to** *Jane.* p54

nice /naɪs/ adj. good: *She's a very* **nice** *person.* p74

no /nəʊ/

1 adj. opposite of yes : *Do you like coffee?* **No**, *I don't.* p7

2 adj. not a/any: *There are* **no** *students in the classroom.* p20

none /nʌn/ not one; not any: *How many people in your class smoke?* **None.** p20

no one /'nəʊwʌn/ nobody. p24

non-smoker /nɒn 'sməʊkə/ n. a person who doesn't smoke. p66

north /nɔ:θ/ n. one of the points of the compass, opposite south. p102

nose /nəʊz/ n. part of the face for breathing and smelling – see picture. p54

not /nɒt/ adv. a word that gives the opposite meaning to another word or a sentence: *He is* **not** *at school, because he* **isn't** (= is not) *well.* p30

note /nəʊt/ n. a short written message: *Mary sent her mother a* **note.** p118

now /naʊ/ adv. at the present time: *We used to live in a village, but* **now** *we live in a city.* p12

number /'nʌmbə'/ n. words or figures like one, two, and three or 1, 2, and 3. p9

o'clock /ə'klɒk/ adv. a word used when saying what hour of the day it is: *What*

time is it? It's four **o'clock** *exactly.* p12

office /'ɒfɪs/ n. a place where business and paper work is done: *She works in an* **office.** p7

often /'ɒfn/ adv. many times: *I* **often** *see her because she lives near me. How* **often** *have you been abroad? Not* **often**, *only twice.* p54

old /əʊld/ adj.

1 not young: *My grandmother is very* **old.** p123

2 the word we use to show our age: *How* **old** *are you? I am eleven years* **old.** p21

on /ɒn/ prep. showing where someone or something is: *I put the book* **on** *the table.* p14

once /wʌns/ adv. one time: *I have been to America* **once**, *but my friend has been more than* **once.** p74

onion /'ʌnjən/ n. food; a vegetable – see picture. p73

open /'əʊpən/

1 adj. not closed: *Banks are* **open** *on Saturday morning only.* p13

2 v. to make something open: **Open** *your book at page 6.* p47

opposite /'ɒpəzɪt/ prep. facing: *The library is* **opposite** *the school.* p75

or /ə'/ strong ɔ:'/ (used when giving a choice): *Will you have tea* **or** *coffee?* p6

orange /'ɒrɪndʒ/

1 n. a round sweet juicy fruit from the orange tree.

2 n. adj. the colour of the skin of an orange when it is ripe; a mixture of yellow and red. p48

orange juice /'ɒrɪndʒ dʒu:s/ n. a drink made of oranges – see picture. p6

parent /'peərənt/ n. a father or a mother. p18

partner /'pɑ:tnə'/ n.

1 a person who is close to another in work, play, etc.: *a dance* **partner**/*a business* **partner**.

2 the person you share your life with. p67

party /'pɑ:ti/ n. a meeting of friends to enjoy themselves, eat, drink, etc.: *a birthday* **party.** p50

pen /pen/ n. an instrument for writing which uses a coloured liquid (**ink**) to make marks on paper. p22

people /'pi:pl/ n. the plural noun for **person**: *I saw a lot of* **people** *at the dance.* p18

perfect /'pɜ:fɪkt/ adj. so good that it cannot be made better: *His reading is* **perfect. perfectly** adv. in a perfect way: *He reads* **perfectly.** p111

perfume /'pɜ:fju:m/ n. a sweet smell; liquid that has a sweet smell: *She was wearing a Chanel* **perfume.** p22

person /'pɜ:sn/ n. (pl. **people** /'pi:pl/) a human being; man, woman or child: *We would like a* **person** *to help us.* p18

photograph /'fəʊtəgrɑ:f/ n. a picture made by a camera.

photo /'fəʊtəʊ/ n. is a short word for **photograph.**

photographer /fə'tɒgrəfə'/ n. a person who takes photographs. p57

pilot /'paɪlət/ n. a person who flies a plane – see picture. p34

pink /pɪŋk/ n., adj. the colour made by mixing red and white. p48

place /pleɪs/ n. a building: *A school is a* **place** *to learn things.* p13

plane /pleɪn/ n. transport by air – see picture. p75

play /pleɪ/ v.

1 to amuse yourself: take part in a game:

He plays football – see picture. p4
2 *to make sounds on a musical instrument: She plays the piano.* p55

please /pliːz/ a word added to a question or an order, to make it polite: **Please** *bring your book to me.* p7

poem /ˈpəʊɪm/ *n.* writing with regular lines and sounds that express something in powerful and beautiful language: *He wrote a poem about war.* p69
poet *n.*: *A poet writes poems.* p68

polite /pəˈlaɪt/ *adj.* (**politer, politest**) having a kind and respectful way of behaving; not rude: *You should be polite to everyone.* p30

politics /ˈpɒlətɪks/ *pl. n.* the study of government. p24

politician /pɒləˈtɪʃn/ *n.* a person who works in a government. p34

poor /pɔːˀ/ *adj.* not having much money; not rich. p85

population /pɒpjʊˈleɪʃn/ *n.* the number of people living in a place: *What is the population of this city?* p103

postcard /ˈpəʊstkɑːd/ *n.* a small card that you often send when on holiday – see picture. p47

poster /ˈpəʊstəˀ/ *n.* a large printed paper advertising something. p106

post-office /ˈpəʊstɒfɪs/ *n.* a place where you can buy stamps, post parcels, etc. p13

potato /pəˈteɪtəʊ/ *n.* (*pl.* **potatoes**) a vegetable found under the ground and cooked before eating. p8

prefer /prɪˈfɜːˀ/ *v.* to like better: *Which of these two dresses do you prefer?* p8

present /ˈprezənt/ *n.* something to give to someone: *He gave his mother a present.* p22

private /ˈpraɪvɪt/ *adj.* belonging to one person or group; not public: *This is private land, you can't walk across it.* p42

problem /ˈprɒbləm/ *n.* a difficult question: *The problem was where to park the car.* p87

pub /pʌb/ *n.* a place to go for a drink. p13

put /pʊt/ *v.* to move to a place; to place: *He put the books on the table.* p56

qualification /kwɒlɪfɪˈkeɪʃn/ *n.* *What* **qualifications** (= special training or knowledge) *have you got for this job?* p106

question /ˈkwestʃən/ *n.* something you ask someone: *You haven't answered my question.* p8

quiet /ˈkwaɪət/ *adj.* having or making very little noise: *The streets were quiet.* p79

quite /kwaɪt/ *adv.* not very much: *He is quite nice but I don't want to see him again.* p109

radio /ˈreɪdiəʊ/ *n.* a machine which receives electrical waves and plays them to you: *He was listening to music on the radio.* p24

rain /reɪn/
1 *v.* (of water) to fall from the sky: *It rained last night.*
2 *n.* (*no pl.*) water falling from the sky: *There was rain in the night.* p78

read /riːd/ *v.* to look at words and understand them: *She read the newspaper.* p5

really /ˈrɪəli/ *adv.* very: *I really liked the film last night.* p109

reception /rɪˈsepʃn/ *n.* the place you go in a hotel to see if there is a room for you. **receptionist** *n.* the person who works in reception. p10

red /red/ *n. adj.* the colour of blood – see picture. p46

religion /rɪˈlɪdʒən/ *n.* belief in one or more gods: *Almost every country has some form of religion.* **religious** *adj.* p66

rent /rent/ *v.* to have the use of or let someone use a house, etc. in return for rent: *My father rents an office in the city.* p114

restaurant /ˈrestrɒnt/ *n.* a place where you can buy and eat food – see picture. p7

retire /rɪˈtaɪəˀ/ *v.* to stop work because of old age or illness: *He retired from the business when he was 65.* p114

rich /rɪtʃ/ *adj.* having a lot of money; not poor. p97

ride /raɪd/
1 *v.* to go along on or in something: *She was riding a bicycle. They rode in the back seat of the bus.*
2 *n.* an act of riding: *He went for a ride in his car.* p114

right /raɪt/
1 *n.* the side opposite to the left side: *The school is on the left of the road, and his house is on the right.* p54
2 *adv.* towards the right side: *Turn right at the corner.* p97

room /ruːm/ *n.* one of the parts of a house separated by walls and doors: *We sleep in the bedroom, and wash in the bathroom.* p117

sandwich /ˈsændwɪtʃ/ *n.* (*pl.* **sandwiches**) two pieces of bread put together with something else in between them: *I made a chicken sandwich.* p11

sarcasm /ˈsɑːkæzəm/ *n.* ironic and unkind words. p125

school /skuːl/ *n.* a place where children go to learn: *Children who go to school are school children.* p15

season /ˈsiːzn/ *n.* one of the four parts of the year; a special time of year: *Summer is the hottest season.* p82

second /ˈsekənd/ *n.* the one after the first; 2nd; *This is the second time I have met him. I came second in the race.* p36

see /siː/ *v.* to use the eyes to know something: *I can see a dog in the garden.* p51

sell /sel/ *v.* to give in exchange for money: *She sold her old bicycle to me.* p27

send /send/ *v.* to cause a person or thing to go somewhere: *She sent me a parcel.* p28

serious /ˈsɪəriəs/ *adj.* not cheerful or full of fun: *He is a serious boy.* p86

service /ˈsɜːvɪs/ *n.* attention to customers: *The service in this shop is always slow.* p74

shave /ʃeɪv/ *v.* to take hair from the face or body by cutting it very close: *My father shaves every day.* p91

shirt /ʃɜːt/ *n.* an item of clothing – see picture. p48

shoe /ʃuː/ *n.* a covering for the foot: *a pair of shoes.* p48

shop /ʃɒp/ *n.* a place where you go and buy things.
shop assistant *n.* a person who works in a shop. p13

shopping *n.* (*no pl.*) buying things: to go shopping. p118

short /ʃɔːt/ *adj.* not very tall; not long: *It's a short distance to school. Mary is much shorter than her mother.* p94

should /ʃʊd/ *v.* (used to give advice). *You should go to bed. You look very tired.* p87

shoulder /ˈʃəʊldəˀ/ *n.* part of the body at

top of arm – see picture. p54

shower /ˈʃaʊə/ *n.* a thing which produces a spray of water for washing – see picture. p54

sincere /sɪnˈsɪəˀ/ *adj.* to mean what you say. p66

sing /sɪŋ/ *v.* to make music with the voice: *She sang a song.* p20

single /ˈsɪŋgl/ *adj.* one only: *A single bed is made for one person.* p20

sister /ˈsɪstəˀ/ *n.* a girl who has the same parents as you: *She is my sister. We are sisters.* p18

sit /sɪt/ *v.* to rest on the bottom of the back: *He sat in a chair.* p57

size /saɪz/ *n.* how big something or someone is: *What size is your house? These shoes are size 5.* p49

skirt /skɜːt/ *n.* an item of women's clothing – see picture. p48

sleep /sliːp/ *v.* to be in sleep; not to be awake: *He slept for two hours.* p25

slim /slɪm/ *adj.* not fat. p66

slow /sləʊ/ *adj.* taking a long time; not fast: *The bus is very slow.* p74

small /smɔːl/ *adj.* little; not large: *I live in a small flat.* p8

smile /smaɪl/ *v.* to turn up the corners of your mouth to show pleasure, approval, etc.: *She smiled when she saw me.* p57

snow /snəʊ/
1 *n.* (*no pl.*) very cold rain, which falls in soft white flakes (= pieces). p78
2 *v.* to come down from the sky: *It's snowing!* p78

soldier /ˈsəʊldʒəˀ/ *n.* a person in the army. p34

sometimes /ˈsʌmtaɪmz/ *adv.* at times; now and then: **Sometimes** *I have coffee for breakfast and* **sometimes** *I have tea.* p108

son /sʌn/ *n.* a male child: *I have a son and a daughter.* p18

sorry /ˈsɒri/ *adj.* a polite way of saying that you are a little sad, or that you cannot do what is wanted: *Did I stand on your foot?* **Sorry**! p4

south /saʊθ/ *n.* one of the points of the compass, opposite north. p102

souvenir /suːvəˈnɪəˀ/ *n.* a thing that is kept to remember a place or an event. p43

speak /spiːk/ *v.* to say words aloud: *Can your child speak yet?* p5

spell /spel/ *v.* to say the letters that make up a word: *You spell dog, D-O-G.* **spelling** *n.*: *His spelling is better than his brother's.* p4

spend /spend/ *v.* to pass or use time: *I spent an hour reading.* p25

sport /spɔːt/ *n.* games and exercise done for pleasure: *Football and running are sports.* p24

spring /sprɪŋ/ *n.* the season after winter, in cool countries. p82

stamp /stæmp/ *n.* put on letters to show how much you have paid to send them – see picture. p16

stand /stænd/ *v.* to be put on your feet: *We stood outside the shop.* **Stand up** (= get to your feet) *please.* p54

start /stɑːt/ *v.* to begin: *I start work at 6 o'clock.* p37

stay /steɪ/ *v.* to live somewhere temporarily: *He stayed with his father while he was ill.* p41

stepmother /ˈstepmʌðəˀ/ *n.* a woman who marries your father but is not your mother: *The children of your stepfather or stepmother are your stepbrothers or stepsisters.* p111

stomach /ˈstʌmək/ *n.* part of the body

where food goes - see picture. p54

stomachache *n*. pain in the stomach. p88

stranger /'streɪndʒər/ *n*. a person you do not know. p68

student /stjuːdənt/ *n*. a person who is learning, especially at a college or university. p20

study /'stʌdɪ/ *v*. to learn about: *I am studying art*. p25

sugar /'ʃʊgər/ *n*. something to make other food sweet: *Do you have **sugar** in your tea?* p6

suitcase /'suːtkeɪs/ *n*. a large bag that you put things in when you travel - see picture. p104

summer /'sʌmər/ *n. adj*. the season, in cool countries, when it is warmest: *a **summer** holiday*. p82

sun /sʌn/ *n*. the large ball of fire in the sky which gives light and heat: *Sit in the **sun** and get warm*. **sunny** *adj. The day was bright and **sunny***. p78

supper /'sʌpər/ *n*. an evening meal. p72

sure /ʃʊər/ without doubt: *I am **sure** that I put the money in the box*. p47

surname /'sɜːneɪm/ *n*. a name that is used by a family, usually written last: *He is called Peter Brown. Brown is his **surname***. p10

sweater /'swetər/ *n*. an item of clothing - see picture. p48

swim /swɪm/ *v*. to move through the water by using your legs and arms: *He **swam** across the river*. p41

swimming pool *n*. a place built for people to swim in. p41

table /'teɪbl/ *n*. a piece of furniture with a flat top and legs: *We eat our meals at a **table***. p129

take /teɪk/ *v*. to carry something to another place: ***Take** the shopping home*. p46

talk /tɔːk/ *v*. to speak or be able to speak: *That child is too young to **talk***. p15

tall /tɔːl/ *adj*. higher than other people or other things: *James is **taller** than Paul, but Richard is the **tallest***. p66

tasty /'teɪstɪ/ *adj*. good to eat, not tasteless: *This pizza is very **tasty***. p66

taxi /'tæksɪ/ *n*. a car with a driver who will take you somewhere if you pay him: *To take a **taxi** to the station* - see picture. p4

tea /tiː/ *n*. a drink - see picture. p6

teach /tiːtʃ/ *v*. to help a person to learn: *Who **taught** you to ride a bicycle?* **teacher** *n*. someone who helps people to learn. p26

telephone /'telɪfəʊn/
1 *n*. (*no pl*.) an instrument for carrying the sound of a person's voice by electricity or radio. p4
2 *v*. to speak to someone by telephone: *I **telephoned** my sister last night*. p10

television /'telɪvɪʒn/ *n*. a large box-shaped apparatus on which pictures appear: *TV is the shortest way of writing **television***. p25

temperature /'temprətʃər/ *n*. the amount of heat or cold: *In hot weather the **temperature** gets very high*. p78

thank you /θæŋkjuː/ said to show you are pleased: ***Thank you** for the present*. p7

think /θɪŋk/ (*past* **thought**) *v*. to have an opinion; believe something: *I **think** it will be hot today*. p69

thirsty /'θɜːstɪ/ *adj*. to want or need something to drink: *I feel **thirsty**. Can I have a drink?* p89

ticket /'tɪkɪt/ *n*. a small piece of paper or card which shows we have paid for

something: *We buy a **ticket** to get a seat on a bus, train or aeroplane*. p44

tie /taɪ/ *n*. an item of clothing - see picture. p48

time /taɪm/ *n*.
1 (*no pl*.) minutes, hours, days, weeks, months, years: *How do you spend your **time** at home?*
2 a special hour or day: *What **time** is it?* p12

tired /'taɪəd/ *adj*. needing rest or sleep. p84

toast /təʊst/ *n*. heated bread for breakfast - see picture. p6

today /tə'deɪ/ *n. adv*. (on) this day: ***Today** is Monday*. p36

toe /təʊ/ *n*. one of the five end parts of the foot - see picture. p54

toilet /'tɔɪlɪt/ *n*. the smallest room in the house! p117

tomato /tə'mɑːtəʊ/ *n*. (*pl*. **tomatoes**) a red juicy fruit that we eat raw or cooked. p8

tomorrow /tə'mɒrəʊ/ *n. adv*. the day after this day: ***Tomorrow** will be Tuesday*. p36

too /tuː/ *adv*. more than is needed or wanted: *He drives **too** fast*. p111

tooth /tuːθ/ *n*. (*pl*. **teeth** /tiːθ/) grows in the mouth - see picture. p54

toothache /'tuːθeɪk/ *n*. (*no pl*.) a pain in a tooth. p88

touch /tʌtʃ/ *v*. to put the hand or another part of the body on or against something: *Don't **touch** that pot; it's very hot*. p54

tourist /'tʊərɪst/ *n*. person visiting a place for holiday. **Tourist Information Centre** *n*. place a tourist goes to get information. p13

town /taʊn/ *n*. a large group of houses and other buildings where people live and work. p96

train /treɪn/ *n*. transport on rails - see picture. p75

travel /'trævl/ *v*. to go from place to place: *to **travel** round the world*. p24

trousers /'traʊzəz/ *n*. an item of clothing - see picture. p48

t-shirt /'tiː ʃɜːt/ *n*. an item of clothing - see picture. p48

turn /tɜːn/ *v*. to change or make something change position or direction: *She **turned** left at the end of the road*. p97

twin-bedded /twɪn'bedɪd/ *adj*. with two single beds. p41

type /taɪp/ *v*. to use a machine to print letters on paper: *to **type** a letter*. p55

ugly /'ʌglɪ/ *adj*. not beautiful to look at: *an **ugly** face*. p111

under /'ʌndər/ *prep*. below: *The cat is **under** the bed*. p41

underground /'ʌndəgraʊnd/ *n*. a railway that goes under the ground. p75

understand /ʌndə'stænd/ *v*. to know the meaning of: *Do you **understand** every word on this page?* p5

up /ʌp/ *prep*. opposite down. p54

usually /'juːʒəlɪ/ *adv*. done regularly: *I'm **usually** at school early, but today I was late*. p117

very /'verɪ/ *adv*. (used to make another word stronger): *It is **very** hot in this room*. p66

wait /weɪt/ *v*. to stay somewhere until someone comes or something happens: *Please **wait** here until I come back*.

waiter *n*. a person who brings food to people eating at a table. p8

walk /wɔːk/ *v*. to move on the feet at the usual speed: *We **walk** to school each day*. p12

want /wɒnt/ *v*. to wish to have something: *I **want** a bicycle for my birthday*. p70

warm /wɔːm/ *adj*. not cold but not very hot: ***warm** water*. p78

wash /wɒʃ/ *v*. to make clean with water: *Have you **washed** your shirt?* p25

watch /wɒtʃ/ *v*. to look at: *I **watched** TV for 4 hours last night*. p25

water /'wɔːtər/ *n*. (*no pl*.) the liquid in rivers, lakes, and seas, which animals and people drink - see picture. p73

wear /weər/ *v*. to have or carry on the body: *She **wore** a pretty dress*. p49

weather /'weðər/ *n*. (*no pl*.) the state of the wind, rain, sun, etc: *I don't like cold **weather***. p79

wedding /'wedɪŋ/ *n*. the ceremony when people get married: *I'm going to my brother's **wedding** tomorrow*.

wedding anniversary *n*. annual celebration of the wedding day. p9

week /wiːk/ *n*. a period of seven days, especially from Sunday to Saturday: *I play tennis twice a **week**. Will you come and see us next **week**?* p13

weekday *n*. any day except Saturday and Sunday. p13

weekend *n*. Saturday and Sunday. p13

well /wel/
1 *adj*. in good health; not ill: *I hope you are **well***. p84
2 *adv*. in a good or satisfactory way: *Mary can read very **well***. p111

west /west/ *n*. point of the compass, opposite east. p102

wet /wet/ *adj*.
1 covered with or containing liquid; not dry: *My hair is **wet***.
2 rainy: *a **wet** day*. p96

white /waɪt/ *adj*. the colour of the paper in this book; very light: *a **white** dress*. p7

wide /waɪd/ *adj*. large from side to side; broad; not narrow. p94

wife /waɪf/ *n*. (*pl*. **wives** /waɪvz/) the woman to whom a man is married. p57

wind /wɪnd/ *n*. air moving quickly. **windy** *adj*. with a lot of wind. p78

wine /waɪn/ *n*. (*no pl*.) an alcoholic drink - see picture. p27

winter /'wɪntər/ *n. adj*. the season in cool countries when it is cold and plants do not grow. p82

woman /'wʊmən/ *n*. (*pl*. **women** /'wɪmɪn/) a fully grown human female. p18

world /wɜːld/ *n*.
1 the earth: *This car is used all over the **world***.
2 all human beings thought of together. p19

work /wɜːk/ *v*. to do an activity, especially as employment: *He **works** in a factory*. p15

write /raɪt/ *v*. to make letters or words on paper, using a pen or pencil: ***Write** your name*. p5

year /jɪər/ *n*. a measure of time, 365 days (or 12 months, or 52 weeks): *She is seven **years** old*. p35

yellow /'jeləʊ/ *adj. n*. the colour of the sun. p48

yes /jes/ opposite no, positive answer. p7

yesterday /'jestədeɪ/ *n. adv*. (on) the day before this day: *It was very hot **yesterday***. p36

yoghurt /'jɒgət/ *n*. food - see picture. p73

young /jʌŋ/ *adj*. not old: *His children are **young** - 4 and 2 years old*. p97

zero /'zɪərəʊ/ the number 0. p9

Grammar index

Numbers are page numbers. LR means Language Review.